Ride for your life. . . .

Trace wheeled his pony and sprang into full flight. They bounded down the back side of the rise in full gallop, Trace bending low in the saddle, trying to avoid the arrows and musket balls that flew after him.

Hoping to gain some ground, he jerked the pony around in a quick turn and charged off in a different direction. It had the desired effect of catching his pursuers by surprise, widening the distance between him and the warriors chasing him—all except for one. Out in front of his brothers, the Sioux anticipated the change in direction and angled across to intercept Trace. He was gaining on him. The determined warrior, war axe in hand, lay low across his pony's neck.

The two of them were outdistancing the rest of the war party, but the lone Sioux brave was almost behind Trace. He looked back into the warrior's face, a mask of scornful fury, his eyes wide in anticipation of the kill, his cheeks adorned with jagged streaks of red and black war paint. His arm was raised to deliver a crushing blow with his stone war axe. Turning, Trace aimed his pistol at the Indian's stomach and fired. He would never forget the look of shocked disbelief that replaced the brave's angry visage as the Sioux rolled off his pony and landed in the grass with a thud. . . .

Wings of the Hawk

Charles G. West

A SIGNET BOOK

SIGNET
Published by New American Library, a division of
Penguin Putnam Inc., 375 Hudson Street,
New York, New York 10014, U.S.A.
Penguin Books Ltd, 27 Wrights Lane,
London W8 5TZ, England
Penguin Books Australia Ltd, Ringwood,
Victoria, Australia
Penguin Books Canada Ltd, 10 Alcorn Avenue,
Toronto, Ontario, Canada M4V 3B2
Penguin Books (N.Z.) Ltd, 182–190 Wairau Road,
Auckland 10, New Zealand

Penguin Books Ltd, Registered Offices:
Harmondsworth, Middlesex, England

First published by Signet, an imprint of New American Library,
a division of Penguin Putnam Inc.

First Printing, August 2000
10 9 8 7 6 5 4 3 2 1

Printed in the United States of America

PUBLISHER'S NOTE
This is a work of fiction. Names, characters, places, and incidents either are the product of the author's imagination or are used fictitiously, and any resemblance to actual persons, living or dead, business establishments, events, or locales is entirely coincidental.

For Ronda

Chapter 1

Young Jim Tracey loved to hunt. Maybe it was because he seemed to have a knack for it. Though only fourteen on this sunny day in the late spring of 1835, he had already proven himself as a marksman. From the age of ten, he had supplemented the family's dinner table with squirrels and rabbits—most of them shot clean through the head with the rifle his daddy had given him. Because of his skill with the old flintlock, it was easy for Jim to persuade his father to let him take a mule up the mountain to see if he could sneak up on a deer.

John Tracey was proud of his son's natural talent as a marksman. Although he took credit for teaching the youngster how to shoot, starting his instruction at an early age, still he knew that young Jim's ability was God-given. It was good for the boy to go off in the woods to hunt. They had been working long hours at the sluice box ever since the winter broke, with not a lot of gold dust to show for it. Besides, they could always use some fresh meat.

John straightened up and, resting his shovel against a haystack-size boulder, arched his back in an effort to ease his aching muscles. He stood there a few moments, watching a young half-breed working with a shovel on the other side of the sluice. Henry Brown Bear was perhaps a year older than his own son, Jim. It was hard to say. John could only guess, and Henry wasn't even sure himself how old he was. He was a good worker, though, and John never regretted bringing him along. When he thought about it, John figured it was best for the boy as well. He had been hanging around the trading post on the Platte, and probably would have turned into another loafer Injun if he had remained there. He was also good company for Jim. The two of them would sit by the fire at night and see who could tell the biggest lies. It made John smile when he pictured his son. *I wish Julia could see how he's growing into a man.* The thought of his wife caused a sharp pang of melancholy to wrinkle his weary brow. *Maybe we won't stay another year, like I said before. We've got a little dust—not enough to buy a farm, but maybe we'll just take what we've got and head back home.*

"Henry, let's call it a day. You've been working pretty hard. Jim ain't the only one deserves a day off."

Henry Brown Bear rested his shovel and straightened up. He gave John a wide, warm smile. John had never seen the half-breed boy in anything but a pleasant humor and he was always willing to work. John knew that Henry had to be tired, but the boy would have smiled just as warmly if he had told him they were going to work on through the night.

In the next instant, Henry's smile seemed to freeze

on his face and his eyes grew wide, staring right through John. He clenched his teeth hard, and he looked as if about to speak, but he made no sound. Instead, he pitched forward, falling facedown in the clear mountain stream. John watched, amazed, thinking at first that the young half-breed was again acting like a clown. He was about to laugh at the boy's antics when he saw the arrow shaft protruding from his back.

Unable to move for a moment, frozen by the sight of a life just taken before him, John Tracey stared in disbelief. It took the snap of an arrow as the shaft splintered on the boulder beside him to shock his muscles into action. He broke from the stream and ran toward the cabin for his rifle. It was too late. He had barely reached the far bank when he felt the impact of the heavy rifle ball between his shoulder blades, driving him to the ground. At the same instant, the boom of the large-bore buffalo gun rolled over his head like a wave of summer thunder. He struggled to get to his feet, but his limbs seemed unwilling to support him. The pounding of his heart hammered in his ears as if that vital organ was going to crash through his rib cage. It was so loud that the sounds of fiendish war cries right behind him seemed way off in the distance, though he knew they were probably scalping poor Henry only a few yards away. John managed to gain his feet, but his chest felt heavy, like a huge stone had been lodged behind his breastbone. He staggered uncontrollably, struggling to escape the hands he could now feel grabbing and clutching at his clothes. It was the last sensation

John Tracey felt in this world before a war axe was buried in his neck.

On a low bluff some fifty yards away, overlooking the clear, rippling stream, a gruff-looking bear of a man stood. His buffalo gun in one hand, he watched the scene without emotion—even with some amusement—as his Blackfoot allies celebrated the kill. After a little while, he picked up his horse's reins and led it down to the scene of mutilation that was now under way. Once the scalps were taken, the bodies were left to rot as the savages busied themselves with ransacking the cabin. He himself had no interest in the spoils of the massacre. Only on second thought did he ask, "Find any little sacks of yellow dust?"

Lame Fox, a solidly built warrior with a long scar across his back, answered, "No." The big white man shrugged his shoulders, not really expecting any. Lame Fox spoke again. "There is another man." He pointed to the edge of the clearing, where some tools were left near the back of the cabin. "See, tracks say three men here."

This interested the bearlike white man, but not enough to cause him concern. He had looked carefully at the two bodies—a man and a boy. He was satisfied. "It 'pears the other one went off up that way on a horse," he said. Lame Fox nodded agreement. "Well, suit yourself on that one. We got the ones that matter."

Always interested in acquiring another horse, Lame Fox called his warriors together. He sent four of them to trail the mule Jim had ridden up the mountain. He, along with the others, would return to their village in triumph with the big white man once they had finished here.

After having left his father and Henry, who were still shoveling gravel into the sluice box, Jim decided to hunt for bigger game than the deer he had set out for. He pushed on through the timberline, up above the trees to the high meadows in search of an elk. The thought of bringing back one of the majestic animals made him swell with imagined pride. He'd show Henry what a mighty hunter he was. But after several hours of searching, he was disappointed to find no sign of elk, or anything else that would make meat for the camp. He decided to call it quits when he heard the powerful report of a large-bore rifle reverberating up through the canyons. *That wasn't Pa's rifle!*

What could it mean? There was only that one shot, but it sounded as if it had come from the valley below, maybe even from the cabin. He prodded the mule, pushing him down the mountain as quickly as he could in an effort to get back to the camp. The mule, having the better judgment of the two, resisted Jim's urging and would go no faster than he deemed prudent. "Damn you," Jim admonished, "can't you do no better than this?" But the mule would not cooperate. So they made their way across the ridges and down into the forest belt at a steady but slow pace, with Jim flailing his arms and kicking the mule's rib cage. The mule simply ignored his antics.

Once they descended the steep slope and were near the base of the firs, the mule relented and picked up the pace to a speed that was too fast to dodge and dart through the crowded pines safely, but Jim was anxious to close the remaining mile to the cabin. At that pace over the rough terrain, an accident was bound to happen. The mule saw the gulch that suddenly appeared before them and tried to swerve to the side, but it was too late. Jim went flying out of the saddle, landing on the near side of the gulch, rolling toward its lip when he hit the ground. He wound up in a tangled ball of juniper at the gully's bottom. The mule slid on his front legs before rolling down the side of another ridge, almost bowling over four startled Blackfoot warriors. One of them reacted quickly enough to grab the frightened animal's reins and bring it to a halt.

Although young Jim was not aware of it yet, the spill had saved his life. Too stunned to move, he lay there wrapped in a cocoon of juniper and berry bushes. He was afraid to move for a few moments, unsure if he had broken any bones. In fact, it amazed him that he did not feel more than slight pain. Lying flat on his back, looking up at the sky from the bottom of the deep gulch, he decided it was time to test his limbs to make sure everything was still sound. Before he could move, however, he was frozen by the sound of voices above him. A moment later, he saw them pass along the rim of the gulch. *Injuns!* Their faces were painted for war, and they were already leading his mule away.

His heart was pounding so rapidly, and so loud, that he feared they might hear it from above. All they had to do to discover him was to glance down into the gulch. He could do nothing but stare, unblinking, at the rim of the narrow gully as they slowly walked their horses past. There were four of them. The shot he had heard must have been fired by them. Maybe, he thought, they shot once at the cabin, and then his father and Henry scared them away. With nothing better to hope for, he decided that was it; his father had chased them away. Holding on to that slim hope, he waited, fearing to breathe, until the four disappeared over the ridge.

He had been lucky. They had not thought to look down at him. However, he had lost his mule, along with his rifle. *But I got my hair,* he thought, and quickly tore his way out of the brambles, forgetting his earlier concern for broken bones. His foremost thought now was to get back to his father.

Making his way as quickly as possible down the lower side of the steep slope above the stream, constantly scanning the terrain ahead of him, Jim was keenly aware of the deafening silence of the pines surrounding him. Every hundred yards or so he stopped to listen, straining to hear any sounds that might alert him to the presence of Indians, hoping that the four who had passed him back up the mountainside were all there were—and not part of a larger war party. His heart was pumping hard, whether from the physical exertion of his haste, or from the thought of finding something dreadfully wrong at the cabin, he could not say.

He struck the stream a hundred yards above the cabin. Cautious now, he slowed his pace and carefully made his way downstream, stepping from rock to rock, pausing often to listen and study the way before him. He smelled smoke—too much smoke for a cookfire. He could feel his heartbeat pounding in his head now, and a cold feeling of dread sent shivers over his body. A few more paces down the stream, and he caught a glimpse of the cabin through the trees. The little bit he could see through the foliage showed nothing amiss. But, glancing up at the treetops, he saw a thin stream of smoky haze drifting overhead. Until then he had heard no sound above the noisy ripple of the stream. Now voices came to him on the wind and he froze in his tracks. It was Indian talk! Not loud screeching or war whoops, but just normal conversation between several Indians. Henry was half Crow. Maybe he was talking with them. That had to be it, for there was neither shooting nor shouting—they were probably Indians looking for food or gifts. Still, he would be cautious.

He left the stream and circled around in order to come up on their campsite from above, on the opposite side of the water. Crawling behind a huge boulder, he slowly raised his head until he could see the clearing and the cabin beyond. What he saw seared an image in his mind that would never completely fade from his memory. Below him, not fifty feet away, the body of the half-breed boy lay still in the shallow water. He knew it was Henry only by the clothes he wore, for his head had been smashed in with a large rock, and strips of flesh had been sliced from his arms and shoulders.

Captivated by the horror before him, he was helpless to move. His eyes wide with fright, he looked beyond the corpse of his friend toward the group of twelve or more savages milling around the tiny clearing. Their horses were grazing on the grass behind the cabin, his father's horse and mules among them. A few of the Indians were making a halfhearted attempt to set fire to the cabin. The back room and a patch on the roof were burning, but the main cabin resisted their attempts. While Jim watched, horrified, they tired of the effort and rejoined their brothers. There was still no sign of his father. As he searched the clearing with his eyes, hoping that his father had managed to escape, he discovered his body.

They had pulled his father's corpse over to a tree and left it in a sitting position, held up by more than a dozen arrows pinning his chest to the trunk. Jim almost cried out. He had to force himself to remain still. His father's scalp had been taken and his head and face were awash in blood. Like Henry, he was identifiable only by the clothes he wore, so brutal was the mutilation he had suffered at the hands of his murderers.

Jim slid down behind the rock, too shocked by the sight to even cry. Dazed, he did not move for several minutes as his brain fought to right itself. After a while, he recovered his senses enough to realize that he could not remain there long without being discovered. He forced himself back up to take another look, totally at a loss as to what he should do. There was no thought of helping his father—it was much too late for that. He wanted to run, but a strong feeling that he should at least take care of his father's body kept him at the boulder. Again, he eased his head above the top of the boulder until he could see the clearing. The actions of several of the warriors gave him cause for more immediate concern. They were scouting around the clearing, pointing at tracks and looking toward the stream. Jim had heard tales of the Indians' ability to track enemies, and his spine went numb when he thought that maybe they were now setting out to find him. There was no more indecision on his part. He decided the best thing for him to do was to run as fast and as far as he could.

Buck Ransom made his way slowly and cautiously through the thick patch of willows that screened the creek bank below the beaver dam. His moccasined feet trod silently through the sparse brush that managed to compete with the willows for the earth's nourishment. Glancing about frequently, a matter of long habit in his chosen occupation, he still managed to focus his main attention on the sandy bank at the water's edge and on the bait stick that was still standing where he had set it. The float was missing. There was no sign of it in the water near the dam, where he would normally expect to find it if the critter had run with it. Gone too was the notch-stick, evidently pulled up and no doubt floating downstream somewhere.

Kneeling on one knee, he remained absolutely still for a long time, listening and watching before leaving the cover of the willows. Buck was cautious by nature, but he was especially alert in Blackfoot country. The country around Pierre's Hole was smack-dab in the middle of Shoshone and Bannock territory, but

Blackfoot war parties frequently raided in the area. And Blackfeet weren't too hospitable toward white trappers. Jim Bridger had counseled against Buck and his partner, Frank Brown, going to South Pass alone. There were beaver galore in the hundreds of streams that etched the Wind River and Sweetwater Mountains, he had said. But it was too dangerous for two free trappers to go it alone, even old hands like Buck and Frank. Buck wouldn't presume to know better than Bridger—Old Gabe was very seldom wrong when it came to trapping and fighting Injuns. But when Bridger had decided to sell out to the American Fur Company the year before, the two old friends had made up their minds they could do better as free trappers. And they figured that though they had kept their hair for more than a few years in these mountains working with a brigade of trappers, it might be a sight easier for just the two of them to keep out of sight from the Blackfeet and the Gros Ventres.

Up to now, they had had considerable good fortune. It was still early spring, and they already had cached several packs of beaver plews. But now there was something mighty curious going on, and Buck aimed to find out what—or who—was robbing his traps. When he felt certain that no one was around, he left the cover of the willows and went down to the water's edge.

Just as before, he found the trap lying on the bank near the dam, the string and float still attached—but no beaver. *Dammit to hell,* he cursed silently and searched the ground for prints or any sign that might give him a clue as to who or what was the thief. He was certain it wasn't the Blackfeet. If they had found his traps, they'd be waiting to ambush him. And if it was a critter, it'd have to be a pretty smart one to take the beaver out of the trap instead of gnawing off everything but a foot.

"Well, we'll see about this," he muttered under his breath, determined to get to the bottom of it if it took all day. He began a careful study of the creek bank downstream. He had already discounted the possibility of a scavenger being the culprit. It had to be a two-legged thief. The puzzling part was, if it was another trapper—one of those thieving bastards from the American Fur Company, maybe—he couldn't figure on getting away with stealing one pelt a day for very long before he caught a rifle ball in his backside. And if it was food he was after, why in hell would he rob beaver traps when the mountains around him were teeming with deer and elk? Buck was determined to find out.

What made the whole thing even more puzzling was the fact that this one particular trap was the only one raided—but it had been raided three days in a row. He continued to search downstream for sign that would tell him where the thief had left the creek, for he was certain the culprit had entered the water some ways down in an effort to hide his tracks. Crossing over, he searched the opposite bank up to the dam, then back downstream again. It took some time, but he finally found a print of a naked foot beside a rotting cottonwood log about thirty yards downstream from the beaver dam.

"Well, now, that is curious for certain," he mumbled and pushed his foxskin cap back so he could scratch his head and puzzle over the footprint. It was a small print, smaller than a grown man's. No boot, no moccasin—just a bare foot. Buck traced the outline with his finger. The way the forward part of the print was deeply embedded, while the heel was only lightly sunk in the wet sand, indicated to Buck that the thief was almost tiptoeing—like his feet were tender. It took only a few seconds for Buck to confirm that the thief had put his boots back on while sitting on the log and then proceeded to leave a plain trail through the trees toward the hills to the west. *Why didn't ya just paint up a big sign that said, "I'm goin' thisaway?"*

From the size of the prints, Buck didn't deem it necessary to wait for Frank to help him go after the thief. Besides, Frank was working his own traps in a stream on the far side of a high ridge that divided the little valley. From the clues he had turned up, Buck already guessed that he was tracking a rank greenhorn. No experienced woodsman would leave a trail through the grass like the one he was now following. And most trappers wouldn't take their boots off and walk barefooted up the rocky bottom of a creek like that.

He paused a moment before following the tracks across an open meadow between the cottonwoods and the base of the hills. Ever mindful of the possibility of an ambush—the trail was so damned obvious that he had to consider that—he studied the belt of fir and pine that ringed the lower hill. *If I get my ass shot off by a damn greenhorn, Frank'll tell every living soul at the rendezvous.* After a few minutes' consideration, he continued, figuring the thief was too inexperienced to set up an ambush.

After a twenty-minute climb up through the pines Buck was wondering if he should have left his horse back on the far side of the creek. His breath became slightly labored as the route steepened, and he was about to scold himself for running a fool's errand when he smelled the smoke of a campfire. Moving more cautiously now, he pushed on. Soon he could see a trail of blue smoke drifting up from a narrow ravine about twenty-five yards in front of him. *Might as well send up smoke signals to ever' Injun in the territory while you're at it.*

Down on his hands and knees, Buck crawled up to the edge of the ravine and positioned himself behind a log. Raising his head slowly, he peered over the log. The scene that met his eyes was just as he suspected. There was a small fire burning brightly in a cramped space between two boulders. Green limbs, only half burned, were the culprits that produced the blue smoke that he had seen some ways back. On the ground not far from the fire were the remains of the missing beavers. Buck shook his head in disgust when he saw the mess the thief had made of butchering the animals. But there was no sign of the thief. That was the last thought that flickered through Buck's mind before the back of his head exploded and everything went black.

When Buck opened his eyes some minutes later, he at first thought he was drowning, as water from his own canteen was poured over his face. The instant his eyes flickered open, the torrent of water stopped, but the next sensation he was aware of was a pounding ache in the back of his head. It felt as if someone had hung a heavy rock from his skull. As his senses gradually returned, he realized that he had been coldcocked, taken completely by surprise. His first impulse was to reach for his rifle, only to find it gone.

"This what you're looking for?"

Still flat on his back, Buck jerked his head to the side, whence the voice had come. He found himself staring into the business end of his own rifle. Sliding his gaze up the long barrel toward the stock, he locked eyeballs with a pair of deep-blue eyes that returned a no-nonsense message to the shocked trapper. Unable to say anything for a moment, Buck stared at his captor, who had taken a step closer, still holding the rifle on him. Finally he sputtered, "Well, I reckon it is. What the hell are you aiming to do with that rifle?"

"I don't know," the boy answered frankly, "I reckon that depends."

"Well, if you ain't aiming to shoot me, how 'bout gittin' that dang barrel outta my face. That there rifle's got a touchy trigger." By that time, the world had stopped spinning around Buck, so he struggled up to a sitting position. The boy backed away a step to give him room to sit up, but he still held the rifle on him. No longer fearing his immediate death, Buck mostly felt irritation, and beyond that, embarrassment. His captor was no more than a lanky, skinny boy dressed in brown homespun, with an unruly shock of sandy hair hanging over his forehead. "What in tarnation did you bushwhack me for?"

The boy shrugged, almost apologetically. "Hell, I thought you was an Injun." Then the sternness returned to his face. "You ought not be sneaking up on people like that." He feigned a threatening motion with the rifle. "I still ain't sure but what you ain't a durn Injun."

"Well, I ain't," Buck replied, gingerly feeling the back of his head, almost expecting to find it cracked. When he found nothing but the beginnings of a large bump, he pulled himself up to sit on the log he had fallen across. Mortified and grumpy, he pushed the offending gun barrel aside and commanded, "Put the damn rifle down." He closed his eyes briefly and rubbed the back of his skull. "What did you hit me with, anyway?"

The boy, still holding the rifle but no longer pointing it at Buck, answered with a glance at a large pine limb lying near the log.

"Damn. It's a wonderment you didn't kill me."

Buck just sat there looking at the boy and rubbing his sore head for a few moments until he suddenly remembered what the whole encounter was about. "What the hell was you doing raiding my traps? Don't you know you could get shot for stealing a man's traps?"

"I was hungry," the boy replied unemotionally.

"Hungry?" Buck grunted. "This country's so full of deer you have to be careful you don't git run over by one. You didn't have to spoil a prime beaver plew, stealing outta my traps."

"I didn't have no gun to shoot a deer." He hesitated. " 'Til now."

Buck's eyebrows flicked up. "Now, hold on a minute, boy. Don't go gittin' no ideas 'bout that rifle."

The boy raised the rifle barrel again as he fixed Buck with a wary eye. "Mister, I don't know who you are. All I know is you come sneaking up on me like an Injun."

Buck studied the young man for a long moment. Young and skinny as he was, he presented a determined front, and Buck decided he would use that rifle if given a reason. But he also saw something else in the deep-blue eyes, something that told him there was no evil residing there. "I reckon you got reason to be cautious at that," Buck said, the gruffness gone from his tone. "But I wasn't sneaking up on you. It don't pay to run around in this country, announcing to ever'body that you're a'coming. If I'da been of a mind to sneak up on you, you'da never had a chance to bushwhack me."

The boy was undecided. This rough-looking, grizzled old mountain man with a face full of silver whiskers was probably up to no ill intent. As he maintained, he was merely looking for the cause of his missing beaver. The boy couldn't blame him for that. But what if he misread the man's eyes? Having recently witnessed a savage assault in this wild mountain country, he was not willing to risk his young neck again. The question was what to do now. Give up the man's rifle—and his own advantage as well? While he was making up his mind, he still trained the rifle on Buck.

Buck, weary of the game by then, asked, "Are you gonna give me my rifle or not?"

"I don't know," the boy answered honestly.

"Don't fret, Buck. I ain't gonna' let this young'un shoot'cha. I ain't got the patience to break in a new partner."

Buck and the boy were both startled by the voice behind them. The boy, seeing Buck's broad grin, turned to discover the formidable figure of Frank Brown standing on the brow of the ravine, his rifle looking square at him. The boy didn't drop Buck's rifle right away, but looked from one of the men to the other, still deciding what his next move should be.

"Go on and drop it, boy," Buck said. "We don't mean you no harm."

The boy hesitated only a moment more before carefully laying the weapon down, propping it against the log Buck was seated on. Then he stepped away while watching intently as Frank moved down the side of the ravine. Buck, realizing the situation had been defused, didn't bother to pick up his rifle. He got to his feet and waited for his partner to make his way down to them.

No one said anything for a few minutes until Frank got to the bottom of the ravine. Wearing a big smile, Frank glanced at Buck briefly before turning his gaze to the young stranger who had held his partner at bay with his own rifle. The grin broadened. Buck didn't make any comment. He knew Frank was going to have his fun with this one, and Frank didn't disappoint him.

"Well, damn, partner," he began, trying to hold a serious expression on his face. "What kinda beaver is this'un? I ain't ever seen one this young before. Ain't got much fur on 'im, has he?"

Buck was too mortified even to attempt to explain how he had gotten in the fix he had been in, so he didn't bother to respond to Frank's wisecracks. He knew he had it coming, so he just sat back down on the log and took it, waiting for Frank to get his fill of it. The boy, for his part, was unsure what his fate was to be at the hands of the two trappers. He thought about making a break for the woods, but decided he wouldn't get far before Frank's rifle ball would catch him.

Frank cast an appraising eye on the rather somber young pup in brown homespun and tattered boots. He was amused to notice the obvious stiffening of the young man's backbone under the scrutinizing gaze. "Well, Buck, what in the big blue-eyed world have you got here?" Turning to the boy, he said, "I'd sure be tickled to hear how you come to be out here in the middle of Blackfoot country. S'pose you tell us." He lowered his rifle and waited for the boy's reply.

The boy stood, feet wide apart, trying to maintain an air of defiance, determined that he would show no fear to the two buckskin-clad mountain men. He had made up his mind that he wouldn't tell them anything. But when Frank laid his weapon aside, and neither man showed any hostile indications, he decided it was in his best interest to be civil. It might be wise if he could join up with the two of them—at least they seemed to know where they were, which was more than he could say for himself. Finally he spoke.

"I was just aiming to get away from the Injuns."

Frank waited for further explanation, but saw that it was not forthcoming, so he prodded. "You must not have wanted to get away from 'em too much, burning that green wood there. You're smoking up the whole Rocky Mountains." While he said it, he started kicking dirt over the boy's fire.

"I was fixin' to tell him that," Buck inserted, still rubbing his sore head.

The boy merely shrugged his shoulders. Frank glanced around at the scattered remains of the beavers. "It's a wonder the buzzards ain't led a war party to you." Suddenly annoyed, he snapped, "What the hell were you raiding our traps for anyway?"

"I was hungry."

"That's all I got out of him," Buck said, slightly amused that Frank was getting a taste of the boy's reticence to expound.

Fixing the boy with a stern eye, Frank muttered, "Three prime beaver plews—wasted." He shook his head, exasperated. "I wish to hell somebody had learned you how to properly skin a beaver." Then he jerked his head back and locked an accusing eye on the young man. "Boy, where's your folks? What in hell are you doing out here?"

"I told you," the boy fired back. "Running away

from the dang Injuns—and I ain't got no folks, leastways I ain't now."

Frank softened a bit at that. "Injuns kill your folks, boy?"

"They killed my pa."

"When?" Buck inquired.

"About three or four days ago."

"Where?" Frank asked.

The boy shook his head. "I don't know." He pointed behind him. "Back yonder in the hills somewhere. I don't know. I've been running, just trying to get away."

"Blackfeet," Buck said.

"Of course they was Blackfeet," Frank snapped, "Who else would they be?" With an involuntary reflex, both men looked around them at the very mention of the word, as if to be sure there were none close by. Turning back to the boy, Frank said, "I still don't know what in thunder you and your pa were doing in this part of the country. It's too far off the main trail. What was you doing, prospecting?" The boy nodded yes. "Didn't find much, I'd bet."

"Didn't find any," the boy quickly replied. There was a modest amount, enough to grubstake a man for a year, maybe. There was certainly no fortune to show for almost a year's backbreaking work. He saw no reason to let on to these two strangers that there was a little pouch of dust hidden in a pile of rocks near the rough cabin that had been home to him for ten months.

Frank studied the boy's face for a long moment, much the same as he would have studied a horse to evaluate its worth. He decided he saw some spunk in the lad. "Well, that there's a familiar song a lot of folks from back East are singing. I'm sorry your pap was kilt, but I reckon that's just part of living out here. What about your ma? The Injuns get her too?"

The boy shook his head. "My ma's back home in St. Louis." He paused to think about it a moment. "I reckon I'd best get back East to take her the news about Pa." As he said it, he couldn't help but recall the last days in St. Louis before he and his father struck out for the gold they were sure was waiting for them in the mountains to the west. His mother was dead set against it from the beginning, but his father had made up his mind. There was no way he could see any hope of owning his own farm unless he found the gold he was convinced he would find in the Rockies. The rumors were rampant. It seemed that every day, some bearded and shaggy dreamer staggered in from the far country telling wondrous tales of gold strikes in the busy streams that sliced through the rocky divides. The fact that these drifters were ragged and penniless did little to discourage his father's faith in the truthfulness of their tales. He was certain that with his ability to work hard, it would take no more than a year—two at the most—to amass a sum equal to ten years' pay from Blunt Brothers Freight Company.

His mother had pleaded with his father to forget about his dreams of owning a farm. She was content to make the most of it there in St. Louis. True, they lived in a tiny house, not much more than a hovel, really, but they had food to eat and he and their elder son, Cameron, had steady jobs at the freight company. But his father was adamant in his decision. No matter how he tried, however, he was unable to make his wife see that there was no future for him or Cameron as long as they worked for meager wages. She pleaded, but there was no changing his mind. So in the summer of 1834, he said good-bye, promising that he would give it no more than two years and then he'd return, no matter what his fortune. He took young Jim with him, leaving Cameron to support his mother until their return. Between his two sons, Jim was the logical choice to make the trek west. He was a born outdoorsman, and folks often commented that Jim had his father's blood in him.

John Tracey was a tall, powerfully built man, and Jim looked to be the spitting image of him. Cameron, on the other hand, seemed to take after his mother's side of the family. Handsome and gentle-natured like his mother, Cameron seemed destined to find his life's work in accounting or clerical work of some kind. Though the two boys were directly opposite in nature, there was a strong affection between them.

There was never any real decision to be made when John Tracey contemplated which son should accompany him in the wild country beyond the Missouri. Jim was eager to go. He had just turned thirteen that spring, but he was strong for his age and unafraid of hard work, and he was already dreaming of the far mountains.

Young James McCall Tracey thought about these things as he stood facing the two grizzled trappers—and the image of his mother, a handsome woman, flashed through his mind. He could still picture her standing in front of their tiny house—Cameron by her side—watching tearfully as he and his father turned their mules toward the dusty road. He would have to go back as soon as possible to take them the awful news. So that all was not lost, however, he decided that it was important to recover the small pouch of dust hidden back at the cabin. It was small compensation for the loss of a husband and father, but by rights his mother certainly should have it.

"I gotta go back and take care of my Pa," the boy stated.

"What fer?" Buck wondered. "I thought you said he was kilt."

"He was. But I need to go back and bury him. I can't leave him for the buzzards." He wasn't sure he could easily find his way back. He had fled, running as fast as he could, much of the time at night. But maybe with the help of these two mountain men, he could retrace his steps. He could give his father a decent burial and recover the pouch. His mother would need that gold.

Frank snorted. "I reckon you took leave of your senses, running around in these woods by yourself. I'm thinkin' we've most likely spent more time in this hollow than we should have. With all the sign you left, I'd say it ain't gonna be long before we have company."

"I'm thinkin' the same thing, partner." Buck got to his feet and picked up his rifle. "I ain't even finished checking my traps."

The boy looked from one of them to the other,

trying to decide what to do. "Well, I gotta go back and take care of Pa."

Frank slung his rifle on his back and motioned to Buck to lead out. "You better come along with us, boy." He paused. " 'Course you can go your own way. Ever' man's free to go his own way out here. But, from what I've seen, I don't think you'll make it too far on yer own. So suit yourself. Only, do it quick, 'cause we're gettin' the hell outta here."

Jim was young, but he wasn't dumb. It didn't take but a second for him to make up his mind. His scalp was a good deal safer with these two ol' grizzlies. "I reckon I'll be obliged to go with you, but I've still got to get back there to take care of my Pa somehow."

Frank was not without compassion and understanding for the boy's concern for his father's body. "First thing is to make sure we ain't run up on by no damn Blackfoot war party. We'll see which way the sun sets the next couple of days. Then, if things is quiet, maybe we'll go back and find your Pa—at least, what's left of him."

The boy's education in survival began almost immediately, as Buck showed him how to cover his tracks as they traveled back across the hills to the creek where the traps had been set. Jim marveled at the way the two men made their way through the trees and along the open ridges. Though both of them were large and bulky in their loose-fitting hide shirts, they seemed to glide through the brush with a fluid motion, constantly scanning the forest around them, eyes darting from tree to tree, boulder to boulder, alert to all sounds and smells. It was obvious to him that Buck and Frank were fully at home in the mountains. And it was equally obvious that he was not. He knew from that moment that he wanted to become as harmonious with the country as they were. But it would not happen right away.

During the first couple of days he was with them, he was constantly made aware of his ignorance of the forest and his greenhorn clumsiness—whether he was causing a minor landslide with a misstep on a rocky slope or breaking limbs while pushing through a willow thicket. They lived in constant danger of Indian attack. This was Shoshone country and, while the Shoshones had been somewhat tolerant in the past, they were beginning to feel the intrusion of too many trappers. It had been a mite safer when the two men had worked for the Rocky Mountain Fur Company, but it was a damn dangerous situation for two free trappers. Keeping their scalps depended upon trapping the streams without the Indians knowing they were there.

To earn his way, Jim helped them work their traps. Buck showed him how to set a trap at the bottom of a beaver slide, set the notch-stick, angle the bait stick over the trap, and daub a little castor on it to attract the beaver. He also helped with the cooking and keeping the camp orderly, while Buck undertook to improve his skinning and butchering skills.

"I don't never want to see you waste a critter like you wasted them three beaver," Buck said. He showed him how to skin a beaver so that the plew was undamaged. He also showed him how to make better use of the carcass. "If you're of a mind to eat a beaver, the meat's all right, cuttin' off strips like you done. But you throwed away the best part." He then demonstrated how to boil the beaver's tail in a pot of water until the skin was soft enough to slit with a knife and peel. Then he took what was left and buried it in the ashes of the fire to bake. When it was done, he watched with amused satisfaction as Jim sampled it. "See what you could have been eatin'?" he said.

"I didn't have no pot," the boy stated dryly.

"Reckon not," Buck said, scratching his head. "Next time you run off from Injuns, carry a pot with you."

On the evening of the second day, after the horses were seen to and Frank had made a wide circle around their camp to be sure there was no sign of any Indians close by, they settled down by the fire. The boy listened silently as the two trappers discussed their season to date.

"I don't know what you're a'thinkin', partner, but I figure I've 'bout trapped out that creek I'm workin'," Buck said.

Frank nodded solemnly and resituated the wad of tobacco in his jaw to give him some room to talk. "Yeah, I reckon we're 'bout done here. I'm thinkin' maybe we ought to work our way back over to the Sweetwater, maybe Wind River."

Buck nodded his approval, then added, "Maybe so."

Frank spit in the fire and waited for the tobacco juice to sizzle. Then he cocked an eye at Jim. "You still set on going back to see to your pa?" When Jim nodded that he was, Frank went on, "I reckon it's safe enough to go find your cabin now. I don't think that bunch that kilt your daddy would hang around there very long." He scratched his chin whiskers thoughtfully. "How many did you say there was?"

"I saw about a dozen at the cabin," Jim replied. "And there was four more up on the ridge."

"Sixteen—twenty at the most," Buck said.

"I wonder what they were doing up here. That don't sound like no big war party." He looked at Jim again. "Were they wearing paint?"

The boy thought for a second before replying. "Yessir, they were."

"War party," Frank said. "What I can't figure, though, is who were they after? There ain't no village anywhere around here for them to be raiding. You reckon they come up here just to get his pa?" This last he directed at Buck.

"Don't hardly seem likely," Buck replied. He glanced at Jim. "More'n likely it was just bad luck you folks was camping where you was."

Nothing was said for another few minutes while Frank sat there thinking about it. Unable to come up with a reason for a war party to be in this part of the mountains, he decided to let it go. "Injuns don't need no reason to make up a war party. Anyway, if you're still of a mind to go bury your pa, we'll start out in the morning." He shifted his gaze toward his partner. "That all right with you, Buck?"

"Hell, why not?"

* * *

After all their traps and plews were loaded onto three of their packhorses, Frank arranged the rest of their possibles on the other one, leaving room for Jim to ride in front of the load. They set out for the narrow ravine where Buck had found the boy. A quick look around told them that Jim's camp had not been discovered, for there were no prints other than theirs from three days before. Satisfied that they were not about to encounter hostiles at any second, Frank and Buck decided it was safe to try to pick up Jim's trail, old as it was, and find the cabin. The boy helped some. He remembered some landmarks from his flight, enough to indicate a general direction. With that to help them, Buck and Frank soon headed across a grassy flat at the base of a steep hill. The boy remembered the place and pointed to a large boulder jutting out of the face of the hill. He had stopped there to rest and regain his breath. They continued on in this fashion for the better part of the day—Jim remembering some point of reference, and the two trappers scouting until they found his tracks. By the end of the second day on the move, they made camp in country that was familiar to the boy. He had hunted this part of the mountains, so he knew that the cabin was only three or four hours away.

Before the sun was directly overhead the next day, they stood on the bank of the stream across from the partially burnt cabin. Jim started toward it at once, but Frank grabbed his mount's bridle and held him back.

"Let's just take a little look here. We ain't in no

hurry." He and Buck sat there looking over the clearing and the slope behind the cabin for several minutes.

Jim, impatient to get his father's body in the ground, pressed the two old grizzlies to act. "Come on, there ain't nobody there."

They didn't move. "Boy, one of the first lessons you need to learn if you're thinkin' on keepin' your scalp in this country, is not to get in too big a hurry. Injuns' stock-in-trade is lookin' like they ain't there." He continued to sit motionless for a few minutes more. Jim noticed that he was watching the horses closely. When the horses showed no signs of sensing others in the vicinity, Frank nudged his mount forward and entered the water. Buck followed, motioning for the boy to trail behind.

Passing around the sluice box, Frank's horse shied away from the first body, still lying half in the water. Frank calmed the animal, holding him steady while he dismounted to take a look. The body was badly decomposed already. He glanced up at Buck, who was still in the saddle. "It's a pretty piece of work, all right." As Jim urged his packhorse up the shallow bank, Frank called out to him. "Boy, are you shore you wanna see this? Me and Buck can take care of your pa for you."

Jim hopped down from the packhorse. "I've done seen 'em once already. I reckon I'm man enough to take care of my pa." It was brave talk, and strictly for their benefit. Inside, Jim could feel his innards twisting in knots as he forced himself to approach the body of his father, still propped against the tree.

He was not prepared for the ghastly sight and had to turn his head away at first, stifling the convulsions that threatened to overcome his stomach. Fighting to calm his emotions, he looked again on the shattered form that had been his father. "I'm sorry I wasn't here to help you, Pa," he whispered, knowing that it was a useless apology. His presence would have hardly mattered in the results of the savage attack.

He was not aware of Buck standing behind him until he felt the old mountain man's huge hand on his shoulder. "It's a mighty hard lesson to learn, boy. Let's git him in the ground and be gone from this place."

Jim nodded and moved aside at Buck's gentle tug on his arm, and Frank stepped in to help Buck with the body. All but two of the dozen or so arrows Jim had seen on that fatal day had been removed. The two that remained were only broken shafts, the arrowheads obviously having been embedded too deeply to remove. Buck examined the shafts carefully, then looked at Frank. "You thinkin' what I'm thinkin'?"

Frank nodded solemnly. "Blackfoot." He unconsciously raised his head a little and looked around him. "Mighty strange to see a Blackfoot war party around these parts. I don't like that a whole lot."

While the two men carried John Tracey's body to the edge of the clearing, the boy fetched the shovels from the side of the cabin, where they still lay. As Buck would point out later, "Injuns ain't got no use for shovels, otherwise they'da stole 'em."

Since the body was already stiff, and impossible to

straighten, it was necessary to dig the grave a little wider at one end—a picture that would always remain in Jim's memory. Once his father's body was in the ground and covered with dirt, Jim could breathe a little easier.

"Who'd you say this boy was?" Buck asked as he and Jim worked on the second grave.

"His name was Henry Brown Bear. He hooked up with us at Deer Creek Crossing on the Platte." Jim paused to consider the premature ending of the half-breed's life. "He wasn't much older than me."

When Henry had been laid to rest, Buck took the shovels and strapped them on one of the packhorses. "Ain't no use leaving three good shovels out here." The Blackfeet had taken everything else of any value. Buck was quick to add, " 'Course, these here shovels is naturally yours, boy." Jim seemed not to hear, as he stood still, staring at the graves.

"We'd best lay some rocks over 'em to keep varmints from digging 'em up," Frank said. "There's a big pile of rocks over there next to the crick."

Jim, still intent upon his father's grave, suddenly remembered. "I'll get 'em," he blurted and moved quickly toward the pile.

"It'll take more than a few," Frank advised and started after the boy.

"That's all right. I wanna do it," Jim insisted, hurrying to get to the stack of rocks before the two men.

Seeing that the old trappers were not going to let him do all the work, he climbed up on the pile and started heaving rocks down behind him. "Here's some good heavy ones," he said and tossed rocks down for them to carry. Then he pulled some of the rocks from the side of the pile, near the bottom, until he uncovered a long, flat stone. When both men had their backs to him, carrying rocks to the graves, he lifted the flat stone and pulled out a small hide pouch from beneath it. Glancing quickly over his shoulder to make sure he was not being observed, he stuck it inside his shirt, letting it ride on his belt. Then he picked up a rock and carried it to his father's grave.

Most of the afternoon had passed by the time the bodies were laid to rest, so they decided to make camp there for the night. "If that's all right with you, boy," Frank said. "If you feel a mite nervous about staying here . . . I mean, if it don't set too well with your daddy being in the ground and all . . ."

"It don't bother me," Jim interrupted. "I ain't got nuthin' to fear from Pa—alive or dead. It's the damn Injuns I'm worried about."

"Good, then—'cause we got good water here and grass for the horses and wood handy for a fire. You don't have to worry about the Injuns, boy. They've done their work here. There ain't nuthin' here they want. Buck, let's get the packs offen them horses."

Buck looked at the boy, then back at Frank. "Why in thunder didn't we take the packs off when we first got here, if you was aiming to make camp, 'stead of letting the dang horses stand around toting 'em all day?"

"Dammit, 'cause I didn't know we was gonna take all day to put them two under the ground. Why didn't you think about taking the packs off?" He started toward the waiting horses.

Buck dutifully followed along after him. " 'Cause you was the one giving all the orders—like you was the *booshway* of this dang outfit."

"Is that a fact? Well, I reckon if we had to wait for you to decide on what we oughta do, we'd still be working for the Rocky Mountain Fur Company!"

"So now it was your idea to be free trappers!"

Jim could not help but smile. The two partners argued all the way over to where the horses were standing.

When they were all settled in for the night, and had had a supper of coffee, beans, and salt pork, the three sat around the fire to let the grub settle. Frank cut a chew off of a plug of tobacco and passed it to Buck. Buck helped himself, then before passing it back, asked Jim, "Have you took up the habit yet?"

Jim curled his upper lip. "No, I ain't. I tried it. Pa give me some once. It makes me sick."

Buck chuckled. "You ain't supposed to swallow it." He paused a few moments while he worked his chew up to a spit. Then he shot a brown stream into the red coals of the fire. It was followed almost simultaneously by a stream from Frank. "I expect, if you stay out here very long, you'll more'n likely learn to chew. They ain't no women, so tabacky is the next best thing to a tit to chew on."

"Well, I reckon I got time before I have to think about that," Jim replied.

Frank lay back, propped on his saddle, studying the boy while he talked to Buck. The kid had a lot of gumption. Watching him the past three days, Frank could tell he had the right kind of sand to make it in the mountains. He certainly wasn't afraid of work. He damn near picked up everything Buck knew about trapping beaver in two days. *'Course, it'll take considerable more time to learn half of what I know.* He thought about it for a while, then interrupted their conversation. "Boy, what have you got your mind set on doing now? Going home?"

Jim didn't answer right away. He thought a few moments about the situation he was in. "I'm obliged to go back to St. Louis and tell my ma and my brother about Pa." He was quiet a moment, then, "I reckon I kinda like trapping beaver, and there's something about the mountains that kinda gets under my hide. I don't know, but before I do anything else, I need to go see my ma."

Frank nodded, understanding. "That's what you oughta do, then. But I don't reckon you got any notion 'bout how you're gonna get to St. Louis, have you?" He didn't wait for an answer. "From what I've seen, your estate consists of three shovels and them ragged clothes you got on." He smiled at the bewildered expression on the boy's face. "I'll tell you what. Now this is all subject to Buck's okay, understand. You can ride with me and Buck till rendezvous, helping out as campkeeper and with the trapping. What plews you trap is yours to keep. That'll give you a month, and that should make you enough plews to buy you a passage downriver on the boat. How's that sound?"

Jim didn't have to give it a lot of thought. "I reckon it sounds fine to me."

"Buck?" Frank turned to his partner.

"Well, I was wondering if I had a say-so in this little contract you and the boy drawed up." He spit in the fire and laughed. "Why, shore, it's all right with me."

"It's done, then," Frank said and grinned broadly at the boy. "And maybe we can fix you up with some buckskins before them rags drop off ya. Might even be able to find you a possibles bag so's you don't have to carry that pouch under your shirt."

Jim flushed. He was glad it was dark so the two trappers couldn't see the red hue that had washed over his face. There was a long silence, punctuated only by the wry grins that adorned the craggy faces of the two trapper partners. Finally Jim responded.

"I reckon I wasn't as slick as I thought. But that little bit of dust is all I've got to show for almost a year of hard work, and I aim to take it to my ma." He hesitated, waiting to see if there were any objections. When there was no comment from Buck or Frank, he reconsidered. "But I guess it's only fair to pay my way if I'm gonna hook up with you."

Buck grunted as Frank said, "No need fer that, boy. You keep your little pouch. Take it home to your ma, like you said. I expect she'll need it, and more besides. Like I said, you can pay your way trappin', same as me and Buck." Buck spit into the fire to make it official. Frank continued, "But you got the right idea about keeping it quiet, and when we get to rendezvous, you best keep it hid fer shore."

It was settled, then. Frank and Buck took on a new partner, if only for a month. The boy was grateful, and wise enough to know that there might not be many of that wild breed that trapped the Rocky Mountains who would be as honest. He fully realized that if they'd had any notions about his little sack of gold dust, it would have been a simple thing to dig a third grave and nobody would have ever been the wiser. He was thankful and considered himself lucky to have crossed trails with Buck and Frank. Still, he didn't get much sleep that night, and every time a limb popped in the fire, he couldn't help but snap his eyes open.

Chapter 2

Julia Tracey stood in the doorway of the modest cottage set back a few dozen yards from the dusty road that led from Milltown to St. Louis. It was not a well-traveled road, but a winding, rutted trace that ran no farther than a mile past her house, ending in a small scattering of hovels around a gristmill. The mill had long since shut down, but the settlement had acquired the unofficial name of Milltown.

It was unusual to see anyone on the road in the early afternoon, most of the traffic consisting of the few souls from Milltown who traveled by foot to work in the city, leaving early in the morning and returning late in the evening. For that reason, Julia Tracey was curious about the fancy rig with the shiny hubs and leather upholstered seat, pulled by two sleek black horses, that had just come into view, a quarter of a mile up the road.

She knew of only one such rig, and that one belonged to Mr. Hamilton Blunt. As the carriage came closer, her curiosity was stirred, and she wondered if the owner of Blunt Brothers Freight was in fact paying her another visit. If so, it would be the second time he had driven out from town this week. Two days before he had stopped in to visit her, saying that he just wanted to see if she was getting along all right, what with her husband gone these many months.

She had assured him that she was getting along as well as could be expected, with her elder son, Cameron, bringing home his pay every week. Though only seventeen, he had taken the responsibility for providing for her until his father returned. He was quite proud of his ability to do so, and she was quick to express her appreciation to Mr. Blunt for giving her son a job. It had been a most pleasant visit from the owner of the freight company. Hamilton Blunt had a reputation as a charmer when it came to the ladies, and Julia found him to be courteous and certainly attentive. She also found it surprisingly considerate that he concerned himself with her welfare, for she knew that he must be an extremely busy man. For that reason, she was surprised to see him driving down her way again.

Perhaps he was not coming to her house and would drive on past, toward Milltown. Just in case, she removed her apron and took a hurried peek at herself in the mirror, smoothing her hair and giving each cheek a little pinch. Then she picked up a ball of yarn she had been working on and seated herself at the table, facing the open door.

In a few minutes' time, she saw the horses reach the hitching post in front of the house. She could now see the imposing figure of Hamilton Blunt as he looped the reins around the side handle of the seat and stepped down. She sat watching the tall, almost regal figure as he paused before the carriage, casually surveying the humble cottage. When he started toward the door, she got up from her chair and went to meet him.

"Mr. Blunt, how nice to see you again, sir. What brings you out here again so soon?"

"Ah, Mrs. Tracey," he said, doffing his wide-brimmed black hat. His generous smile reflected his pleasure in seeing her. Then, as quickly as his broad smile had flashed, he turned it off and assumed a most serious countenance. "I'm afraid it is my sad duty to be the bearer of bad news. Your son—"

"Cameron?" she interrupted, her pleasant smile fading to a concerned frown.

"Yes, Cameron." He reached out and placed his hand on her arm. "I'm sorry to have to be the one to bring you bad news, but I didn't want you to hear it from someone else." He could feel her body stiffen. "Cameron's met with an accident." She inhaled sharply, almost gasping. "It happened at work. It couldn't be helped."

"How bad . . . is he all right?" she stammered, pressing both hands over her mouth to suppress her anxiety.

"I'm afraid he's dead."

She would have fallen had he not been quick to grab her by the shoulders to support her. She could make no sound at first, staring at him with eyes wide in shock, unable to believe what she had just heard. When he nodded his head, confirming the truth of what he'd said, she sobbed uncontrollably. He pulled her close to his chest, holding her tight to his body.

While she cried out her anguish, he consoled her. And when she was in control enough to listen, he told her how her son had been killed. It was a freakish accident, he explained. Cameron had been helping to load several large freight wagons. "One of the mule teams bolted, frightened by something—I don't know what. Cameron couldn't jump out of the way in time, and he was struck down." He had to pause when she swooned again in grief. After a few more minutes, during which time Blunt continued to hold her close and stroke her hair with his hand, she became calm once more. He continued, "You should know that I'm pretty sure it happened so fast that he never suffered. It was over so quick, nobody could help him." He continued to stroke her hair and the back of her neck. "Cameron was a good worker, a smart boy. I had great plans for that boy."

When Julia had recovered sufficiently, she poked up the fire in the kitchen stove and put some coffee on to boil. Then she sat down at the table with Hamilton Blunt, appreciative for his visit, despite the tragic news he brought. She would never have guessed from the reports of John and Cameron that Hamilton Blunt could be so compassionate and considerate.

Blunt went on to explain that he had taken the responsibility to have Cameron's body transported to the undertaker, thinking it more kind to do that than to arrive at her house with the body of her dead son. When she registered mild alarm, he was quick to assure her that he would pay all the funeral expenses, including burial in the church cemetery next to his own family plot. She was almost overwhelmed by his generosity. When she expressed concern over how she could ever repay him, he insisted that she should let him worry about that.

"When my husband returns, perhaps he will have been fortunate enough that we will be able to repay your generosity." Then, thinking about the circumstances that had prompted John to leave Blunt Brothers, she added, "I hope you hold no ill will against my husband for leaving your employ."

"Not at all, Mrs. Tracey—may I call you Julia?" She nodded. "Why, I greatly admire his courage. It takes a great deal of ambition to risk the hazards of that savage part of the world." He patted her hand and held it as he went on. "If John is lucky and finds his fortune, and if he wants to repay me when he comes home, why, that'll be fine too. But I want you to know that it isn't necessary."

She could not believe his generosity. There was no way that she could have paid Cameron's funeral expenses. Then the thought struck her—without Cameron's wages, how would she live? Studying her face as closely as he had been, he must have guessed the thought that had caused her expression of sudden distress.

Still holding her hand, he said, "I don't want you to worry about a thing. You hear?" He gave her hand a little squeeze. "I've already taken the liberty to set up an account for you at Trotter's General Store. You can get whatever you need, whenever you need it. He'll send me the bill."

At first she was speechless. When she could find words, she exclaimed, "Mr. Blunt . . ."

"Hamilton," he interrupted.

She flushed. "Hamilton. I can't ask you to do that."

"It's already done. No need to trouble your pretty head about it."

"I don't know what to think. I declare, you must be an angel, right here on earth."

He squeezed her hand again.

Two months had passed since the interment of her son. The little cottage on the Milltown road had begun to close in around her as she spent the lonely nights wondering if she could stand it until John and young Jim returned from the West. The days were not so bad, for she found any number of ways to busy herself. But the nighttime—from the early-evening hours when Cameron used to come heavy-footed through the door, tired and hungry, until she finally found the solitude of sleep—was the hardest time.

The only person she could count as a friend was Nettie Bowen, whose husband, Travis, had worked in the freight yard with John. But she only saw Nettie once or twice a week, when she would make the two-mile walk to Trotter's Store. Nettie and Travis lived in a little white house about a hundred yards short of the store.

Travis had acted a little peculiar when Julia asked about Cameron's accident. He plainly had no desire to talk about it. When Julia pressed for details, Travis explained that he was not in the freight yard when it happened. In fact, no one was in the yard but Tyler Blunt, the youngest of the three Blunt brothers. Travis insisted that he didn't know any more about the accident than she did. He sought to avoid any discussion about it, and after the funeral it seemed that he even avoided her. She thought his behavior strange, but then, Travis Bowen was a somewhat peculiar man anyway.

Hamilton Blunt's visits became more frequent, a fact that surprised Julia, for she had expected to see very little of him after his magnanimous gestures. He would show up at odd times during the week, usually with a gift of some kind. She protested that he need not waste his time checking on her, but he insisted that he needed to satisfy himself that she was all right. He often expressed his concern about the fact that she was living alone. She assured him that while it was painfully lonesome, she would manage, and that her husband and younger son would soon return.

Then one hot July day, she received another visit from Hamilton Blunt. His sober expression when she answered his knock immediately alarmed her. It was the same expression he had worn when he came to tell her about Cameron.

"Julia, I don't know how to tell you this," he started. Knowing it was tragic news, she clutched her hands to her chest. He shook his head soberly. "It seems that I'm destined to be the bearer of sad tidings for you."

"What is it?" she pressed. "Is it John?"

He nodded gravely. "I'm afraid so. One of the trappers came in from the Wind River country yesterday." He took her hands in his. "Julia, John's been killed—the boy, too."

"Jim! Oh, no!" she cried. "There must be some mistake!"

"I'm afraid not, Julia. We've known this trapper for a long time. He's completely reliable, and he knew your husband—called him by name, John Tracey. He said John and the boy were panning for gold on a little creek in the mountains. They were attacked by Blackfoot Indians. He and the boy were both killed. The trapper saw the bodies himself."

Julia was devastated. Her entire family had been destroyed, all within a two-month period. Suddenly her limbs would not support her, and she started to swoon. Blunt helped her to a chair and dipped a glass of water from the bucket for her. She took a few sips and then pushed it away. Overcome with grief, she bowed her head and sobbed. All the while, Hamilton stood over her, stroking her shoulders and back.

"Julia, I can't stand to see you suffer like this." He reached down and gently lifted her chin so she could look at him. "I want you to come and live in my house. I won't take no for an answer. It's not good for you to be alone at a time like this." She looked at him, bewildered, unable to think beyond her sorrow. He persisted. "Come on, get what things you need. You're coming home with me right away. I'll send someone back to get the rest of your things tomorrow."

* * *

Morgan Blunt leaned back in his chair until it rested against the wall and propped his feet on the corner of the wide walnut desk. He took a long pull on his cigar and exhaled a dense blue cloud that rolled across the desk toward his younger brother. Tyler grinned, showing teeth already yellowed from chewing tobacco almost constantly from the time he was twelve. He sat down on the corner of the desk and helped himself to one of the dark-leafed cigars from the ornately embossed cedar box. Spitting his plug into the brass spittoon, he lit the cigar from a candle on the desk. He puffed furiously in an effort to generate more smoke than his brother. When the door opened, neither brother bothered to take notice.

"Get your behind off my desk," Hamilton Blunt ordered in a gruff, scolding tone. Tyler, grin still in place, took his time getting to his feet. Hamilton took one hand and raked Morgan's feet off of the desk. "And keep those damn dirty boots off my desk. I swear, you two aren't fit to live indoors." He sank down heavily in his leather armchair.

Morgan leered and righted his chair. "I swear, brother, what are you in such a rank mood for? You ought to be a happy man. Right, Tyler?" He winked at his younger brother, who widened his grin in reply. "You got what you want, don't you? Your sweet little bird's in the nest."

"That's a fact," Tyler chimed in. "She's a right pretty little thing too. If she was younger, I might wanna try some of that myself."

"You watch your mouth," Hamilton warned. He

would stand for just so much of his brothers' insolence—and they knew it. There was no question who gave the orders in the family. Hamilton had always been the driving force, as well as the brains, behind the fortune he had amassed for the family. But they also knew he would have to stand their chiding because they were his brothers—and, more importantly—they knew too much about the dealings of Blunt Brothers Freight Company.

"That's right, Tyler," Morgan said. "Watch your mouth. Show a little respect for a widow in mourning."

Hamilton ignored the sarcastic tone. "Are you sure LaPorte took care of that business?"

Morgan smiled. "I'm sure." He picked up a sack that had been lying beside his chair. Reaching in, he pulled out a couple of grisly strips of flesh, a shock of thick hair attached to each.

"Goddamn, Morgan, put those damn things away!" Hamilton blurted out. "Don't ever bring things like that in my office."

Morgan laughed. Tyler giggled delightedly. "Lemme see 'em, Morg." Morgan dropped them back in the sack and threw it across the desk to his younger brother. Tyler dove into the sack like a child with a bag of candy.

Hamilton took a moment to watch his youngest brother, shaking his head in disgust. Then he turned his attention back to Morgan. "You're sure LaPorte got the right ones? Because I've already told her they're dead."

In a serious tone, Morgan replied, "Yeah, I'm sure.

LaPorte's seen John Tracey before, working in the freight yard. He took his Injuns up there and found his little gold mine. Those scalps are the receipts for the money I paid him. Don't worry, your little bird is a genuine widow." Morgan had no qualms about committing murder. He had done it before, but then it was to eliminate competition. He was more concerned with Hamilton's obsession for the wife of one of his employees. Morgan wondered how long this passion would last—probably no longer than it had with his first wife. *Poor Constance,* he thought, with no earnest compassion for his brother's late wife. *She made the mistake of getting fat.* He almost laughed when he thought of the unfortunate woman's last days—so ill and not knowing why. She finally succumbed, almost two years to the day before Hamilton brought Julia Tracey to his house.

If there was a weakness in Hamilton Blunt, it was his obsession for certain women. Not content to satisfy his desires with the likes of Madge Pauley—who worked as a barmaid and was always ready to perform a service for a modest fee—Hamilton cast his roving eye on the rather handsome features of Julia Tracey. Once that happened, nothing would stop him from gaining his prize.

Hamilton considered Morgan's answer for a moment, then nodded his head, satisfied. "I want to be damn sure there were no mistakes." He shifted his gaze to Tyler. "Like that first job."

Tyler, busy amusing himself with the scalps until then, dropped the grisly trophies back in the sack and took issue with his brother's barb. "What do you mean? You said that little bastard should have an accident. Well, he damn sure had an accident, didn't he?"

Hamilton looked at him with the patient look of a man accustomed to dealing with idiots. His young brother was wild, with a generous dose of evil, but noticeably lacking in brains. "He was supposed to look like a wagon ran him down. The way you bashed his head in with that axe had the undertaker asking a helluva lot of questions—like why there were no wheel marks on his body."

Tyler shrugged his shoulders impatiently. He had already been scolded for this. He thought it unfair to bring it up again. "Dammit, you wanted him dead. Well, he's dead—and ain't nobody said nothing about it."

"Are you sure Travis Bowen didn't see anything?"

Tyler, irritated by his brother's worrying, shot back, "I told you he didn't. Hell, I sent him to change a team of mules. He didn't see nothing." He paused, then added, "He better not have, if he knows what's good for him."

Chapter 3

Jim moved silently through a thicket of chokecherry bushes that had been picked clean of their fruit by birds—a fact that held no interest for him at that moment. His attention was focused on the young black-tailed deer drinking at the edge of the creek. Carefully placing one foot before the other, he moved through the bushes without shaking a leaf. Closer now, he stopped to test the wind to make sure it had not changed on him. Satisfied that he was still downwind of the animal, he resumed stalking it, making his way slowly down the bank, using a stand of willows as a screen. He had managed to close within twenty-five yards of the deer when the animal sensed the danger. It suddenly lifted its head up from the water and snorted. Jim knew it would bolt within seconds. He would have no better opportunity for a shot. He slowly raised the pistol and took careful aim. The deer took two nervous steps backward, jerking its head from side to side, seeking to locate the danger it sensed.

The pistol cracked and emitted a puff of smoke that sent the deer bounding over the low brush, the pistol ball sailing harmlessly over its head. Frustrated to the point of anger, Jim threw the pistol at the deer as it disappeared into the trees on the far side of the creek. "Damn you!" the boy cursed at the offending firearm. "I got a good mind to leave the damn thing in the bushes. Can't hit anything with a damn pistol unless it's setting on the end of the barrel."

In spite of his frustration, he dutifully searched through the low shrubs until he found the pistol. It belonged to Buck, otherwise he might not have bothered. "I could have throwed my knife and had a better chance of hitting him," he mumbled as he cleaned the dirt off the weapon. He had lived to regret pushing his Pa's mule down that slope—for more reasons than one. But the reason that rankled him this day was the fact that he had lost his rifle when he and the mule parted company.

Without realizing it, he was developing skills that would prolong his life in the mountains—and in such a short time that Buck and Frank often commented on it when the boy wasn't around. Jim didn't realize that not many men, Indians included, could have sneaked up to within twenty-five yards of that deer to even consider trying a shot with a pistol.

With a rifle, he could have easily killed the deer and provided meat for the camp. Buck and Frank hunted, and never failed to provide plenty to eat. But it was important to the boy to contribute to the food stores as well. More than that, it was in his nature to hunt, and he decided on that day that he was going to find himself a more accurate weapon than Buck's pistol. He knew it was out of the question to ask to use one of their rifles. A mountain man would as soon loan you an arm or a leg. Besides, this was still Blackfoot land. A trapper couldn't chance working his traps without his rifle. In fact, a mountain man looked upon his rifle as a more intimate partner than a wife. Both Buck and Frank carried Hawken rifles—percussion cap, not flintlocks—and Jim had often cast an envious eye upon the fine pieces with their octagonal barrels. "I'll just have to make me a bow," he announced and started back toward camp.

"I heard the crack of that pistol a while back," Frank said when the boy walked back into camp. He winked at Buck. "Where's the meat? Did you need some help toting it back to camp?"

"It was a buffalo—I was so hungry, I ate it on the spot."

Frank snorted a laugh. "You been spending too much time with Buck. Your lies are getting bigger ever' day."

Jim sat down by the fire and helped himself to a cup of coffee from the kettle nestled in the coals. After he was settled, he pulled the pistol from his belt and examined it. "I can't get close enough to anything to hit it with this thing." He reached out to return it to Buck.

Buck pushed it away. "You keep it on you. It's better than nuthin' if a Blackfoot sneaks up on you."

Jim stuck it back in his belt. He sat there drinking his coffee, thinking for a long time. No one spoke in the drowsy dusk of the evening, the only sound the low sizzle of a burning limb. After a while, Jim decided what he was going to do. "I'm gonna make me an Injun bow," he announced.

His statement piqued Frank's interest. "That right? You ever shoot a bow?"

"Nope."

"How do you know you can hit anything with a bow any more than you can with that pistol?"

"I reckon I can learn. Injuns can shoot pretty dang good with 'em. If they can, I can." Jim wasn't just making big talk. He sincerely figured he could do most anything he made up his mind to.

"You ever make one?"

"Nope, that's the part that's got me worried a little bit."

Frank launched a long brown tobacco stream into the fire, barely missing the coffee kettle. "Well, I have. A Crow by the name of Little Bull showed me how to make a bow, and the arrows too, at rendezvous on the Snake River. Musta been four year ago." He spat again. "Trouble was, I never could hit nuthin' with the damn thing."

"I remember you dang near hit Ollie Finster with it," Buck chimed in. " 'Course, you claimed you was trying to hit a cook pot 'bout ten yards to the left of where Ollie was settin'." The recollection of it caused Buck to throw his head back and laugh. "Ol' Ollie was set on whuppin' your ass. Said you was tryin' to murder him. You was doin' some mighty fast talking that day to cool ol' Ollie down."

"Ollie was old, but he was tough as a pine knot," Frank added, thoughtfully.

Jim's interest had been sparked. "Will you help me make one?"

"I reckon."

When they split up the following morning to work the traps, Frank told the boy to keep an eye out for a good young ash, as this was the wood of choice for a stout bow. Buck allowed as how he would keep an eye peeled as well. It was close to the time when they would pack up and head for the Green River, where the rendezvous was to be held that summer. Though they were still trapping a few streams, they were not finding prime plews. Summer fur wouldn't bring as much as winter pelts. For that reason, much of their time was spent scouting out likely spots to trap in the late fall and the following spring. Consequently, Buck and Frank were not adverse to spending a little time hunting for the proper wood for the boy's bow.

When the perfect piece of mountain ash was found, Frank showed Jim how to fashion a bow about four feet in length. He backed it with tough strips of buffalo sinew to give it strength, and he wrapped strips of hide around the middle for a handle. He used some more sinew to make the bowstring. Jim was pleased with the result. The hardest part, he found, was making the arrows. Frank used the same ash wood for them. He said the Crows used a piece of horn with a hole in it to fashion a smooth, uniform shaft. The slender limbs were forced through the hole, leaving a round, straight shaft. They had a piece of horn, so Frank bored a hole in it with his knife until it appeared to be about the right size. It was crude, but the finished product was not that bad, considering the artisans. Feathers were tied in slits on one end of the shaft to make the arrow spin, and a chiseled quartzlike stone provided the arrowhead.

When it was done, Frank held it up for Buck and the boy to see. He was tolerably pleased with the finished product. "Well, boy, there she is. I ain't making but one. You seen how to do it, you can make the rest yourself."

For the rest of the days they remained in the Sweetwater country, until they set out for rendezvous, Jim worked on his arrows. As soon as he had made four, he began experimenting with his new weapon, practicing until darkness made it too difficult to recover the arrows. Just as with a rifle, Jim seemed to have a natural feel for the bow, and he soon became expert enough to hunt with it. He came to almost prefer it to a rifle because its silence allowed him to take one animal without scaring off the one next to it. Watching him stalk a deer, Buck was fairly astonished when Jim made a kill shot from a distance of fifty yards. He exclaimed to Frank that night, "Maybe we better git ourselves a dang bow."

"Maybe so," Frank answered, laughing, "but I don't wanna wait for an Injun to git inside fifty yards before I light up his behind."

Despite the fact that he had recently lost his father, it was a good time for Jim. If ever a boy knew for sure where his destiny lay, it was Jim Tracey. The high mountains were where he belonged—of that he was certain. Trapping with Buck and Frank, he had almost forgotten his self-imposed obligation to return to St. Louis when the day came to leave for rendezvous.

Jim's first sight of rendezvous was overwhelming. To the boy, it looked to involve as many folks as the city of St. Louis. It was one huge, sprawling cauldron of redmen and white, trappers and savages, traders and merchants, even some missionaries. In fact, there were several thousand Indians, their tipis spread along the river, and at least two hundred trappers. Everywhere he looked, there were solemn-faced warriors; Indian maidens with shy, searching eyes; woolly mountain men too long in the hills; horses, dogs—it was one giant circus.

They rode through the encampment until Buck and Frank spotted some of their old companions from the Rocky Mountain Fur Company. After a round of hooting and hollering, backslapping and handshaking, they set up camp alongside their former partners in the trapping business. These were all company men, working for Jim Bridger just as Buck and Frank once had. It was much like a great family reunion. Jim was swept up in the spectacle of it all.

This was the time for drinking whiskey and blowing off steam that had built up over the long winter and spring. But it was also a time to sell plews, trade horses, buy new supplies, and catch up on the news—who had gone under, who had quit and gone back East. It was a time to find out what value a man's year of hard labor was worth after the many hours spent wading in freezing-cold streams up to his waist, while trying to keep an eye out for bloodthirsty braves.

On the second day after their arrival at rendezvous, Jim went with Buck and Frank to negotiate the sale of their harvest. His modest pack of plews seemed skimpy when compared to those of his two partners, but it wasn't a bad showing for a greenhorn with only a month's trapping experience. And it would earn enough to buy him some buckskins and a pair of moccasins to replace his worn-out boots.

Buck introduced him to Bill Sublette, who had brought a load of supplies all the way from St. Louis. "Bill, this here young man is working with me and Frank. He's got some plews to sell."

Jim had no idea what his pelts were worth. He was thrilled to get any amount for them. Buck and Frank, on the other hand, were somewhat disappointed. Prime pelts had gone for as much as six dollars the year before. Now Sublette was offering only five for winter fur, four for summer—and this in spite of the fact that it had been a bad year for beaver. Most of the trappers had not been as fortunate as the two partners. This accounted for the subdued tone of the camp this year, Frank told him. The boys didn't have much left over after buying supplies for the coming year. There was still some drinking and wild carrying-on, but not like in years past. Still, it was wild enough to suit young Jim, and the party never stopped. All night long the loud talk went on, punctuated periodically by gunshots and occasional drunken brawls.

One day Buck's friend and former employer, Jim

Bridger, decided it was time to end his many years as a bachelor, and he took the daughter of a Flathead chief as a wife. Buck decided to celebrate this occasion properly by drinking all the whiskey in camp. He might have done it, too, if Frank had not been matching him drink for drink until sometime before daylight when Frank slid under the table, dead to the world. When Jim came into the big tent that had been set up as a saloon, Buck was standing in the center, holding on to the tent pole with one hand and an empty jug with the other. Jim looked around him. Bodies were strewn everywhere in various positions. It looked for all the world like the aftermath of a massacre. Buck stared at the boy with eyes glazed as if he had been staring into the sun. It was apparent that he did not recognize Jim.

"You 'bout ready to get some coffee?" Jim asked, not sure if Buck could actually hear him or not. His eyes were open, but he continued to stare right through Jim. "Come on, Buck. I made a pot of coffee and I cooked some side meat." Buck said nothing, but continued to stare. "Where's Frank?" As soon as he said it, he noticed Frank's body under the table. He looked back at Buck, waiting for some response. Buck's eyes flickered, the only indication that he was alive, then the contents of his stomach spilled out of his mouth and down the front of his shirt. That was enough for Jim. He turned and left the tent.

It was well after sunup when the two trappers came staggering back to camp, both soaked to the skin. Ben Broadhurst, who owned the makeshift saloon, had hired a couple of trappers to carry all the drunks out and throw them in the river. Most of them sobered up enough to wade out of the water. A few were swept downstream, where they were pulled from the current by some of the Indian women who were collecting water for cooking. Buck, since he was the only one on his feet, was left where he stood. But after Frank was carried out, he decided to leave too—a decision probably made with the only brain cell that hadn't been pickled. He was on his way back to the camp when he fell in the river. He was one of the bodies fished out downstream by the Flathead women—one of whom he proposed to during the rescue. It must have been tempting, for Buck must have presented a splendid picture of mature manhood at that point, but the lady declined. It wouldn't have worked out anyway. It turned out that she was the mother of the woman Jim Bridger took for a wife, and that would have made Buck Jim's father-in-law.

Buck was sick for two days. Frank was looking for some hair of the dog that bit him before sundown that very day. He kept trying to persuade Buck that a drink of whiskey was what he needed to settle his stomach down, but Buck couldn't stand the sight of the jug, heaving violently each time Frank held it under his nose.

"I swear, Buck, you must be gittin' where you can't handle it anymore."

"Hell," Buck groaned, "who was the last man standing?"

All during that second day after the party, Buck groaned and complained that he had gotten too old to participate in such tomfoolery. He allowed as how he never intended to take another drink as long as he lived. By the following day, he began to believe he was not going to die after all. That night, he bought another jug.

Jim Bridger's wedding celebration left Buck with a cloud of melancholy hanging over his head. He had cause to reflect on his wild and lonely life in the mountains and regretted the fact that he had never taken a wife for himself. Man was meant to have a mate, he reasoned, and his life was closer to the end than it was to the beginning. That kind of thinking can lead a man to do irrational things. And, when a jug of frontier whiskey is added to the mix, anything can happen.

Buck may have been content to drink away his sorrows and vomit up his melancholia, along with the contents of his stomach, the next morning, had it not been for the presence of an Indian woman. She was a fair-sized woman, by no means a savage beauty. But to Buck, in his advanced stage of intoxication, she was the fairest flower of the plains. The only problem, and one Buck considered minor, was that she was in the company of an evil-tempered trapper named Badeye MacPherson. Badeye was not the man's given name, of course. It was a naturally assigned moniker due to a failing eye that was covered by a black patch.

Frank noticed his partner's brooding as Buck continued to consume the contents of his jug, starting a fresh fire in his throat just as soon as the flames from the previous gulp abated. He followed Buck's stare across the large tent and saw where his focus rested. "Buck," he said, "I see trouble brewing. You might better get your mind on somethin' else." When Buck continued to stare without answering, Frank sighed and said, "I reckon you're gonna do it."

"I reckon I am," Buck replied and struggled to his feet. He reached out to steady himself on Frank's shoulder.

"I'll tote the pieces back to camp," Frank said.

"Obliged," Buck replied and shoved off, setting an unsteady course across the grass floor of the tent, toward the woman.

The Indian woman, a member of the Snake tribe, was seated on Badeye's lap, cheerfully pouring whiskey down his throat. She looked up quizzically as Buck approached, then smiled at him. It was indication enough for Buck that she had as much as said, "Howdy, handsome stranger. Please take me away from this one-eyed mountain goat."

Buck grabbed the woman by the arm and pulled her up from Badeye's lap. His senses dulled by alcohol, Badeye sat there for a moment before he brought his good eye to focus on Buck. When it finally registered in his mind, he bellowed, "Hey, what the hell do you think you're doin'?"

Buck stated simply, "I'm takin' the woman." He turned and started staggering back to Frank, towing the frightened woman in his wake.

"The hell you say!" Badeye roared and lunged to his feet. But he was a good deal drunker than he thought, having sat there drinking for several hours. He was too drunk to walk, in fact. Had he not stumbled into Buck and the woman, he would have surely gone down on his face. Having collided, the two woolly mountain men grappled drunkenly, each trying to throw the other to the ground. They would have both gone down, but for the woman holding both of them up.

There was a temporary pause in the drinking by the others around as everyone watched the comical performance of the two struggling trappers, who looked more like two grizzlies performing a mating ritual. What the fight lacked in fury, it made up for in sound. Both combatants grunted and strained, cursed and screeched—added to the high-pitched scolding from the woman—until a sizable crowd from outside was attracted to the contest.

"To the death!" Badeye exclaimed dramatically as the two parted for a new start, his knees wobbling uncertainly.

"To the death!" Buck echoed and swung his fist, trying to land a punch on Badeye's jaw.

The blow missed Badeye but landed flush on the mouth of the Indian woman. There was not much force behind it, but enough to make her take a step backward and blink.

"Beg your pardon, ma'am," Buck offered as politely as he could.

She put her hand to her lip and wiped the blood away. The blood served to infuriate her, and she hauled off and slapped Buck on the side of his head, sending him reeling across the tent and crashing into a table of card players. They cleared out of the way just in time to avoid becoming part of the show when Badeye dived on top of Buck.

On the floor now, the two struggled and wrestled for advantage. First Buck was on top, then Badeye. The Indian woman found a broom and proceeded to administer a steady drumbeat on whichever body was on top. And so it went, until everybody there wearied of the contest, especially the two principals. Finally Buck prevailed, being considerably bigger than Badeye. He managed to pin Badeye with his arms underneath him, holding him there by his knees. With one forearm pressing Badeye's neck to the floor, Buck drew his skinning knife with his other hand. "Now, by God," he said, while panting for breath.

That was when Frank stepped in. Up to that point, no one had been hurt, except for the woman, who had a split lip. Frank was sober enough to know that Buck would not ordinarily want to do any real harm to Badeye. Besides that, someone had told him during the fight that the woman was Badeye's wife, and he knew Buck wasn't aware of that. "Hold on a minute, partner," Frank said and grabbed Buck's wrist.

Buck jerked his head around, his face a mask of fury until he saw it was Frank. Then he grinned and said, "I'm gonna take the bastard's scalp." The statement caused a couple of Snake warriors seated at the edge of the tent to start "Ki-yi-ing."

"Buck, you don't wanna do that," Frank insisted. "That would put a terrible hardship on ol' Badeye. Besides, that there woman you're fightin' over is Badeye's wife."

"It is?" Buck seemed genuinely astonished.

"It is," Frank confirmed. "Looks to me like you got the best of it, anyway. You don't need to scalp him." He looked down at Badeye. "You've had enough, ain't you, Badeye?" Badeye, his one good eyeball frozen on the gleaming knife blade only inches from his forehead, nodded vigorously. "See there, Buck?" Frank went on. "It's all over. You can let him up."

Buck was uncertain. He had the upper hand and he was a little reluctant to relinquish it. But it was true that he was plum wore out from the exertion. "All right," he said finally. "Maybe I won't take his scalp." He jerked his wrist out of Frank's grasp and held the knife close under Badeye's nose, turning the blade back and forth, taunting him. He wanted some trophy for his victory, and if he couldn't take the scalp, he would take something else of importance. "You can keep your mangy scalp, but I'm taking this." He jerked the eye patch off Badeye's head and held it up, twirling it in the air. Badeye was too exhausted to protest. After some cajoling, Buck was persuaded to get off of Badeye, and Frank led him outside the tent, where they found Jim waiting for them.

"What was all the ruckus?" Jim asked.

"Nothing much. Buck was just trying to get married again."

Frank helped a stumbling, muttering Buck remain upright while they headed for their camp. When they walked by the river, Frank pushed Buck in.

Just as it had the time before, the morning sun

found Buck in a heap of misery. He claimed to be even sicker this time, and before the morning was many hours old, he had thrown up several times. Jim made him some strong coffee, and by the time the sun was halfway across the river valley, he was able to sit up and eat some boiled deer meat. When Frank returned from a little parley with Bill Sublette, Buck was resting on his saddle, examining his trophy.

"When you gonna give that thing back to Badeye? I seen him walking around with a rag tied around his head." Frank helped himself to a cup of coffee and found a place to sit.

Buck continued to study the eye patch as if it had some mystical power. "I don't know that I will," he finally answered. "Did you say he was walkin' around?" Frank nodded. "Damn," Buck muttered. His attention back on the eye patch, he said, "You know, Frank, I know I was mighty drunk, and I don't remember a helluva lot about last night. But one thing I do remember—when I took this here eye patch offen Badeye, there was a bright blue eyeball staring right at me." When Frank showed no special interest in this profound discovery, Buck expounded. "I'm tellin' you the truth! There wasn't no empty hole there, like that half-breed over there at Laramie last year. You know, the one got his eye gouged out by that big feller, LaPorte?"

Frank glanced up when he realized Buck was waiting for some reaction to his statement. "Well, what about it?"

"I been thinkin'. Maybe ol' Badeye's bad eye ain't bad a'tall."

"Thunderation, Buck, what the hell would he wear the damn patch for if his eye was good? I swear, sometimes I think that damn whiskey's done pickled your brain."

Buck was not easily dissuaded. "Maybe ol' Badeye's smarter than you think. Maybe he's been saving that one eye, keeping the sun out of it, protecting it, in case the other one goes bad."

"Wagh," Frank bellowed. He looked at Jim and shook his head, laughing. "I swear, Buck, even this here fourteen-year-old young'un knows better than that. Give the damn patch back to the man."

Buck scratched his beard thoughtfully. "I think I'll keep her a while yet. It might be a right smart thing to save one of my eyes with this thing." He placed the patch over his left eye and tied the string behind his head.

Much to Frank's disgust, Buck wore the eye patch for the rest of the day before finally admitting that it restricted his eyesight too severely. That evening he sent Jim to return his trophy. There was one positive result from Buck's drinking sprees—Jim resolved to never take up the evil habit. He didn't care for the prospect of the gut-wrenching sickness that Buck seemed doomed to suffer time and time again.

When all the trading was finally done, the rendezvous began to break up. There were still several hundred people camped by the river when Jim came to his two friends to tell them he was leaving.

"I reckon I'm gonna' go back East to see my ma. Mr. Sublette said I could go with him to help with the mules." He looked fondly at the two old trappers. "I reckon you know I'm much obliged to you for letting me tag along with you. I hope to see you again someday."

"Why, shore you will, boy," Buck said. "We can always use a partner as smart as you are. Can't we, Frank?"

"That's a fact. Take care of yourself, boy, and if you get back out this way, give us a holler."

"I will," he said and turned away, hurrying to join Sublette's party.

Chapter 4

It was late summer by the time Jim arrived in St. Louis. He had been gone a year, but so many things had happened that it seemed like much longer. During that year, St. Louis had changed into a bustling, boisterous town, still growing monthly. But it had not kept pace with the boy of fourteen who had seen things that most boys his age never see. He had trapped the icy mountain streams and lived under the stars. And he would never be the same, content no longer to be a part of the busy, noisy city that he had returned to.

Although he now felt hemmed in by the congestion of the town, he knew where his responsibilities lay, and he had resigned himself to staying here and helping his brother provide for their mother. Since his father was dead, Cameron was now the head of the family, but it was Jim's duty to help him. Maybe he would seek a job in the freight yard with Cameron. Perhaps, with the sack of gold dust he was bringing, he and Cameron could start a nest egg that might one day grow to enable them to acquire the farm his father had always dreamed of. His own dreams of snow-capped mountains, clear mountain streams, and forests teeming with every kind of critter imaginable would have to wait.

These were the thoughts that filled Jim's mind as he made his way down the dusty wagon trace toward the little settlement of Milltown. He had been walking for almost two hours when he rounded the curve a quarter of a mile above the house. He could see it now. At once, a feeling of dread descended upon his shoulders, and he pictured his mother's face when he told her of his father's death. It was going to be the hardest thing he ever had to do, harder even than burying his father. As much as he wanted to see his mother and brother, he wished now that he had stayed in the mountains. But that would have been even more cruel, letting them wonder what had happened to them. He had had no choice but to come home and take care of his mother.

Within a hundred yards of the house now, he strained to see if he might catch a glimpse of his mother. Cameron would be at work still. Cameron had been a bit lax in keeping up the outside of the place, he noticed. The little yard was filled with weeds, and the garden had grown knee-high in grass and thistle. This wasn't like Cameron. Maybe he had been working long hours and could not take care of the place properly. *Well, I'm home now. Together, we'll get things back in shape.*

Closing the last few yards, he jumped the ditch and started up the short path to the house. It was then that he suddenly sensed that things were not right. He could tell before reaching the door that there was no one home. The feeling was confirmed when he tried the latch and found it locked. He knocked on the door. "Ma," he called out several times, but there was no answer. Odd, he thought, to find the door locked. It was never locked, not even when his mother walked to the store. They had never bothered because it was a simple task to open a window and enter as you please. Then he realized that the windows were all closed. On a day as warm as this one, surely one or two would be open.

He entered through a side window near the chimney. As he had expected, the air was hot and stale inside. The windows had been closed up for some time, by the look of things. Standing in the center of the front room, he looked around him. Nothing seemed to be missing. The table, the chairs, the sideboard, the rug his mother had hooked from rags, all there as he remembered. But where was his mother? He ran his finger across the corner of the table, leaving a trail in the dust. "Ma?" he called out again.

He walked through the kitchen and opened the back door, looking out toward the well. Like the front yard, everything was overgrown with weeds. There was little doubt that his mother and brother had gone, but where? He entered the little room off of the kitchen where he and Cameron slept. From the dust on the bedstead and small chest, it was obvious that Cameron had not been there for some time. The straw pallet that had been Jim's bed was rolled up in a corner of the tiny room.

Finally he went into his mother and father's bedroom. The room was dark and musty, the air heavy with the scent of dust and moldy clothes. He opened a window to let some fresh air in. It didn't help. The room had been closed up for too long. Looking around, he discovered that his mother's things were gone. His father's were undisturbed.

Totally at a loss, he sat down on the bed and puzzled over his predicament. They had gone. That much was clear to him. Still, he thought, he could wait there just in case Cameron might show up, though he had a feeling he wouldn't. He glanced out the window. The sun was getting pretty low in the trees. It was too late to look for his family today, even if he knew where to look. The only person he could think of who might be able to help was his mother's friend Nettie Bowen. He decided to stay the night and go back up the road in the morning to the Bowens' place.

Finding nothing to eat in the house, he supped on some dried buffalo jerky from his pack. He still carried his bow that Frank had made, but in this civilization there was nothing to hunt. Jerky would do, he thought. Still, some strong black coffee would sure have tasted fine. There was a candle on the mantel over the fireplace, but he didn't bother to light it. The darkness suited him, and when the sun finally disappeared beyond the row of poplars behind the house, he unrolled his old pallet in the middle of the front room and went to sleep.

Accustomed to getting up before daybreak, he was somewhat surprised when he awoke to find the sun peeping through the front window. He half expected to find his mother there, but when he sat upright and looked around, he realized that he was still alone. He picked up his little pack of belongings and took one long look around the room before leaving. An object on the end of the mantel caught his eye, reminding him of something his father had repeated many times at the rough little cabin by their placer mine. *Dang, I wish I hadn't gone off and left my pipe.* Jim smiled when he recalled it. And there it was—right where his father had left it. Jim stepped over to the mantel and picked up the pipe. His father had loved that pipe. He had carved it from a çherrywood limb, and he always claimed that there wasn't a pipe made that smoked sweeter. Jim held the bowl up to his nose and sniffed the pungent aroma left by many hours of burning tobacco leaves. Then dropped it in his pocket and, taking one more quick glance around, went out the front door.

Retracing his steps of the day before, he walked back up the road toward Trotter's Store. It was still early when he approached the homely little brown shingled cottage with rose bushes framing the front door. He was only halfway up the path when the door opened and Nettie Bowen stood gazing at him, her eyes squinting as if to improve her focus.

"For goodness' sakes," she exclaimed. "Jim Tracey, is that you?"

"How do, Mrs. Bowen. It's me, all right."

"Sweet Jesus! We heard you was dead, you and your pa too. And here you are, big as life. Praise the Lord!"

Jim was totally confused. As far as he knew, no

one here could possibly know that his father had been killed. "No, ma'am, I ain't dead. I don't know who could have told you that."

Suddenly a frown crossed Nettie's face as a sobering thought came to her. "Your Pa—then he's all right too?"

Jim shook his head slowly and dropped his chin. "No, ma'am. Pa's dead."

There was almost a hint of relief on Nettie's face, which puzzled the boy. Her smile immediately returned. "Have you had any breakfast? You look like you ain't had nothing to eat in a week. I declare, I saw you walk by the house yesterday and I didn't even recognize you—dressed up like a wild Indian like that. Come on in the kitchen and I'll fix you some breakfast."

That sounded wonderful to Jim. But he said, "No, thank you, ma'am. I don't want to trouble you."

"Nonsense. Get yourself in this house. I bet you ain't had a decent meal since you and your pa set out for that wilderness." She stood back, holding the door open for him, and motioned him in.

Gratefully, Jim accepted. As hungry as he suddenly became when the prospect of eggs and hominy was suggested, he was still anxious to find out what had become of his family. "Mrs. Bowen, I went down to the house, and there's nobody there. Can you tell me where Ma and Cameron are?"

Turning a big iron skillet back and forth to spread the grease evenly, she cocked her head sharply and fixed him with a steady gaze. "You don't know about your mama, do you, son?" She set the skillet aside on the corner of the stove and sat down at the table facing him. "And nobody's told you about Cameron?" He shook his head no.

So, seated at the kitchen table, he listened, hardly able to believe what he was hearing. Nettie Bowen told him of his brother's accidental death in the freight yard and of Hamilton Blunt's generous gestures to help his mother. He listened in shocked silence as the numbing reality set in that he had lost his father and brother in that one tragic summer.

"Where's Ma?" was his one simple question when she paused.

"She's gone to stay at Hamilton Blunt's big house. Truth of the matter, I ain't seen her since Cameron's funeral. But Mr. Trotter told me that Hamilton Blunt drove down to your house and took her home with him." She got up to start his breakfast again. "You gonna be all right? I mean, if you feel like you wanna cry or something, there ain't no shame in it."

"I'm all right. I don't cry," he stated, staring unblinking at his folded hands on the table.

She broke four eggs into the skillet and stirred them up together. "Folks thought it was pretty decent of Mr. Blunt to take care of your ma, what with your pa getting killed—and Cameron—and you too, they thought."

"Yessum, I reckon." One thing still puzzled him, though. "Mrs. Bowen, how did they know my pa got killed? How could anybody know that?"

"I don't know. When I talked to your mama at Cameron's funeral, she didn't know much about it herself. I think she said some scout or buffalo hunter, somebody like that, brought the word back." She put on a bright smile for him. "Anyway, ain't she gonna be overjoyed when she sees you?"

A very confused and troubled young man left Nettie Bowen's house and set out for Hamilton Blunt's palatial estate on the hill overlooking the freight yard. It was a walk of about three miles, so Jim had time to do a lot of thinking. For the most part, he tried to sort out the puzzling events that had ended with his mother living in the house of his father's former employer. It was hard to accept the fact that Cameron was dead. Nettie Bowen had said that a loaded freight wagon ran him over. That was hard to believe—Cameron was an extremely careful young man. He'd be the last person Jim would figure to be the victim of such a freak accident.

Things looked busy at Blunt Brothers when Jim passed the office building and took the small winding road that led up the hill to the house. Hamilton Blunt had built a large white home that reflected his opulent tastes, with wide porches spanning the front and sides of the building. To Jim, it had always seemed like a great white castle hovering over the freight yard below. Blunt's wife had had very little to say about the design of the house, according to what Jim's father had told him. In fact, she only lived in the house a year before she suddenly became ill and died. Looking up at it now, Jim felt the cold, impersonal character of the structure. Grand as it was, there was no warmth in its facade.

Standing before a corner window of the freight office, Hamilton Blunt stared intently at the lanky youngster dressed in animal skins. He didn't say anything until the boy turned in at the driveway to the house.

"Morgan, who the hell is that?" He didn't wait for his brother to come to the window. "Is that that damn Tracey whelp?"

This captured Morgan's attention right away. "What? Where?" He got up and joined his brother at the window. "Damn. I don't know."

"He's supposed to be dead," Hamilton growled.

They moved to a side window to watch the young man's progress up the drive. "It couldn't be young Tracey," Morgan said. "LaPorte said he was dead. He wouldn't have any reason to lie about it."

Hamilton exhaled loudly, irritated. "I'm going up to the house. You stay here till I get back."

Julia Tracey thought at first that she was looking at a ghost. She rose to her feet, forgetting the ball of yarn in her lap, ignoring it when it fell to the floor and rolled across the room. She rushed to the window and strained to see if the gangly young boy approaching the house was a trick her mind was playing. *No—it was Jim!*

For a moment she thought she might faint. Her head began to spin, and she grabbed the window sash for support. "Jim?" she heard herself whisper, still finding it difficult to believe that her son had returned. He had almost reached the bottom step of the porch before she recovered and hurried to the front door. As she rushed out to the porch, he looked up to see her.

"Ma!" he exclaimed and bounded up the steps two at a time. She hugged him tightly, released him to look at him for a few moments, then pulled him to her again. "I'm sorry, Ma. I'm sorry about Pa," he blurted. "There wasn't nothing I could do." He suddenly felt guilty about coming home without his father, a feeling that he had somehow let her down.

"I know, Jim, I know. What could you do? You're just a boy." She held him at arm's length again. "They told me you were dead too." She looked him up and down as if to make sure he was all right.

"Well, I ain't. I'm home now. I can take care of you. We can go back home."

A frown creased her brow, and she said, "We'll have to talk about that. You heard about Cameron?"

"Yes, ma'am." He lowered his head and said nothing for a moment. "I reckon I'm the man of the house now." He forced a smile. "Don't worry. I've got enough to take care of us for a while, till I can find work. We'll be all right."

They both turned then at the sound of a horse galloping up the path. Hamilton Blunt jerked the jet-black stallion to a halt, his hooves plowing up miniature dust clouds in the sun-baked dirt. Blunt had thrown a leg over his horse's back before the animal came to a full stop. He dismounted only a few feet from the bottom step.

Jim had often seen his father's employer, but not up close. He was surprised to see how big the man was. Dressed in English riding britches and a white shirt with a black string tie, he presented a formidable figure. He flashed a wide smile as he ascended the front steps and joined them on the porch.

"Well, well," he said, "now isn't this a wonderful sight for a mother's eyes?" He turned his smile fully toward Jim's mother. "This is Jim, isn't it?" Turning back to Jim, he said, "We thought you were dead, boy."

Jim explained how he happened to escape the fate his father had met when the war party attacked their camp. He apologized once more to his mother for not being in camp to help his father.

"I doubt it would have made any difference," Blunt said. "Did you get a look at any of them, boy? Were they all wild Indians? That's what we were told."

"Well, I didn't see all of 'em, but they were Injuns all right. Blackfoot, Buck said—that's a feller I was trapping with."

Blunt put his arm around Julia's shoulder and pulled her close to him. She flushed slightly, looking a bit uncomfortable when she saw the look in Jim's eye. "Well, Julia," Blunt said, "I know you will get some comfort knowing Jim here is all right." He turned his smile on the boy again. "Has your mother told you about us?"

Seeing the startled look on Jim's face, his mother said, "Not yet, Hamilton. I haven't had time."

"Then it's time we told him. Jim, your mother and I are going to be married."

The announcement staggered Jim. He stepped back, recoiling from the impact of the words. "You're what?" he exclaimed, not really knowing what to say. When his mother smiled and quietly nodded, the boy suddenly felt sick inside. "Why, Ma?" Then, trying to bring her to her senses, he pleaded. "You don't have to do that, Ma. I'm back now. I'll take care of you."

"It's not a question of having to—" Hamilton Blunt started.

"Don't listen to him, Ma," Jim interrupted. "You don't have to marry nobody. Let's go home. I'll take care of you."

"Son, you don't have a home to go to anymore—" Blunt started once more. This time Jim's mother interrupted.

"Let me talk to him, Hamilton. It's an awful lot for a fourteen-year-old boy to understand."

"As you wish, my dear. I've got to go back to the office now anyway, but I'll see you at supper."

Jim stood there trembling with hurt and anger as Blunt descended the steps and stepped up in the saddle. He fixed the boy with a stern look before pulling the black's head around and kicking his heels into the animal's sides.

"Ma, why are you doing this? You don't want to marry that man."

She took his hand and led him to a chair and bade him to sit. Patiently, she tried to explain. "Jim, I know it must be hard for you to understand. But when your father was killed, and then Cameron—and you, I thought—I was alone in the world. I had no place to go and no way to support myself. Hamilton Blunt came to my rescue, Jim. He was there when I needed someone desperately. I couldn't afford to stay in the house. Where could I go?" She looked away, a wistful look in her eye. "He was kind enough to offer his home, and after a while . . ." She didn't finish the statement. "Well, you don't know Hamilton like I've come to know him, Jim. He's a kind and generous man, and quite charming." She took his hands in hers. "You'll see. Wait till you get to know him better."

He pulled his hands away. "Ma, I don't want to hear you talk like that. Pa ain't been dead more'n three months. How could you even think about getting married?"

"Sometimes you do what you have to do, Jim." She tried to cheer him up. "Why, it'll be a good thing for you, too. Hamilton is a very wealthy man. There may be opportunities for you."

"There won't be no opportunities for me. I'm John Tracey's son and that's who I'll always be. I don't want nothing to do with that man. I'll make it on my own, and if you do the right thing, you'll come on home with me."

"I'm sorry, Jim. I'm staying here."

Jim was angry. He couldn't understand his mother's attitude. To him, it was an insult to his father for her even to be in Blunt's house. It didn't look right, and the thought of Hamilton Blunt stepping in and taking his father's place made him feel sick inside. He prayed that wherever his pa was, he wouldn't see what had come to pass. Exasperated with his mother and at a loss as to what he could do about it, he got up to leave. "I'm going home—

to our house," he emphasized. "Maybe when you quit acting crazy, you'll come on home."

"Jim," she called out, but said nothing more when he turned his back to her and did not respond. It tore at her heart to see him act this way. He was too young to understand that she couldn't depend on a boy of fourteen for support. She stood, wringing her hands as she watched her only surviving son striding determinedly down the path. *I'll speak to Hamilton,* she thought. *Maybe he can talk to the boy.*

Hamilton was already determined to talk to the boy, but it was not going to be the kind of talk Julia was praying for. He stood at the side window of his office, watching for Jim to return from the house. When the boy reached the main road, Blunt walked out to intercept him as he passed in front of the freight yard. "Jim, boy," he called out, affecting a friendly smile, "let's talk a minute."

Jim had already seen more of Mr. Hamilton Blunt than he cared to that day, but it appeared it was going to be difficult to avoid additional conversation. "I best be getting home," he mumbled, hoping to avoid the confrontation.

Blunt was a big man, and it seemed to Jim that he purposely stood as tall as he could in an effort to intimidate him. The smile remained fixed on his face, however, as he confronted the boy. "Jim, I think there's some things you should understand. You love your mother, don't you, boy?" Jim did not respond. "Sure you do, and you want what's best for her. I know you do. I know it's hard on you, losing your pa and all. But your mother has a chance to have a much better life than what your pa could have ever given her. Now you have to be a big enough man to get out of her way and let her be happy."

He paused and leveled a steady gaze at Jim, gauging the effect of his words. When there was no noticeable change in the boy's expression, he attempted to convey a benevolent facade once more. "You've grown up quite a bit since the last time I saw you. Looks to me like you're about ready to get out from under your mama's petticoat and be off on your own. There's not much work for a young man starting out around here. Maybe you'd have better luck if you tried the city."

Jim looked at the man who was said to have been so kind to his mother. He decided right then that he didn't like Hamilton Blunt—and not just because he was set on marrying his mother. There was something about the man that made Jim skeptical of everything he said. When he realized that Blunt was waiting for an answer from him, he said, "I think Ma will change her mind and come on back home, so I reckon I'll just stay."

He turned and started to leave, but Blunt caught him by the shoulder and spun him around. "Look here, boy. I'm trying to be nice to you. But if you don't have enough sense to read my message, let me put it plain to you. I don't want you around here. Your mama doesn't want you around here. So I'm advising you to get the hell out of here and find someplace else to live—the farther from here, the better."

Jim snatched his shoulder free of the powerful hand that pinched into it. "Now I'm advising you. Don't *ever* lay your hand on me again." He backed away, keeping a wary eye on the imposing man. "And I reckon I'll go where I damn well please."

"You little snot," Blunt growled as the boy walked briskly away from him. *We'll see if you stay or not.*

Jim had a great deal of thinking to do. He had been defiant toward Hamilton Blunt because he didn't like the man—and he sure as hell didn't like for anyone to tell him to get out of town. On the long walk back to his father's house, he thought about the meeting he had just had with his mother. She was genuinely glad to see him—he was certain of that. On the other hand, there seemed to him a part of her that saw his return from the dead as inconvenient. When he recalled his mother's last words to him, and the look in her eyes when she spoke them, he was struck with the cold realization that she was content to stay with Blunt. It was a bitter potion to swallow. He shook his head, trying to rid his mouth of the taste of gall.

By the time he reached the rough little cottage on the Milltown road, his mind was laboring with the decisions he struggled with. He was of a mind to take the gold he had brought back and head back to the West—look for Buck and Frank. *But it was his mother!* Maybe he should take up living in the house, and when she saw that he could take care of them, she would come home. Blunt had said Jim couldn't pay the rent. Well, he didn't know about the pouch Jim had hidden under the front porch the night before. He still wasn't sure what he should do, but he made up his mind that he would stay there for a few days—if only because Blunt had told him to leave.

Having made a decision, at least for the time being, he spent most of the day cleaning and dusting. The house had been neglected since his mother had moved her things to Blunt's house. Maybe, he thought, his mother might come by to see if he was here. If she did, he wanted things to look nice. After he had done about as much as he could to improve the appearance of the place, he decided he'd better get up to Trotter's before the merchant closed for the day. There was nothing to eat in the house, and he had had nothing since Mrs. Bowen fixed him breakfast.

After making sure there were no curious eyes around, he reached under the corner of the porch and took a small amount of dust from the sack. The thought struck him that it might be pretty risky to leave that much gold lying around. For want of a better solution at the moment, he crawled back under the porch a little farther and scraped out a hole next to one of the stone posts. When it was covered up and smoothed over, he deemed it safe enough for the time being.

He was beginning to fear that he had waited too long to walk up to the store, but he was relieved to find Mr. Trotter still there. There were a couple of customers milling around when he walked in. One of them was a lady he did not know. The other was a man who appeared to be looking at a harness on the far side of the store.

"Well, I'll be!" Mr. Trotter exclaimed. "I heard you were back from the dead, young fellow. Welcome home."

"Thank you, Mr. Trotter." Jim nodded politely to the smiling storekeeper. "I need some things. I can pay for them."

Jim browsed around the store while Mr. Trotter waited on the lady. His mind was occupied with thoughts of the items he was going to need if he decided to stay in the house. It occurred to him that he needed a horse and a rifle. He wondered how much his pouch of gold would convert to in dollars. What if it wasn't as much as he needed? His thoughts were interrupted when he almost bumped into the man looking at harnesses. "Beg your pardon, sir," Jim offered.

"Hello, Jim," came the subdued reply.

Surprised, Jim glanced up at the man's face. "Oh! Hello, Mr. Bowen." After his initial surprise at bumping into Mr. Bowen, his next thought puzzled him. Travis Bowen had probably been his father's closest friend. They had worked together at the freight company for years. It struck Jim as odd that the man hadn't greeted him as soon as he walked in the door. It even appeared that Mr. Bowen had purposely remained over behind the harnesses. Jim wondered if he would have spoken at all if Jim hadn't practically cornered him.

"I heard you was back," Bowen said softly, his words carefully chosen as if someone was eavesdropping. "I'm real sorry about your pa. He was a good man."

"Yessir. Thank you, sir."

Bowen fumbled for words. "And about Cameron," he added. "But I'm glad to see you're all right, son."

Travis Bowen had always been outspoken and friendly in the past, a man who enjoyed a good joke and liked to tease youngsters like Jim. But now, the man suddenly seemed so sober. Jim supposed it was out of respect for the deaths of his father and brother. He was about to tell Bowen that he had had breakfast at his house that morning when Bowen suddenly blurted out a quick good-bye, abruptly dropped the harness and headed for the door, saying he had something at home he had to attend to. *Damn! He acted like I smell bad or something,* Jim thought.

Bowen paused just before going outside. With his hand on the doorknob, he turned back toward the boy. "Jim—be careful, son." When the boy seemed mystified by his warning, Bowen fidgeted a moment more before adding, "If I was you, I'd stay well clear of the freight company." Then he was out the door, leaving the boy to puzzle over his strange behavior.

The lady soon finished with her purchases, and Jim was left alone with Mr. Trotter. "Well, Jim, what can I do for you?" Trotter asked.

Jim explained that he needed a few things right away and the only currency he had was in the form of gold dust. He then produced the small amount he had tied up in the rag. Trotter took it and examined it under a glass he kept behind the counter. After a few moments of serious study, he pronounced it to be the genuine article and poured it on a scale to weigh it. "You've got about thirty dollars' worth here. What do you wanna do with it?"

Thirty dollars! That seemed like a lot of money to Jim for not much more than a good-sized pinch of the yellow dust. His mind immediately started working on multiplying it times the pouchful he had hidden. "Uh," he stammered, "can you set me up a line of credit?"

"Sure I can," Trotter replied. "Have you got more of this somewhere?"

Jim hesitated before answering. His father had always said that Trotter was an honest man. Jim decided he could safely confide in the man. "Yessir, and I'd sure like to get it changed into something I can spend."

"I can do that for you—set you up with a line of credit or give you cash money, whatever you want. Now, I might not give you as much as you'd get from the bank's assayer. But I'll be as honest as I can. I know what an ounce of gold is worth today, and I believe my scales are fairly accurate." He knew what the boy's situation was, suddenly on his own and probably with no idea what his gold was worth. Trotter thought it would be best for Jim to bring his dust to him before some dishonest scoundrel found out about it and cheated the boy.

When Jim left Trotter's, he enjoyed a great sense of relief. His mind filled with thoughts of his father and brother, he walked down the lonely road to Milltown, determined to cook himself a supper of the salt pork he had just purchased and get a good night's sleep. Tomorrow he could think about making plans.

He saw the smoke long before he reached the curve in the road a quarter of a mile above the house. A thick black column rose straight up over the treetops and hung like an omen of doom in the still evening air. Jim's heart began to pound, and he immediately broke into a run, anxious to make the turn in the road where he would be able to see his house.

At the bend, his worst fears were confirmed. The spectacle that greeted his eyes caused his mind to reel for a moment in disbelief. The house he was born in—his father's house—was engulfed in a blazing ball of fire. He ran as fast as he could, straining for breath by the time he reached the front path. The heat from the inferno forced him to back away to the road again. There was no thought of putting out the fire, or of saving anything inside. All was lost.

As he stood there, helplessly watching his boyhood memories melt away in the intense heat of the flames, several people came running from Milltown, drawn by the smoke. There was nothing anyone could do but stand by and watch. A few people offered their condolences to the young boy, who stood with his shoulders drooping, his eyes locked on the flames.

It didn't take long. In less than two hours the fire had consumed everything save some smoldering, smoking lumps of timber, bits of metal and glass, and the blackened stone fireplace. A few of the spectators hung around after most of the crowd had gone, sifting through the ashes with their boots, looking for anything of value. There was nothing to be salvaged, though. When the last of them had finally given up and returned to their homes, the boy was still seated on the ledge of the well, staring at the ashes.

At approximately the same time Jim discovered his father's house in flames, his mother stood at the front door of the huge white house overlooking the freight yard. She watched Hamilton Blunt as he rode into the yard, dismounting and handing the reins to the stableboy. He wore a stern expression on his face, but immediately switched to a broad smile when he looked up and saw her.

"My, but aren't you a mighty pretty sight tonight," he said, taking her hands in his and gently kissing her forehead.

Julia blushed. She was still unaccustomed to Hamilton's verbal bouquets, especially at her age. Her life before John's death had been hard, and she and John had never had room for frills. There was love, certainly. She never questioned it. But there had not been tenderness for many years. It was not that John would not have given it, it was just not in his nature to do so.

In truth, Julia was not quite sure what to do with herself since moving into Hamilton's house. She had supposed that she would take over the housekeeping and cooking, but Hamilton informed her that he intended to keep the woman who had cooked for him ever since his wife died. As for the housekeeping, the woman's daughter came in twice a week to clean and do the wash. At first the thought of such luxury threatened to overwhelm Julia, but it was an easy matter to become accustomed to it. When she had asked Hamilton what he expected her to do all day, he had replied that she had only to make herself beautiful for him. She felt like a girl of sixteen again.

He put his arm around her, and they walked into the front hallway. She stood back and watched him while he took off his hat and hung it on a knob by the door. *He is a handsome devil, in a rakish sort of way,* she thought. Almost as if reading her thoughts, he parted his lips in a wide smile and ran his fingers through his thick, silver-flecked hair to shake out the indentation his hatband had left. She had never seen a man as impressive as this man who wanted her for his wife. She had to shake herself mentally to recall her wandering thoughts and ask the question that had burdened her mind.

"Hamilton, I wonder if . . . I mean, do you think you could talk to Jim? I think he's just upset and confused. He's so young, and an awful lot has happened so quickly. I think, if he just had an opportunity to get to know what a wonderful person you are . . ." Her voice trailed off, her eyes pleading.

"I'm sorry, darling," he said, trying to match the concern in her eyes with that of his own. "I have already tried to talk to Jim once, when he left here. I swear, I don't know what's wrong with that boy, Julia. I told him that all we wanted to do was to help him get over his grief—told him he always had a home here with us if he wanted it. He told me he would never live with me—got downright nasty about it—threatened to kill me and called me . . . well, I don't think it proper to repeat such language to a lady. I told him I didn't appreciate some of the remarks he made about you, his own mother, for goodness' sakes. He acted like he might become violent, so I had no choice but to leave him be. I'm sorry, darling. I tried, but I'm afraid there's no hope."

Chapter 5

Tired and discouraged, Jim lay down near the smoldering ruins. The ground was warm and hard, baked by the fire. Ignoring the rumblings in his empty belly, he gave in to his weariness and slid into the comforting arms of sleep.

He awoke the next morning, surprised to find that the sun was smiling down on a perfect day, oblivious to the tragic blow his life had once again suffered. He sat up, stiff from his night on the hard ground, and looked at the still-smoking remains. He had never felt more alone in his young life. Almost giving in to his despair, he nevertheless reached down deep inside his soul and summoned the strength to overcome this new tragedy. Hamilton Blunt had been right about one thing, he decided. It was time for Jim to become a man. So resolved, he scolded himself for acting like a child and got up on his feet. "It's gonna take a heap more than this to run me out," he announced, already entertaining suspicions that the fire was no accident.

As he started poking around in the charred ruins of the house, the thought suddenly struck him—*the gold!* In the chaos of the night before, he had completely forgotten the bag buried under the porch. His eyes immediately focused on the stone pilasters, standing now like scorched stumps among the charred timbers. Which one was it? It was not as easy to tell now that the porch and house were no longer standing. He determined it to be the third one in from the front and started to toss charred debris out of his way. Before clearing the timbers from around the pilaster, he stopped and studied the short stone column. The ground around it had not been disturbed, and he was sure that the pouch of valuable dust was safe and untouched by the flames. Knowing it was risky to carry that much gold dust around with him, he decided it best to leave it buried, since the heat of the fire had baked the ground hard, leaving no evidence of the hole he had dug. He couldn't think of a safer place to keep it until he needed it.

That decided, he thought to tend to his empty stomach next. He still had a little money in his pocket, and a line of credit at Trotter's, so he set out for the store once again. As he hopped across the ditch by the road, he caught sight of something that caused him to pause. It was a hoofprint, and a recent one, too. As far as Jim remembered, none of the spectators there the night before were on horseback. Wary now, he searched the ground around the house, and found many more hoofprints. Suspicions that he'd had earlier seemed to be confirmed. His house had definitely been visited by several riders the day before. There was little doubt that he had been burned out deliberately.

His initial feeling was one of anger. It was obvious to him that Hamilton Blunt was set on destroying his life. *Well, he's got another think coming,* he thought, determined to fight back—although at the moment he had not the slightest idea what he could do about it. Hamilton Blunt was a powerful man, too powerful to be challenged by a fourteen year-old boy. "He still ain't gonna get away with it," Jim muttered and set out for Trotter's again.

He had not quite reached Travis Bowen's house when a rider loped into view. When he was close enough to make out the man's features, Jim recognized Tyler Blunt, the youngest of the Blunt brothers. Jim knew him by sight only, but his father had told him that Tyler was a young rakehell, good only for heavy drinking and barroom fights. Jim moved to the side of the road to give the horse room to pass. But Tyler steered his large gray directly toward the boy, reining up in front of him.

"Well, now, lookee here," Tyler greeted the boy sarcastically. "If it ain't the Tracey young'un. Hey, boy, I heard you had a little fire down your way last night—thought I'd come take a look at it myself." He nudged his horse closer to Jim, forcing the boy to back up a step. "Don't leave you with much cause to stay around here no more, does it?"

Jim didn't answer. He stepped around the gray's head and continued walking. There was a sharp ache in the pit of his stomach that had nothing to do with hunger, and the blood in his veins felt like ice water.

Without having any proof of it, he knew for certain that this sneering son of a bitch was directly involved in burning down his house. There was no doubt that Hamilton Blunt had sent Tyler to make sure Jim was getting out of the county.

Tyler pulled his horse around and circled back in front of Jim again. "Hey, boy, I ain't through talking to you. Don't you go walking away from me, or you'll feel the business end of this whip." Jim stopped, only because the big gray was again pressing against him, forcing him back. "Where do you think you're going, anyway?" Tyler taunted.

"I reckon where I'm goin' is my own business, and none of yours," Jim said, meeting the bully's gaze straight on. "Now, get that damn horse off of me."

"Listen here, you little turd, you better be on your way outta this part of the country. If I see you around here after today, you just might have a little accident yourself. You understand me?" He pulled on the big gray's reins, forcing the horse to sidestep, pushing Jim toward the ditch.

Jim felt the tremendous weight of the horse bearing down on him, the powerful muscles of its neck and withers forcing him over. He drew his knife and gave the animal a quick jab behind his front leg. The gray screamed and sprang backward, went stiff-legged for a couple of bounds, then bucked his hind legs up in the air. The sudden explosion of movement caught Tyler by surprise, causing him to lose the stirrup on one foot and grab the saddle horn to keep from being thrown.

"Damn you!" Tyler roared when he once again

had the horse under control. He pulled the pistol from his belt and was starting to aim it at Jim when he heard a voice behind him.

"Jim, is that you?" Nettie Bowen called out from her front doorstep.

Teeth clenched, his face twisted with rage, Tyler hesitated. He looked at the woman and then back at Jim. "You're lucky this time, boy. But your luck has run out. If I see you around here again, I'll nail your hide to the barn." He put the pistol away, wheeled his horse around and kicked the animal into a gallop, scowling at Nettie Bowen as he passed.

Jim stood there for a few moments, watching until Tyler had disappeared around a bend in the road. He had no doubt that Tyler would have shot him if Nettie Bowen had not been there to witness it. Now that the incident was past, he was aware of his trembling hands, shaking from both fear and anger.

"Come here, Jim," Nettie called. She waited on the step until he walked up to her door. "I saw what happened. What on earth was he doing? It looked like he was trying to run over you or something."

"He's wantin' to run me out of the county, I reckon," Jim answered.

"For goodness' sakes, what did you ever do to him?" When Jim just shrugged his shoulders, not really wanting to discuss it, she didn't press the issue. "You stay away from him. That Tyler Blunt always was a troublemaker. I don't know why Hamilton puts up with him." She paused and gave Jim a stern look. "Have you had any breakfast? I'll bet you haven't."

* * *

Hamilton Blunt looked up from his desk when he heard his brother open the door. "Well, did you take care of that piece of business?"

Tyler shrugged, still hot about the incident on the Milltown road. "Yeah, I took care of it. I told you that this morning. There ain't nothin' left over there but a hole in the ground, and I just put the word to the little bastard a while ago."

"He's still around this morning?" Hamilton was disappointed to hear that. He had been sure the boy would be scared enough to run. "He doesn't seem to get the message any too well, does he?"

Tyler grinned. "He's damn sure got the message now. I woulda got rid of the little snot for good if ol' lady Bowen hadn't stuck her nose into it."

"If he goes, let him be. I just want him out of here." Hamilton was ruthless in getting what he wanted, but unlike his brother, he was willing to let the boy live if he didn't ever have to see him again. He wasn't about to have any whelp of John Tracey's around to remind him of his wife's former husband.

"You don't have to worry about that little rat anymore. I aim to see that he's out of the way," Tyler said. "I'll ride out that way tonight to make sure he's gone."

Jim stayed away from the ruins of his house for the remainder of the day. He thought it best to wait for darkness before going back to dig up his gold. He spent a good deal of the afternoon in heavy thought, rethinking his plans to make a home there on the Milltown road. The more he thought about it, the less certain he was that his mother would choose to leave Hamilton Blunt's house. Yet he was reluctant to believe she had chosen to forget his father and her two sons for a life as the mistress of the huge white house overlooking the freight company. Maybe he should try to lease some acreage with his gold, try farming like his pa had dreamed of doing. Yet even as he thought it, he knew that farming was not the life for him—not since his heart had heard the call of the mountains.

At dusk, he made his way down the Milltown road once again to recover the pouch buried beside the pilaster. By the time he reached his ravanged home, it was already getting dark, but the stone supports stood out in the dull light. He approached the third one from the front and started clearing away the tangle of charred timbers that lay beside it. The smell of smoke was still heavy in the air. When he had moved the debris, he dropped down on his knees and used his knife to break up the baked dirt. In only a few minutes' time, he felt the top of the elk-hide pouch. His body suddenly tensed when he heard a sound behind him, and then a voice.

"Just like I figured. The little rat came back to his nest." There was no mistaking the sarcastic voice of Tyler Blunt. "Looks like you're trying to dig another burrow, little rat. Make sure it's big enough, 'cause it's gonna be your grave."

Jim turned around to face him, still on his knees. Tyler was no more than ten feet from him, his pistol pointed at Jim's head. There was no time to be scared. The boy glanced right and left, desperately searching for some means of escape. There was none. Tyler had the drop on him for certain. It was then that Tyler noticed the skin pouch in Jim's hand.

"What you got there, boy? Come on outta there and let's see what you dug up. Don't get up!" he warned. "Crawl outta there on your hands and knees." Tyler backed up a couple of steps from the blackened ruins, keeping the pistol leveled at Jim's head. While Jim did as he was told, Tyler kept up a steady stream of banter, obviously enjoying baiting the boy. "I warned you, didn't I, boy? I told you to get your scrawny little ass out of this county. But here you are, back after I told you what would happen to you. Now you know what's gonna happen? They're gonna find you in the morning with a hole right between your eyes. Now hand me that poke you're holding."

He reached down and snatched the pouch from Jim's hand, surprised by the weight of it. "Hot damn, what you got in here, boy? Gold? It's got some weight to it. And you had it hid under the porch. If I'da known that, I'da burned this damn shack down sooner." Though it was too dark for Jim to see it, there was a broad grin across Tyler's face at the prospect of being paid for doing something he'd do every day of the week for free. He kept Jim on his hands and knees while he hefted the sack, speculating as to its weight. "How much is in here, boy? You might as well tell me. You ain't gonna care in a few minutes anyway." When Jim refused to answer, Tyler whacked him across the head with the pistol barrel. The blow snapped Jim's head to the side, cutting open his cheek, but it was not hard enough to render him unconscious. Tyler wanted the boy completely aware of what was happening to him. It made the execution more enjoyable for the sadistic Blunt.

The blow from Tyler's pistol made Jim's head ring, and he could feel the blood flowing down his cheek. The longer Tyler taunted him, the less scared and the more angry he got.

"Why don't you beg me to spare your worthless life?" Tyler teased. He was clearly disappointed in the boy's calmness in the face of death.

"Why don't you kiss my ass?" Jim replied.

That did it for Tyler. He grabbed a handful of Jim's hair and pulled him up from his knees. He pressed the barrel of the pistol against Jim's forehead and growled, "Good-bye, you little turd. Say hello to your brother for . . ." The pop of the pistol was followed immediately by a heavy grunt from Tyler as Jim suddenly knocked the pistol away from his forehead with one hand, while coming up under the larger man's breastbone with his long skinning knife.

Tyler staggered backward in shocked disbelief, staring wide-eyed with horror at the bone handle protruding from his midsection. He grabbed it to try to pull it out, but the movement of the blade caused him to scream in pain. Forgetting the boy, and everything else but the searing agony in his gut, he staggered a few steps forward before sinking to his knees, his eyes staring wildly. Hardly believing what had just happened, himself, Jim wasted no more time. He pulled a short piece of charred timber from the ruins, and with as much force as he could put behind it, he swung it at Tyler's head repeatedly. Each blow made a hollow sound, like thumping a gourd, as the timber bounced off Tyler's skull. Jim became frantic. It seemed the stabbed man would never go down. He was plainly unable to defend himself, yet somehow he remained on his knees, groaning, his head rolling back and forth. Jim clubbed him once more, and finally Tyler rolled over on the ground.

The shocking reality of what he had just done suddenly struck Jim and he sank down on one knee, unable to take his eyes off of the dying man. *What if he ain't dead? What if he gets up again?* Jim realized he was trembling. He wanted to run, but his stubborn rational mind forbade him to leave without his fortune and his knife.

Unable to approach Tyler, Jim sat down in the dirt several feet away and waited, hoping Tyler would die soon. Tyler was no longer moving, but he was still whimpering quietly, no longer clawing at the knife embedded in his gut. After almost an hour had passed, Jim began to worry that he might be found there by some of Tyler's friends. Jim knew he could stay there no longer, but he couldn't take the chance that Tyler might recover somehow. He had to make sure.

Reluctantly, he dragged himself to his feet and went to the pilaster where his gold had been buried. He worked at one of the heavy stones until it broke free. It weighed at least thirty or more pounds. It should do the job, he thought. The thought of what he was about to do made him queasy inside, but he was determined to do what had to be done.

Lugging the heavy stone in both hands, he stepped cautiously toward the dying man. Standing directly over Tyler's head, he lifted the stone up as high as he could. He stood there, poised to deliver the lethal blow, when he realized Tyler was already dead. Relieved, he backed away and dropped the stone on the ground, his strength suddenly drained.

His thoughts turned toward flight. He had killed Tyler Blunt. Surely, the sheriff and the Blunts would be after him. He had to get as far away from St. Louis as fast as he could. Someone would surely be looking for Tyler come morning. It wouldn't matter if Jim had killed him in self-defense. Hamilton Blunt wouldn't care. He'd be out to hang him. His adrenaline pumping with thoughts of escape, Jim hesitated no longer. He rolled Tyler's body over with his foot and, with both hands, yanked his knife free from Tyler's gut. He picked up his pouch of gold dust and ran toward the road. In his haste, he almost ran into Tyler's big gray horse, tied to a shrub by the side of the road. Without hesitating, he pulled the reins loose and jumped into the saddle. The gray accepted him willingly and responded instantly to the heels jabbing into its flanks.

Riding as fast as the gray could gallop, Jim headed up the dusty road, putting the grim scene at the burned-out cottage behind him. Off to his right, a big yellow moon floated just above the tops of the poplars, throwing long shadows across the darkened road. An avalanche of thoughts threatened to bury the young boy's mind as he tried to figure out what he should do. To his mind, he had done no wrong. Why should he run? There was always the chance that no one would ever know who killed Tyler Blunt. He thought about that for a few minutes, then rejected the idea. Hamilton Blunt had to know Tyler had gone to see Jim, and he had probably sent him out there himself. The Blunts ran the whole county. What chance did Jim have of proclaiming his innocence? He had no choice but to run.

His decision made, he spurred the horse onward. He felt his pocket to make sure his pouch of dust was still there. It was going to be the start of a new life. He would need to outfit himself to return to the mountains, where a soul could lose himself for good. Maybe he could find Frank and Buck again.

He would have to convert his dust to hard cash, and at the moment he only knew one place to do that—Trotter's. He trusted the storekeeper to treat him fairly. The problem was he couldn't afford to wait for the store to open in the morning—he would just have to wake him up. The next thing to cause him concern was Tyler's horse. Up to that point, he didn't feel he had done anything wrong in defending his life. But if he kept the gray, he could be charged with horse stealing. He decided to leave the horse with Mr. Trotter.

Trotter lived upstairs over the store with his wife and two daughters. When the big gray slid to a stop, Jim leaped down from the saddle, taking the back steps two and three at a time. "Mr. Trotter!" he yelled repeatedly while banging on the door. He kept knocking until he saw the glow of a lamp in the window. A few moments later, he heard the creaking of the floorboards on the other side of the door. Finally, the door opened, and Mr. Trotter stood in the doorway, still in his nightshirt.

"Who is it?" Trotter asked. "Jim? Is that you?"

"Yessir. I'm real sorry to bother you, but I can't wait till morning. I have to leave tonight and I need some money." He held his pouch up so Trotter could see it. "I wouldn't bother you if it wasn't real important."

Trotter hesitated momentarily. He was a patient man, and he had always liked the young Tracey lad, but it was the middle of the night. He was reluctant to leave his soft bed to accommodate a young boy in what might or might not turn out to be a real emergency. "What happened to you? That's a right nasty-looking cut on the side of your face."

"I just got my head bumped. It ain't much," Jim offered in explanation.

After studying Jim's face in the glow of lamplight, Trotter finally gave in. "All right," he said. "Let me get my pants on." He disappeared back into the house, reappearing a few minutes later with his nightshirt stuffed into his trousers. Jim could hear the muffled voice of Mrs. Trotter complaining to her husband. "Just go on back to sleep," he heard Trotter say. "I'll be back in a minute."

At the bottom of the stairs, Trotter paused. Holding the lamp up so he could take a closer look, he said, "That looks like Tyler Blunt's big gray."

"Yessir," Jim replied. His mouth suddenly went

dry and he tried to swallow the knot in his throat. "Yessir," he repeated. "I'm gonna have to leave him here with you if you don't mind. I didn't steal him. I just borrowed him for a little while."

Trotter looked at Jim, his curiosity fully primed. Knowing Tyler Blunt's disposition, he figured it highly unlikely that the boy had Tyler's permission to ride his horse. "Are you in some kind of trouble, son?"

"Yessir," Jim stammered. "I've got to get away from here right now. I ain't taking the horse because I ain't no thief."

Trotter decided not to push the boy for any more information. Jim had obviously gotten himself in some kind of trouble with Tyler Blunt. Everyone in the county knew Tyler to be an arrogant, sadistic son of a bitch, and if something had caused him to come to grief, then he probably had it coming. Trotter deemed it prudent to have no knowledge of why Jim Tracey was in such a hurry to leave town. "Come on, then," he said. "You're going to need more than a few things if you're hightailing it for good."

Chapter 6

Logan stood on the rough planks of the wharf, his feet widespread, his arms folded across his chest, his gaze fixed intently on the boy standing before him. Aside from the moccasins and deerskin trousers, everything else the boy had looked new—his Hawken percussion rifle, the powder horns, pistol, and possibles bag. Jim had sought Logan out, seeking passage on his keelboat for the trip up to Council Bluffs. If he had ever seen a greenhorn, Logan was sure he was looking at one now.

"So you're looking for passage to Council Bluffs, are you?" He glanced around behind the boy, expecting to see some adults. "You by yourself?"

"Yessir."

Logan grinned. "Run off from home, did you?"

"Nossir. Ain't got no home."

"That so?" Logan stroked his chin thoughtfully while he continued to eyeball the boy. "Look's like you got yourself outfitted up pretty good. You sure you ain't in some kind of trouble back home?"

Jim was losing patience with the interrogation. "Mister, the only trouble I got is trying to find out if I can ride upriver on your boat. I can pay for my passage."

Logan laughed in spite of himself, recalling a day many years before when he left home himself to set out on his own. He wasn't much older than this lad. "Well, I bet you can. But let me give you a little advice—don't be telling folks around the river that you got money."

"I didn't say I had a lot of money. I just said I had enough to pay for a ride on this boat." That wasn't entirely true, for his little poke of gold dust had converted into a sizable fortune. He had enough for his passage plus enough to purchase a couple of good horses when he got to Council Bluffs. Most of it was sewn inside the deerskin shirt he carried in his pack.

"You got folks meeting you at Council Bluffs?" Logan asked. When Jim explained that he didn't—that he planned to go overland from there up the Platte—Logan thought it over for a few seconds. "All right, what the hell. You can go along. And if you make yourself useful, you can go for half the usual rate."

"Yessir. Thank you, sir."

Logan continued to study the young man standing in front of him for a moment more as if still deciding. "What's your name, son?"

"Trace . . ." Jim blurted, then checked himself.

"Trace?" Logan replied. "Trace what? Is that your last name?"

Jim had to think fast. It wouldn't be smart to give his real name in case word had spread about Tyler's death. He hesitated a moment before adding,

"McCall—Trace McCall." It seemed fitting that he use his father's last name and his mother's maiden name.

"All right, then, Trace, you can stow your possibles over there back of those barrels. But you're gonna have to keep an eye on 'em yourself. If something turns up missing, don't come blubbering to me."

Jim thanked him and went to stow his possessions. It was unnecessary for Logan to warn him to watch over his pack. He was a different young man returning to the mountains than the one who had journeyed down to St. Louis with the sorrowful message for his mother. There was something about killing a man that leached the boyhood right out of a body. Jim knew his weapons and the beaver traps he had purchased from Mr. Trotter would make the difference in his living or dying in the harsh mountains. He positioned himself behind the long mound of cargo in the middle of the boat while Logan barked out orders to the twenty keelboatmen.

The bowline was cast off, and the square sail was run up the mast. There was only a slight breeze, but it was enough to push the boat away from the wharf. The polemen hustled to pick up their poles from where they had been neatly stacked along the sides of the boat. Once everyone was in place, the sternline was cast off and Jim's journey up the Missouri was under way.

The gentle breeze served to ease the strain on the polemen as they set their poles in the muddy current, probing for the bottom. They were a sordid collection of river rats, these boatmen, and Trace vowed anew to make sure his belongings never left his sight. Logan kept after his crew, cajoling, then cursing, showing no sympathy for their labor. He was not totally without feeling, however, for he put in to shore early that first afternoon after making barely four miles. It was enough to sweat most of the whiskey out of the men from the previous days in town. Logan didn't tolerate any liquor on his boat, except that which might be on board as cargo. But he fully expected the men to drink all they could find at each end of the trip.

As soon as the boat was secured, the crew split up into several smaller groups, each around its own fire. Jim was invited to sit down at the fire of the only other paying passenger on board. The man introduced himself as Rufus Dees. A good portion of the cargo was his responsibility, he said. He had a string of six mules waiting in Council Bluffs to transport his goods to Fort Laramie. This sparked Trace's interest, since Fort Laramie was his planned destination after leaving the boat.

"Settin' out on yer own, are ye?" Rufus Dees asked as he ground up a handful of green coffee beans.

"Yep," was all Trace replied, eyeing the round little man carefully. He could see nothing sinister in the man's eyes, but one could never be sure. He decided Rufus was making polite conversation and nothing more.

"Where be ye a'headin'?" He hardly took his eyes off the beans he had rolled in a cloth as he pounded them on a rock. When Trace didn't answer, Rufus looked up and smiled. "I don't aim to be nosy, boy. Where you're headin' is your own business."

Trace flushed slightly. He had hesitated, wondering if this seemingly harmless little man was already scheming to relieve him of his new rifle. "No, sir," he quickly replied. "I was just wondering myself where I was going. I figured I might go to Fort Laramie—see if I can hear something about some friends of mine."

"Laramie, eh? Well, like I said, I'm takin' supplies up there." Rufus put his coffee on the fire to boil, and took a slab of salt pork from his pack. He liked what he saw in the quiet lad, and he was of a mind to ask him if he wanted to go overland to Laramie with him. Six mules were a handful on the trail. Though Rufus could handle them alone—he'd done it many a time—it sure made life easier if you had a little help. Besides, if the boy could hit anything with that new Hawken that never seemed to leave his hand, it wouldn't hurt to have another rifle along. He decided he'd watch him for a few days before making up his mind—see how the boy handled himself. "You got anything to eat?"

Trace nodded. "I got some jerked meat."

"Jerked meat?" Rufus snorted. "You'd best eat with me. Jerky is what a man eats when they ain't nuthin' else. I hope you got more in that pack than jerky. We're liable to be on this boat for a month and a half or more."

"I aim to hunt," Trace replied. "I brought some coffee and a few staples. This ain't the first time I've been to the mountains."

Rufus went to his pack again. "I got some potatoes I'm fixing to fry up. The missus give 'em to me. Figured I could eat 'em for a few days, but it looks like they're already goin' rotten. We might as well cook 'em up tonight and have us a feast."

Trace was grateful for Rufus Dees's hospitality and happily helped him dispose of his little sack of potatoes. Their bellies full, they made their beds by the fire. Trace went to sleep propped up on his pack, his rifle clutched securely in his arms, listening to the low murmur of the boatmen as they talked around their fires.

The next day saw them twelve miles farther up the river. At day's end, Logan picked a spot to camp near a heavily wooded slope. After Trace helped secure the boat, he took to the woods to see if he could find something for supper. Rufus had the fire blazing and the coffee ready when Trace returned to camp with three fat rabbits to repay Rufus for the potatoes. Rufus was to find in the following days that the young man with his Hawken never failed to bring back something to cook. Before the trip was over, they had formed an unspoken partnership. Trace provided the meat, Rufus did the cooking.

Riverboat travel was not an easy means of transportation for Logan and his crew. The river was not as wild in late summer as it was in the spring, but still there were snags and sandbars to negotiate, as well as periodic Indian attacks, which usually proved to be more of a harassment than a full-scale assault. Of greater aggravation were the insects and the river itself. It seemed that too often, the river was too deep for the poles and the current too swift for the oars, leaving no means to propel the craft except by hauling it along by ropes from the shore. On these days, they sometimes made little more than three or four miles.

Trace was beginning to wonder if they were going to make it to Council Bluffs before winter. Not content to sit idly by as his new friend Rufus did, Trace pitched in and helped the crew pull the boat along. Sweating in the late-summer sun, he would sometimes wonder about the purpose of the huge square sail, lufting on the mast in the continuous absence of any wind. As fall approached, however, he saw more days when a breeze would attempt to fill the sail. Still, it never seemed to help a great deal in propelling the heavily laden craft.

From the first day after leaving St. Louis, Trace had noticed that the boat rode bow-high in the water. It appeared to him that the boat would ride more level if most of the cargo hadn't been loaded toward the stern. One day, while the men were working hard to pull the boat around some snags, Trace questioned Logan about it, saying that if some of the cargo was shifted toward the bow, it might make their job a little easier. Logan replied that the boat was loaded that way for a reason. "If you load her bow-heavy, and run up on a sandbar, you'd never get her off until you unloaded the damn cargo."

Morgan Blunt rode in silence, his solid frame rocking in the saddle in rhythm with the gait of his late brother's horse. He had always admired the big gray, and had once tried to trade it away from Tyler. Tyler wouldn't part with the horse for anything. He had often joked about it, saying, "I'll leave him to you in my will. You can have him when I die." *Well, brother, it looks like I didn't have to wait as long as you thought.*

He felt no remorse for having callous thoughts about his brother's demise. There had never been any feelings of closeness between the brothers, and Morgan had felt no real sense of sorrow when Tyler was killed. Anger, yes, and a sense of humiliation that one of the powerful Blunt brothers had been murdered by a sniveling brat. Hamilton had been furious when some men brought Tyler's body to the house. He ordered Morgan to find the boy, no matter how long it took. Being the eldest, Hamilton was always the one who called the shots. More than that, he controlled the money. Blunt Brothers Freight was, in reality, Hamilton Blunt. The brothers' names were on the company signboard merely because of Hamilton's largesse. Morgan knew that and accepted it. He and Tyler were there to do Hamilton's dirty work, just as he was doing on this day.

He glanced behind him at the two riders following him with the packhorses they led. The three of them carried enough guns to discourage any Indian raiding parties they might encounter on their way to find Joe LaPorte. The packhorses carried trade items that LaPorte would use to pay his band of savages—mainly muskets, blankets, whiskey, and gunpowder.

Morgan felt certain that Jim would head west in his flight from St. Louis. So he had checked the docks, asking all the shippers if they had seen a boy of Jim's description. One had recalled seeing a boy, outfitted with rifle and pack, who had sought passage to Council Bluffs. But his name was not Jim Tracey. According to the boat's papers, it carried two passengers, named Dees and McCall.

No matter, Morgan thought. Jim would most likely head toward the frontier, and if he did, LaPorte and his Blackfeet would find him. The best place to start looking for LaPorte would be Fort Laramie. When he wasn't trading or raiding with his savages, he usually liked to hang around Fort Laramie to get away from his Blackfoot wife. Laramie was a busy trading post, with lots of squaws from several tribes—all were welcome, except the Blackfeet, who were constantly at war with most of the other tribes.

The remaining days of summer dragged slowly by, and the first signs of fall appeared in the trees along the riverbanks. The boiling-hot afternoons gave way reluctantly to cool evenings when Trace could feel comfortable in his deerskin shirt again. By the time Logan confirmed that the settlement beyond the bend was Council Bluffs, the company of boatmen had already seen a light frost.

"Mighty early for first frost," Rufus observed. "And after a summer as hot as this'un's been. I wouldn't be a bit surprised if we ain't in fer a hard winter."

Trace peered up at the sky, looking for signs of winter. Thoughts of mountain beaver streams were racing through his mind, and he felt an urgency to hurry. Trappers would soon be striking out for favorite streams they had scouted out during the summer, looking to trap when the beavers had their winter fur. Rufus could see the excitement in Trace's eyes when the boy talked about his plans to become a free trapper. He had seen it before, the lure of the far mountains. When it got in a body's blood, man or boy, there was nothing to do but follow the call.

"I was thinking I might talk you into staying on with me after we git this here load out to Laramie. They's a heap of folks needin' supplies out yonder, and they's more ever' year. I won't try to fool you—you ain't gonna git rich driving mules. But it'll make you a good living."

Trace was surprised by the offer. He counted Rufus as a friend by then, but he couldn't tell him that it might be a little too dangerous for him to be in St. Louis on a regular basis. People were looking for him there, and even if there was not a constant threat from the law and Hamilton Blunt, driving mules was not enough to fill his hunger for the mountains. He expressed his gratitude to Rufus for considering him worthy of partnership, but explained that he had to decline. He had made up his mind to trap, and he had already invested in the equipment necessary for the job.

"I suspected as much," Rufus said. "You've done heared the hawk's cry, ain't ye?" He smiled and placed his hand on the boy's shoulder. "Well, I hope you find what you're a'lookin' fer. You're a right smart boy, Trace, and the offer still stands anytime you change your mind." Rufus didn't hold out much hope that Trace would change his mind, however. He had seen it before—the lure of the high mountains—and he saw it in this young man's eyes now. Trace had heard the cry of the mountain hawk, calling out his name, and Rufus knew the boy was bound to answer.

Trace appreciated Rufus's offer, but he was pretty certain he wouldn't be changing his mind. He had sorely missed the mountains ever since he left Buck and Frank on the Green River. Maybe he *had* heard the cry of the hawk, as Rufus put it. Whatever the reason, he knew that the closer to the mountains he got, the faster his heart beat.

As soon as the boat was tied up, they started unloading the cargo. Trace helped Rufus stack his supplies in a big pile by the landing. When it was all on the bank, Rufus left Trace to watch over it while he went to the livery to fetch his mules.

"You better bring more than six mules," Trace called after him. It looked like an awful lot of supplies when it was stacked up in one pile.

Rufus looked back and laughed. "Oh, I'll get it all on my mules. Don't you worry 'bout that."

A couple of hours later, Rufus returned, riding one mule and leading six others. The two of them set to loading the animals, and when it was done, Trace still marveled that every last bit of the load was securely packed on the six mules. Rufus knew his business. The loads were carefully balanced on each mule, covered with hides, and securely lashed.

There was still the matter of acquiring a couple of horses for Trace, one to ride and one to carry his traps and gear. Rufus took him at his word when he maintained he had the money to purchase his horses.

He offered to lend the boy a mule, however, in case Trace might have underestimated the cost. But Trace insisted that he had made provisions for buying his horses, so the best Rufus could do was tell him where he could buy them.

"Now, I'll tell you who to see. His name's Gus Kitchel. He owns the stable where I keep my mules. Gus knows horseflesh about as good as anybody in the territory—and I seen some stout-lookin' stock there this morning. But, mind you, Gus is in it fer the money, same as ever'body else. So keep a sharp eye on him and you'll be all right. I'd go with ye, 'cept I'd rather a man pick his own horses. I'll wait here till you get back."

Trace left Rufus busy making himself a pot of coffee and set out for the stable. It was half an hour's walk, and along the way Trace ripped the money out of the inside of his deerskin shirt. It was considerably lighter when he put it back on.

Approaching the stables from the corral side, Trace paused to look over the horses before seeking out the owner. After a few minutes, he picked out a couple of spirited mounts that caught his eye. He had just started toward the stable door when it opened and a man walked out to meet him. Trace remembered his mother remarking once that when two people had been married for many years, they often began to look like each other. With that thought in mind, Trace figured that Gus Kitchel must have been dealing with horses all his life. He was a lanky man. A slouch hat was pulled so far down on his head that the brim pushed his ears out to the sides. A face as long as winter featured a prominent nose that ended with a small mouth and no chin to speak of. If there ever was a man with a horse face, Trace was looking at him.

"Hello, young feller," Gus greeted him. "Rufus said you might be coming by." He offered his hand and Trace shook it.

"Mr. Kitchel," Trace acknowledged.

"Rufus said you'd be needin' a couple of horses."

"Yessir. I like the look of that bay over there, and maybe that paint." He looked at Kitchel. "That paint looks like an Injun pony. I don't reckon he'll cost as much."

Gus grinned. "You know good horseflesh when you see it, don't you, boy? Them's two good horses, all right. I don't keep nuthin' but good stock. I recollect Rufus said you was set on headin' to the Rockies. Trappin', he said."

"That's a fact."

"Well, then, I think I might have a horse you'd be interested in. Take a look at that blue roan over there. Ain't that a fine-lookin' animal?" Trace admitted that it was. "That there's a mountain horse, trained to work in the mountains. You ride that horse, and you'll be the envy of ever' trapper in the territory."

Gus threw a rope on the roan and led him over to the gate. Trace was no expert on horses by any means, but he looked the horse over as best he could, watching for any obvious flaws. He could find none.

"You won't have to break him, either. He's ready to ride." He pushed his hat back a little and scratched a tuft of sandy-gray hair. "Now, to be honest with you, son, I'd have to ask a little more for that horse than the paint. You was right, the paint is an Injun pony, and this here roan comes from pure-bred stock. But you'll thank me for it when you're climbing them high mountains."

Trace decided to trust the man's word, and he made a deal for the blue roan and the bay. Gus, to show his heart was in the right place, threw in a saddle and bridle and a coil of rope. The saddle was old, but Gus had put a new girth strap on it. He picked up the saddle and threw it on the bay. "Best ride the bay a day or two. He ain't been rode in a while and might need a little smoothin' out. The roan'll take the lead line all right."

Gus held the bridle while Trace climbed aboard. The bay stamped his hooves and sidestepped a few paces, but settled down quickly enough. Trace took the lead line from Gus and headed out the gate, leaving the horse trader to count his money.

The bay felt good underneath Trace. He fell in with the horse's gait right off, and when he nudged him with his heels, the horse responded without hesitation. Trace was relieved. In hindsight, he knew he should have ridden the horse before he bought him. But now he felt confident and ready to head back to the mountains. He had never owned a horse before, and he couldn't suppress the pride he felt as he loped along the narrow wagon road. Looking behind him, he felt an added satisfaction at the sight of the blue roan, its head high, tugging at the rope.

After admiring Trace's newly acquired horses, Rufus got on his mule and led the string out on the trail.

There were still a few hours of daylight left, and Rufus decided they might as well get started. Leading the blue roan, Trace brought up the rear. They rode until dusk before making camp by a small stream.

The next day Trace saddled the roan. Gus had advised riding the bay for a couple of days, but Trace decided the bay wasn't as rusty as Gus figured. The roan was a handsome horse, broad and muscular, and as gentle as Gus had promised. Trace's spirits were soaring as he followed the mule train all day. In the late afternoon they reached a wide creek where Rufus said he always camped on his way to Laramie. There was still considerable daylight left, but Rufus said there was no good water for half a day beyond, so they made camp early. Trace, impatient with the slow pace of the mule train, longed to feel the wind in his face with a good gallop. He pulled the roan around the mules and kicked his heels. The horse did not respond right away, and Trace had to kick several times more before the roan made a move. Finally he took off at a hard gallop, Trace yelling and spurring him on. He pulled him up hard at the edge of the creek, and the roan slid to a stop in the soft sand.

Trace dismounted, whooping and laughing, full of the thrill of a fast horse. Then just as quickly, he stopped laughing. Something was wrong with the roan. Trace would almost swear he saw the horse stagger before walking to the edge of the water. Trace watched in shocked confusion as the horse, wanting to drink, could not because it was wheezing too hard for breath. When Rufus came up with the mules, he found Trace puzzling over the animal.

"Well, I'll be . . ." Rufus started. "That horse's wind is broke. He's been rode into the ground."

Trace stood staring at the tortured animal. "No wonder he wanted me to ride the bay for a couple of days."

"That damn Gus bamboozled you." Rufus quickly added, "Could of happened to anybody, Trace. There wasn't no way to tell, without you riding him hard like that. That damn Gus—probably figured you wouldn't do more than walk behind them mules." He shook his head as he walked all around the wheezing horse. "He might be able to walk all the way to the Pacific Ocean. But if you git jumped by any Injuns, you might have to ask them to chase you at a walk."

Trace felt sick inside. It was hard for him to go to sleep that night, thinking about the money he had thrown away, getting taken for a greenhorn as soon as he set foot off the boat. He had worked hard for that money, and his father had died for it.

The morning air was cool when Rufus threw his blanket back and sat up. There was a soft mist rising from the dark water of the creek that gave the cottonwoods on the far side a veiled, ghostly appearance. He stretched and yawned. "Time to git up, Trace." There was no answer. He looked across the smoldering campfire and saw that Trace's blanket was missing. Finding that strange, he got up and looked around. The boy had gone. His pack and his horses were gone as well. *Well, I'll be . . . lit out on me. And I never heard a thing.*

Gus Kitchel pulled his boots on over his long johns and headed for the stable. He paused outside the little one-room shack he called home and broke wind, applying sufficient pressure to obtain the desired resonance. Satisfied, he continued to the stable. He barely glanced toward the corral when something caught his eye. "What the hell . . ." he muttered. The blue roan was quietly standing in the corner of the corral.

Confused, he stood there staring at the horse for a few moments before going into the stable. He pushed the door open wide enough to step through and then turned to close it. When he turned around again, he was met with the barrel of a Hawken rifle only inches from his long nose.

"God a'mighty!" he blurted, his heart in his throat. "Hold on!" He backed up against the closed door. "Now, hold on a minute, son. I didn't mean to cheat you, I swear. Take any horse you want, just take it easy with that rifle." Trace did not reply, but continued to hold the rifle on him. "You can have your money back. I won't even charge you for a different one."

Trace finally spoke. "I don't want my money back. "You're the only thief around here. I'll pay for my horse." He stepped back to give the trembling man a little room, the Hawken still leveled at him. "Now go throw a rope on that paint."

Gus didn't have to be told twice. He cut the paint

out from the other horses and slipped a rope over its head, all the while throwing cautious glances at the determined young man still holding the rifle on him. He nodded toward the bay tied to a post near the barn. "You want me to tie this'un onto the saddle?"

"No, just give me the rope and open the gate," Trace said.

When he was mounted, he walked the bay toward the gate, where Gus was holding the paint's lead line. Taking the rope from the terrified man, Trace nudged the bay lightly and rode out the gate. Gus Kitchel stood by the gatepost, shaking his head, thankful to still be alive.

Rufus Dees woke up the next morning to find Trace rolled up in his blanket on the other side of the fire. "Damn," he mumbled, "I didn't even hear him come in."

Chapter 7

Rufus led the way, following the Platte River to Fort Laramie, a journey he planned to make in two weeks or better. Trace rode behind on the paint, leading the bay. He had assumed that Rufus would want him to lead three of the pack animals while Rufus led the other three. But Rufus insisted that the mules would trail just fine. They had done it many times before. This suited Trace, as it afforded him an opportunity to occasionally string the bay behind the last mule, leaving him free to range out to the sides and work the paint a little.

Trace was satisfied that he had bought two good horses with his money. He found that while the bay was as good a horse as a man could hope for, the paint was the more nimble of the two. In a race, the bay might nose ahead of the paint after a mile or so, but the paint would beat the bay out of the gate and could cut as quick as a rabbit. Riding across the endless expanse of prairie, Trace was soon free of worrisome thoughts of the Blunts and St. Louis. The only things that occupied his mind were the horizon before him and the river that led to the mountains.

On the third day out, Trace spotted a Pawnee hunting party on the far horizon while he was ranging away from the mules. He quickly guided his horse down into a gully and dismounted. Leaving the paint to nibble at the grass, he crawled back up to the edge to see if the hunting party had spotted him. About a quarter of a mile away, the Pawnees gave no indication that they were aware of his presence. They continued on, riding in a direction that would cross Rufus's intended trail if they held to it. He looked back to see how close the mule train was. There was no sign of Rufus, but Trace knew he couldn't be far behind the slope that he had crossed moments before when he had first seen the Pawnees.

Scrambling back down to the gully, he jumped on the paint and, riding low beneath the crown of the slope, hurried back to warn Rufus. He met him near the foot of the slope, about to lead the mules up it.

"Injuns!" Trace called out as he galloped up. "Keep them mules below the rise."

Rufus was immediately alert. "Where?" he replied, looking right and left. Trace told him there were about six or seven and they would most likely cross their trail about a mile ahead. Rufus, relieved to find that an angry horde of redmen was not about to descend upon him, slid his rifle back in its deerskin sheath. "Pawnee, I expect—probably a hunting party. We'd best hold up and give them a chance to clear our path." There was little danger as long as the hunters did not discover their presence.

During the days that followed, there were a couple more incidents when small hunting parties were sighted at a distance. Trace always seemed to spot the Indians before they saw him, and Rufus soon came to appreciate his sharp-eyed young friend. Each time Rufus had made the solitary trek to Fort Laramie in the past, he never failed to count himself a fool for making the trip alone, counting on sheer luck to save his neck. He truly wished the boy would consider throwing in with him, even though that would make the trip only one shot safer. The safest thing to do was to wait until a sizable train made up in Westport or Council Bluffs, with twenty or thirty teamsters for protection against the Pawnee and the Sioux. But that was not Rufus's style. He was an independent businessman. This way he could make a trip whenever it was convenient for him, and he had always felt that a smaller train like his would be less likely to attract the attention of a large hunting party. Small parties of five or six hunters did not cause him concern. He carried two rifles and two pistols, enough to discourage a party of that size.

The days were still comfortably warm for the most part, but the nights brought a crisp chill that made the campfire feel real friendly. At dusk after the horses and mules had been brought in close to the fire and hobbled, Trace would ride out and take a wide circle around their camp to make sure there were no uninvited guests lurking about. It was a habit acquired during his time with Buck and Frank. When Rufus commented that Trace seemed overcautious, Trace expressed his astonishment that Rufus never took such precautions himself. "You're wearing your scalp a little loose," he told him.

By the time Chimney Rock appeared in the distance, Rufus had—without realizing it—relinquished all responsibility for selecting campsites and line of travel to the boy. In addition, Trace provided meat when he deemed it safe to fire his rifle. Rufus had begun to wonder how he was going to make it back to the Missouri without the companionship of the alert young man.

The journey almost over, Trace began to feel excitement welling up in him again. In two days' time they should sight the wooden palisades of Fort Laramie. Most of the trappers would have scattered into the mountains for the fall season, but someone at the fort should be able to tell him where Buck and Frank were trapping. He had made up his mind during the ride from Council Bluffs that he would cast his lot with the two old buzzards. Pleasant thoughts of trapping filled his mind when he topped the rise and found himself facing three Sioux warriors.

They were as startled as he was. When Trace reined back hard on the paint, sliding to a dead stop, they did likewise. In that same instant, Trace saw fifteen or twenty warriors at the bottom of the rise behind the three—all painted for war. He remembered then that Rufus had said the Cheyenne and the Sioux were making war on some of their old enemies during the past summer—as well as all white men. Time stood still as the boy stared wide-eyed at the savages, the Sioux staring back in wonder at this white boy so near the banks of the Platte. The fact that Trace did not immediately turn and run probably saved his life.

Thinking there were perhaps many white men on the other side of the rise behind the boy, the Sioux hesitated—surely the white boy was not alone. The three braves in front began talking among themselves, and then one of them gave the sign of peace. Trace returned the sign, and the Sioux moved forward to meet him. He could feel their eyes examining his Hawken rifle and pistol. Backing the paint slowly while still keeping an eye on the approaching Sioux, Trace knew he was going to have to make a run for it. He had learned enough from Buck and Frank to know that the Indians were peaceful just as long as it took them to find out how many men were with you. When they topped the rise and saw that he was alone, the whole mad horde would be swiftly upon him.

This was a war party, ready for mischief, probably on their way to steal horses from the Pawnees, their old enemies. It was just Trace's misfortune to get caught in the middle. There was always the chance that they would simply pass him by, having more important business to take care of. Yet Trace knew the folly of that line of reasoning as soon as the thought passed through his mind. No lone white man was safe on the prairie. He could feel his scalp tingling already.

Frank had said that Indians respect bravery in a man, so you must never show fear in confronting one. Trace thought about that as he continued backing toward the top of the rise. His better sense told him that they might respect him if he attempted to stand before them, but he would also be respectably dead. His fears were confirmed when he reached the summit. One of the Sioux could contain himself no longer. He suddenly notched an arrow and let it fly, the shaft narrowly missing Trace's head. Like a signal, the brave's action triggered loud whoops from the warriors behind him, and they whipped their ponies into a gallop. Trace calmly raised his rifle and knocked the foremost warrior off his pony. Outraged, the war party charged up the rise like a swarm of angry hornets.

Trace wheeled his pony, and the paint sprang into flight without any encouragement. They bounded down the back side of the rise at full gallop, Trace bending low in the saddle, hoping to avoid the arrows and musket balls that chased after him. He was thankful for the roughness of the terrain that prevented his pursuers from taking dead aim. Trace still held his rifle in his hand but he did not attempt to reload it while galloping over the gullies and knolls, afraid he might drop the weapon in the process. With his free hand, he managed to slide the Hawken's rawhide sling over his shoulder and draw his pistol from his belt.

Hoping to gain some ground, he suddenly jerked the paint around in a quick turn and charged off in a different direction. It had the desired effect of catching his pursuers by surprise, widening the distance between him and the warriors chasing him—all except for one. Out in front of his brothers, the Sioux anticipated the change in direction and angled across to intercept the speeding paint. He was well mounted and gradually gained on Trace. Trace glanced back to see the determined warrior, a war axe in his hand, lying low on his pony's neck. There was no time to be frightened. Trace called on his pony for all the speed he could give him, but the paint could not match the speed of the Sioux brave bearing down on him. Trace wished he had ridden the bay that day.

When he chanced another look behind him, he could see that the two of them were outdistancing the rest of the war party, but the lone Sioux brave was almost behind him. Not willing to risk a missed shot with his pistol, Trace waited until the Indian pony's neck was abreast of the paint's rump. He looked back into the warrior's face, a mask of scornful fury, his eyes wide in anticipation of the kill, his cheeks adorned with jagged streaks of red and black war paint. His arm was raised to deliver a crushing blow with his stone war axe. Trace aimed his pistol at the Indian's stomach and fired. He would never forget the look of shocked disbelief that replaced the brave's angry expression as the Sioux rolled off his pony and landed in the grass.

His situation was improved, but only by a little. Seeing the second of their number fall victim to the fleeing white man caused the war party to drop back in the chase. But the pursuit was quickly taken up again with renewed fury. Trace, realizing that he could not risk leading the savage mob back to Rufus and the mule train, veered once again and headed directly north, away from the river.

It was a horse race now. The thing Trace was not sure of was the paint's endurance. He had never fully tested it, and he longed again for the bay. Still, the little pony maintained a steady gallop, stretching out across the rolling plains. Glancing behind him, he could see his pursuers still coming on, maintaining the pace but not closing the distance. How much longer could his horse hold out? He could see flecks of foam flying from the animal's mouth already. He glanced back again. He was not outrunning them. He had to go to ground.

Veering from his course once more, he headed the pony toward a narrow defile at the base of a hill, the Sioux no more than a hundred yards behind him now. The tired horse almost stumbled as he scrambled over the side of the gulch. Trace leapt out of the saddle immediately. He scrambled back up to the brow of the defile, hastily measuring powder and selecting a lead ball. After seating the ball and patch with the hickory rod, he laid the rifle aside and loaded his pistol. Satisfied that he had done all he could do for himself, he took up his Hawken and prepared to die.

The Sioux raced down to the flat before the hill, and charged toward the defile in which Trace had taken cover. Suddenly they pulled their ponies to a stop, still seventy-five yards away. Their ponies dancing and eager, the warriors appeared to be discussing something among themselves as they held their restless mounts back. Trace was puzzled by their hesitation. *They've already lost two of their number. They must have a helluva lot of respect for my rifle,* he thought.

He could have easily picked off the leader at this close range, but he decided to wait and see what they were going to do. Why didn't they advance? He looked to his right and left, thinking they might be waiting while some of their friends crept around to rush him from the sides. He couldn't spot anyone. Still they waited. A few minutes more passed, and then, to Trace's astonishment, the Sioux started slowly backing away. Maybe they had seen Rufus coming along behind and decided to go after him first. Maybe they simply respected his firepower and had decided not to lose any more warriors. He began to feel confident again, thinking that maybe he had faced down the entire band. He looked back quickly to make sure his horse was all right. When he did, a shadow caught his eye, causing him to glance up. There, on the crest of the hill behind him, was a long line of fifty or more warriors, silently sitting their ponies, watching the retreating line of Sioux.

Saved from the frying pan moments before, Trace was now in the fire for sure. In a panic, he scrambled across to the other side of the gully and prepared to meet an attack from the other direction.

Staying as low as he could, he raised his rifle and aimed at the warrior in the center of the file. The others all seemed to be watching him for a signal, so Trace figured him to be the leader. He remembered stories told by the trappers that sometimes a whole war party could be totally demoralized by the death of their war chief. Reluctant, however, to trigger the chaos that his shot was bound to ignite, Trace hesitated, deciding to let them fire the first shot. It occurred to him then that they had given no sign that they had even spotted him below them in the narrow passage. Instead, they seemed intent upon the party of Sioux, who now looked slightly disorganized, as if deciding what to do.

Trace lowered his rifle. He looked hard at the silent line of warriors above him and decided they were Crow. Even if they did sight him, he would be of little interest to them at this point, when a small band of their traditional enemies was before them. Badly outnumbered, the Sioux made their decision. Suddenly they turned and bolted toward the river. Trace heard a chorus of war whoops above him, and the Crows immediately swept over the crest of the hill in hot pursuit of the fleeing Sioux.

Trace was totally confused, uncertain what his course of action should be, caught as he was between two warring tribes. It appeared that he was out of danger for the moment. He watched wide-eyed while the band of Crows charged down the hill to the left of his position, ignoring him while yelling and whooping after the Sioux. When the last of the line had descended and were racing across the flat, Trace led his pony out of the defile and jumped into the saddle. He pointed the paint toward the side of the hill and angled across the path of the retreating Indians. His one thought now was to cut back toward the river to try to intercept Rufus, who must have heard all the commotion and was no doubt seeking a place to hide.

Racing along a wide ravine, he emerged upon the open flat, only to discover the battle had reversed its momentum. The large band of Crows was now on the run back toward him. Beyond them, toward the river, he could see what looked like an army of Sioux chasing them. "Sweet Jesus!" Trace exclaimed, looking around him in a frantic effort to find cover somewhere. Off to his left, there was a line of trees that indicated a stream. He headed straight for it.

The beating of his heart seemed to be in rhythm with the pounding of the paint's hooves in the sandy bank of the stream as he searched for a place where the bank was steep enough to protect him and his horse. Hearing the cries of the retreating Crows only yards behind him, he guided the paint down in the shallow water where a cottonwood leaned out across the stream.

Hastily tying his pony's reins to a willow whip, he crawled back to the base of the cottonwood to a position from which he could fire. To his immediate dismay, the retreating Crows had the same notion he had. Within seconds, the now disorganized band of fleeing warriors descended upon the bank of the stream. Warriors yelled to each other, horses screamed protests, lead balls snapped overhead. The desperate Crow ponies jumped and slid down the banks, seeking cover from the fierce pursuit. As quickly as possible, the riders were off their ponies and scrambling to defensive positions behind the banks. Painted warriors fell in on either side of Trace, only a few yards away, their bows ready to repel their enemy. They apparently took no notice of the white boy in their midst.

Like his unlikely allies, Trace was more concerned with the charging mob of Sioux, and he leveled his Hawken and took aim. The foremost of the attacking Sioux were now within two hundred yards of the stream. Trace set his sights on the lead man and squeezed the trigger. The Hawken spoke and the Sioux warrior rolled backward off his horse. Trace quickly reloaded. As he did, he glanced briefly to his right to meet the astonished eyes of the Crow warrior beside him. Clearly, the Crows had never seen a rifle with the long-range accuracy of his Hawken. There was no time for introductions. Trace aimed again and knocked another Sioux off his pony.

The second kill caught the attention of many of the other Crows in the stream, and out of the corner of his eye, Trace could see first one and then another of the embattled warriors as they craned to see from where the deadly fire was originating. Ignoring them, he reloaded as quickly as he could and fired again. Three enemies dead, and the Sioux were not yet in range of the Crows' bows and muskets.

Equally as confused as the Crows, the Sioux slowed their charge somewhat when three of their number were killed before they were within fifty yards of the stream. Clearly, their attack was disrupted, for one of the dead was their war chief. The assault continued, but without its initial resolve. The Crows, on the other hand, saw their wavering as a sign of defeat. One among them, an older warrior with three eagle feathers in his long graying hair, leapt up and yelled a challenge to his brothers, admonishing them to rise up and kill the hated Sioux. Almost as one, the Crows rose from the banks, their war cries splitting the air as they sent a deadly rain of arrows toward the approaching Sioux.

In the confusion that followed, Trace was not sure

what had actually taken place, or when he decided to join in the countercharge. He only remembered that he fired his rifle as fast as he could reload it amid the swarm of arrows and musket balls until everything went black.

"How long will you drag this white boy with us?" Yellow Bear asked. He stood gazing down at the injured young man on the travois. "It has been two days and still he babbles like a crazy man. I think he is already in the land of the spirits. It is only his mouth that won't die. I think we should leave him here."

Buffalo Shield listened patiently to Yellow Bear's words, well aware of the young warrior's distrust of all white men. He, too, looked at the young boy lying on the travois. He looked to be no older than his own son, Black Wing. "He fought beside us against the Sioux. It would not be right to leave him. It was his rifle that turned the Sioux attack when it looked like they might overrun us at the stream."

Yellow Bear scowled. "It was not the white boy who made the difference—it was that rifle. Anyone could have done it with the medicine gun."

Buffalo Shield gently reminded, "You tried to shoot the gun and could not get it to fire."

"The gun is useless," Yellow Bear retorted, a look of disgust on his face. "There is no flint to make the powder burn. The boy must have broken it."

"We'll keep it with him anyway. Maybe he knows how to fix it," Buffalo Shield decided.

Yellow Bear stood a few moments longer, staring

down at the injured white boy. "His head is broken," he concluded, and turned to mount his pony. "We have rested long enough. It's time to get started again. If you want to continue to take care of this dead white boy, it is for you to decide. If it were up to me, I would leave him here and take his horse. It is a fine-looking animal."

Buffalo Shield made no reply, but prepared to get on his horse. After he was mounted, he picked up the reins on Trace's pony and joined his fellow warriors on the trail north, leading the injured boy on the travois. He had been very impressed with the unusual young man who had joined in their fight with the hated Sioux. The strange new gun the boy carried reached out and killed two Sioux warriors before they were even in range of the few rifles the Crows had. His people had not had guns for very long, but they knew how to use them. This boy's weapon used powder and ball, like theirs, but the piece that held the flint was not there. Buffalo Shield was confident that the boy could explain it, if he ever came back from the land of the spirits. He believed the boy's unusual skill with the rifle was caused not by any strong medicine he possessed but merely by this new gun that they had not seen before. Buffalo Shield was interested in any new gun that would kill an enemy from two hundred yards away. He had decided to look after the sick boy until he either recovered or died. The boy deserved that—he had fought well. He had no one to look after him, anyway, for Buffalo Shield was sure that the white man's body they had found scalped near the river must have been the boy's friend—maybe his father.

For two days, as the Crow war party journeyed northwest, on their way back to their village on the Powder River, Trace bounced along on the travois—sometimes sleeping, sometimes murmuring incoherently on the edge of consciousness. Buffalo Shield was about to admit that Yellow Bear had been right, that it had been useless to drag the boy this far. But on the morning of the third day of their journey, when Buffalo Shield bent low to observe his patient, he was met by two wide blue eyes staring up at him.

Trace was at once alarmed. Upon awakening after what seemed a deep sleep and finding himself staring eyeball to eyeball with a Crow warrior, he was certain he was about to be scalped. He started to bolt upright, only to be stopped by a stabbing pain in the back of his skull that sent flashes of lightning before his eyes. He realized then that he had been injured. He sank slowly back down on the travois, aided by the gentle hand of the Crow warrior.

"Ah, you are back," Buffalo Shield said, smiling at the boy. "We thought you might be dead." The puzzled expression on Trace's face told him that the boy did not know his language. "Do you understand my words?" he asked. Again there was no response. Buffalo Shield continued to gaze upon the injured white boy for a few seconds longer before smiling reassuringly at him and rising to his feet. He turned to his son, Black Wing. "The boy does not speak our tongue. Go and ask Big Turtle to come make talk with him."

In a few minutes Black Wing returned, followed by a short, solidly built warrior. "So the white boy is not dead after all," Big Turtle said. He walked up close to Trace and stared down at him. "He looks like he is still a little crazy from that musket ball that bounced off his skull."

"It's hard to tell," Buffalo Shield replied. "He doesn't talk, or even groan—and I don't think he understands our tongue. Maybe his head was cracked."

Big Turtle looked back at Trace and smiled. To Buffalo Shield he said, "We'll find out." Speaking now in broken English, he knelt down close to Trace and asked, "Can you understand my talk?" Trace's eyes lit up at once, and he nodded his head. Big Turtle continued. "Can you talk?"

Again Trace shook his head yes, then said softly, "Yes."

"Good," Big Turtle said, nodding vigorously. He turned to Buffalo Shield. "Good," he repeated in the Crow tongue. Buffalo Shield nodded in response.

Big Turtle explained to Trace that he had been grazed by a Sioux rifle ball and had been asleep for a long time. Trace's memory of the fight near the Platte slowly returned to him, and he remembered shooting his rifle repeatedly, but nothing after that. Big Turtle explained that Trace was struck down from behind by a Sioux warrior, who was just about to reload and finish the boy off when Buffalo Shield sank an arrow into the Sioux's heart.

Trace shifted his gaze to the tall, lean warrior standing over him and smiled. To Big Turtle, he said,

"Tell him thank you." After waiting while Big Turtle relayed his thanks, Trace asked, "Am I a prisoner?"

Big Turtle quickly flashed a wide smile. "No, you are welcome guest—big medicine—shoot gun that kill far off." He nodded toward Buffalo Shield. "His name Buffalo Shield. He take care of you for two days. Not sure you alive or dead."

"Two days?" Trace gasped. "Have I been laying here for two days?"

Big Turtle nodded. "Three, counting today."

"Damn," Trace exhaled, then remembering, "Rufus!" His eyes wide in alarm, he asked, "There was another white man, driving a mule train—is he . . . ?"

"Dead," Big Turtle affirmed. "Sioux find him."

Trace sank back. This news was distressing. He felt a deep sadness for the loss of Rufus Dees, who had been so kind to the young boy setting out on his own. Then another thought struck him. "You say the Sioux killed him?" Big Turtle nodded. "Did they take everything?"

Big Turtle shrugged. "Reckon so. When we find him, there was nothing else."

The Sioux had obviously made off with all of Rufus's supplies, as well as his own bay horse, his traps and supplies, and the extra ammunition for his rifle. The thought of being unarmed caused him to glance sideways—at least the Crows had let him keep his Hawken and the lead and powder.

While Trace was silently contemplating his present situation, Big Turtle related their conversation to Buffalo Shield. When Buffalo Shield asked a question,

Big Turtle turned to Trace and asked, "What is your name?"

"Jim . . ." he said without thinking, then quickly added, "Trace."

"Jim Trace?" Big Turtle asked.

"No," Trace replied, "just Trace—my name's Trace." It might not be important that this wild band of Crows knew his real name, but there was no use taking the chance that they might pass it along to some white man. As feeble as he felt, Trace decided he was lucky to have been picked up by the Crows. When he thought about it, there could be few places better to hide from the Blunts than with a band of Crow Indians.

After having been unconscious for two days, Trace was badly in need of nourishment. Buffalo Shield and Black Wing soon brought him food and water. Rebounding with the healing capacity of youth, Trace spent only one more day on the travois before he was able to discard it and ride his horse again. Though his head still felt a little fragile, it was better on the paint than on the jolting travois. Most of the time, Black Wing rode by his side. Trace took an instant liking to the son of Buffalo Shield. He had a constantly pleasant disposition, and the two boys, while unable to talk to each other, still managed to communicate to some extent through nods, smiles, and gestures.

In the evening, Big Turtle would talk to Trace. He explained away the confusion Trace had felt when caught between the two warring tribes. The smaller group of Sioux that Trace had accidentally encountered were waiting to entice the Crows to chase them into an ambush, laid for them by the larger force of Sioux warriors. The Sioux were returning from a horse-stealing raid in Crow country, and the Crow war party, led by Yellow Bear, had been riding to overtake them.

Big Turtle said it was lucky for them that Trace had surprised the Sioux, getting them to chase after him, for it had brought them out in the open. Buffalo Shield, upon seeing the band of Sioux that chased Trace into the defile, counseled Yellow Bear to reconsider attacking the smaller party. He argued that this was not the same party of Sioux that had stolen their horses—they had no extra horses with them. But Yellow Bear had blood in his nostrils and would not wait. He led the charge down the hill and after the Sioux, only to be met by the larger band, waiting in ambush along the riverbank. They were lucky to escape with only a few dead. Buffalo Shield maintained that the main reason the Sioux decided to break off the attack on the disorganized Crows taking shelter in the stream was the rifle of the white boy.

Trace realized then why he was a welcome guest and being treated cordially by all the braves. All except one, that is—Yellow Bear. During the ride back to the village on the Powder, Yellow Bear presented nothing but a scowling face to Trace. Big Turtle said it was because he had a strong resentment toward all white men. He considered them inferior. Big Turtle himself was barely tolerated by Yellow Bear because of his own family history. Big Turtle told him that his father had been a white trapper who hunted for the Hudson's Bay Company. His father lived with the Crows until his death at the hands of a Gros Ventres warrior. But the fact that most warriors believed Trace and his medicine rifle were the reasons they had defeated the Sioux at the stream, only added to Yellow Bear's resentment of the young man.

The party of Crow warriors, along with the lone white boy, were on the trail for two more days before descending a line of low-lying bluffs that bordered the Powder River. On the opposite side of the river, in a grove of cottonwoods, Trace saw the lodges of Red Blanket's village. The camp stretched along the riverbank for what Trace estimated to be at least a quarter of a mile. At that moment in his young life, it seemed to be as far from St. Louis as the moon was from the earth. No one would find him here.

Through Big Turtle, Buffalo Shield invited Trace to come to live in his lodge with him and Black Wing. Black Wing smiled broadly, nodding vigorously, as Big Turtle translated. Trace accepted graciously, but voiced some concern as to what Buffalo Shield's wife might think of the arrangement. Buffalo Shield was quite puzzled that the boy would think Dull Moon would object. In fact, when told of Trace's part in the fight with the Sioux, Dull Moon was honored that he would come to her tipi.

Over the next few days, Trace was introduced to a way of living that was much to his liking. The simple, honest openness of the Indians' way of dealing with life's daily decisions appealed to Trace. They ate when they were hungry, slept when they were tired. When the grass was grazed out and the game became scarce, they packed up and moved to a new place. It seemed a natural way of life, one that he immediately embraced.

Trace's reputation as a marksman was established soon after he joined Red Blanket's village when he participated in a hunt for buffalo. The nights were becoming chilly by then, and the women of the village were busy working hides and drying meat for the fast-approaching winter. Buffalo had been sighted only two days' ride from their camp on the Powder, so the entire village packed up and moved north. Having fully recovered from the nearly fatal blow to the head, Trace was eager to join in the excitement of the hunt. He had never hunted buffalo, though he had heard Buck's tales of killing the great beasts of the prairie.

Black Wing was as eager to introduce Trace to the excitement of the tribal hunt as Trace was to go. He was helping Trace adorn his pony with bright jagged slashes of lightning in red and black paint when Yellow Bear rode by.

"So you go on your first buffalo hunt," he observed in a dry tone bordering on sarcasm. "How do you think to kill the buffalo? You have no weapon."

Although Trace was learning the language rapidly, he was unable to catch all of Yellow Bear's words. So Black Wing answered for him when he saw that his friend did not understand. "He will use his gun, the one that killed the Sioux warriors."

"Huh!" Yellow Bear snorted. "The gun is no good. It won't shoot anymore. He has broken it."

Trace, listening carefully, and watching their gestures as they talked, guessed what Yellow Bear's remarks concerned. Big Turtle had told him of Yellow Bear's earlier comments about the gun that no longer had flint to ignite the gunpowder. He held his Hawken up and pointed to it with his other hand, gesturing that it was big medicine. Yellow Bear snorted contemptuously and wheeled his pony, riding rapidly away.

A short distance away, readying his own horse for the hunt, Buffalo Shield had paused to watch the brief meeting. He was confident in the belief that the white boy would make the gun shoot. He would keep Trace close to him during the hunt, for he was curious to see how the boy would make the rifle fire again. Watching the two young boys preparing for the hunt brought a smile to the old warrior's face.

Scouts had been sent out ahead to find the buffalo and to determine the best plan of attack. They returned to the camp, which was now packed up and on the move, to report their findings. The most efficient way to kill as many animals as possible—stampeding the herd over a cliff—was not an option because of the absence of such terrain. Since the country near them offered no natural places to box in the buffalo so they could be slaughtered easily, it would have to be done on the run. Each hunter would fly into the herd and kill as many as he could from a galloping pony. This was the method that pleased Black Wing most. It was by far the most exhilarating.

Trace and Black Wing fell in with the other hunters and rode out to where the animals had last been seen. The scouts, leading the way, signaled for quiet as they made their way around a low line of hills that prevented the beasts from sighting them. Downwind of the grazing herd, the Crow hunters circled around until they were abreast of the largest concentration of the animals. They waited while six other braves came up from behind the herd to drive the buffalo toward the waiting hunters.

They waited for what seemed like an eternity to Trace. Finally the sound of musket fire broke the stillness, accompanied by the whoops of the riders coming up from the upper end of the valley. The hunters moved into position, straining to hold their skittish ponies back. Trace checked his load and seated the lead ball properly. Then he reached into his bullet pouch and retrieved a percussion cap. Buffalo Shield, watching the young man closely, muttered, "Ahh . . ." when he saw the small copper cap placed in position. *Yellow Bear will not be pleased with this,* he thought, smiling.

Red Blanket warned the anxious hunters to be patient and instructed them to hold their nervous mounts until the foremost buffalo had passed their position. Trace could see the herd now, so many that they filled the broad valley from side to side. As Trace watched in awe, the beasts in the rear started to run, causing those directly in front of them to bolt into those ahead of them. And so it progressed, like a great wave that begins slowly, picking up momentum until it crashes on the shore.

Red Blanket held his hand up, holding his hunters until the buffalo were within range of their bows and muskets. In the excitement of the moment, a young hunter behind Trace, struggling to keep his horse from backing into the hunter behind him, accidentally discharged his musket. A couple of hunters in the rear, thinking the signal had been given, charged over the crest of the hill, straight down toward the valley. Red Blanket tried to stop them, but it was too late. The leading buffalo turned and stampeded away from the waiting hunting party.

There was no choice but to follow and join in the chase. Hunters raced to get within range of their bows and the poorly made fusees, the muskets many of the Crows had traded from the Hudson's Bay Company. Trace gave the paint his heels, and the little pony tore off across the valley after the thundering herd. When he had closed the distance to within an effective range for his Hawken, he looped the reins around his saddle horn and brought the rifle up. They were such huge targets, how could he miss? He squeezed the trigger and dropped a large cow from a couple of hundred yards away. He reloaded as quickly as he could while hanging on to the racing pony with his knees. Another shot, and another buffalo tumbled, and again he reloaded. Still, they were not close enough for the Crow hunters to shoot.

By the time the main body of hunters had closed within range of their weapons, Trace had accounted for four of the huge shaggy animals. He was caught up now in a wild torrent of grunting dark bodies, veering right and left in a crazed panic, while daring Crow riders—their naked torsos painted with their own individual designs—darted in and out, loosing their deadly missiles. And then suddenly, on an unseen signal, the hunt was over. Trace pulled up and watched as the stampeding beasts turned down a narrow draw and thundered out of sight in a cloud of dust.

In spite of the premature warning that had set the herd off too soon, it was a successful hunt. A carnival atmosphere now descended upon the valley as the women and children began skinning and butchering the fallen beasts. Hurrying to the great dark mounds, the women were quick with their knives. The children waited eagerly for choice hunks of the still-warm livers, laughing delightedly at the blood-smeared faces of their playmates. It was all a fascinating spectacle to Trace.

To his surprise, Trace found himself the object of considerable attention. Many of the men came up to him to pat him on the shoulder and express admiration for his shooting. They were curious to examine the Hawken rifle, nodding to each other with smug expressions of approval. Of these hunters, Buffalo Shield was the most interested. He called Big Turtle to come and talk to Trace.

Trace explained that the rifle was an improvement over the older flintlocks, and he showed Buffalo Shield the small percussion caps that replaced the flints of the weapons that some of the braves were using. The rifle's much greater range was not due to the percussion cap, though, he explained. The Hawken was a rifle of enviable accuracy and power, far beyond that of their muskets.

"We have not seen a gun like this before," Big

Turtle said, as he ran a finger along the octagon-shaped barrel. "You're the first white man we've seen in a long, long time. Are all the white trappers carrying these new guns?"

"Well, no," Trace replied, "not all of 'em—but all that can get their hands on one."

Trace came to realize a general acceptance by Red Blanket's village after the hunt. Red Blanket, unlike Yellow Bear, held no deep hostile feelings toward the white man. He merely felt it prudent to avoid him whenever possible. In Trace, he recognized the potential to become a Crow brave, and he welcomed the boy and his rifle. Yellow Bear, on the other hand, was still unbending in his distrust for anyone of pale skin, and continued to show his contempt for the boy by ignoring him.

Chapter 8

In the fall of 1835, Fort Laramie was the major trading post between the Missouri and the Rockies. Jim Bridger had seen that potential when Bill Sublette and Robert Campbell built it, only a year before, and this was the reason he and his partner, Tom Fitzpatrick, bought it from them. The fort saw a wide variety of clientele passing through its front gate—trappers, hunters, traders, and Indians of several tribes. They traded animal skins for the luxuries the white traders offered; blankets, guns, powder, steel axes—and whiskey. All manner of men rode into Bridger's fort, some good, some bad. It was a man of the latter character that Morgan Blunt sought on this chilly afternoon in late September.

He sent his two men to ask around for Joe LaPorte among the small groups of trappers still lingering near the whiskey barrels, while he searched the camps outside the wooden palisades. There were not many trappers left around the fort. Most were free trappers who, being their own bosses, were getting a late start, for whatever reason. Bridger's company of men had long since left for the headwaters of the

Yellowstone. Morgan walked up to two old mountain men who were arguing over the proper method of tying a pack on a mule.

"Dammit, Frank, I reckon I know how to tie on a side pack. I reckon I've done it enough."

"Is that a fact?" Frank shot back. "Well, whose mule raked a sack of flour off on a pine tree near Henry's Fork?"

"I swear, Frank, that was three year ago. Ain't you ever gonna let that rest? I ain't so shore that weren't you that tied off that mule, anyway."

"The hell it was. I recollect that little loose knot of your'n, crossing it over the top to try to keep the slack out of it." He was about to go on when he realized that the rather large man with dark, scowling eyes had stopped behind Buck and was waiting to speak. "Howdy," he said, looking past Buck.

"I'm looking for Joe LaPorte. Have you seen him?" Morgan Blunt asked.

Frank eyed the stern-faced stranger for a moment before answering. An Easterner by the look of him—a trader, maybe. Frank wondered if the frown on the man's face was a permanent feature. It appeared that his countenance had never been graced by a smile. "Joe LaPorte?" Frank echoed. "No, I'm happy to say I ain't seen him."

Buck, never one to hesitate to pry into another's business, turned to scrutinize the stranger. It had been his experience that few white men confessed to having dealings with the notorious mountain man the Indians called Big Bear. "I heared a feller say he seen LaPorte hanging around that Injun camp over yonder." He gestured toward a group of Sioux lodges downriver a few hundred yards. "What are you lookin' fer that skunk fer? Somebody musta been murdered."

Morgan's scowl deepened. "What I want him for is my business." Then, realizing that he might need additional information from the two trappers, he grudgingly added, "No offense meant."

"Why, 'course not, stranger," Buck returned, studying the man as he would a scorpion crossing his path. "A man's business is his own."

Morgan attempted to smile in an effort to put the trappers at ease. The strain on his facial muscles was obvious. "The storekeeper said two trappers came to the rendezvous this summer with a young boy, about thirteen or fourteen, but the boy went back to St. Louis." Morgan paused, closely watching the eyes of the two men facing him. "His name's Jim Tracey. He should have been back here by now. Have you seen him?"

Frank quickly answered, "Don't recollect seeing anybody by that name. Do you, Buck?"

"Don't recollect," Buck replied.

"How about McCall?" Morgan asked.

"Nope," Buck answered. "You lookin' fer two boys?"

Morgan shook his head impatiently. "No, one boy—I just figured he might be using another name." Realizing it might sound a little strange to them, he said, "Jim's my nephew. I'm supposed to meet him out here." He was attempting to maintain an innocent facade, but his impatience was beginning to split the seams of his demeanor.

Buck was confident he could tell a maverick when he saw one, and he didn't like the look of this Easterner. Glancing at his partner, he saw a mirror image of his own thinking in Frank's eyes. He wasn't sure who this man really was, but he felt certain he was not the boy's uncle. He didn't feel obliged to tell Morgan anything at all, especially if he was in league with Joe LaPorte.

"So you're saying you haven't seen the boy," Morgan said, his dark eyes brooding under heavy eyebrows. "But Bridger's clerk in there says he's pretty sure you two had a boy with you at the rendezvous. How do you account for that?"

Buck's eyes narrowed. "Mister, I don't have to account fer nuthin'." The two men stood glaring at each other for a long moment before Morgan Blunt abruptly turned on his heel and headed toward the Sioux camp.

"I don't think he believes you, Buck," Frank said with a quiet chuckle.

"He does seem to be in a bit of a huff, don't he?" He pushed his hat back and thoughtfully scratched a shock of white hair. "Wonder why the likes of that coyote is lookin' fer Jim?"

"He must have got hisself in some kind of trouble in St. Louis."

Buck nodded his agreement. "Well, we ain't seen him since he left to go back East, and that's a fact. If he's come back, I kinda figured he'd look us up."

"Maybe so," Frank sighed. "Well, we're already

two days behind Bridger. We'd best get these mules packed and head out."

Morgan Blunt walked between the tipis, looking right and left, peering at the Sioux women busy at their cookfires. Most of the men were milling around the courtyard inside the fort, trying to trade skins for the many precious and exotic things the white man offered. Near the end of the row of lodges, he saw two Sioux men lolling drunkenly outside a tipi. *LaPorte,* he thought. *If he ain't in there, he's been there.* He walked brazenly up to the entrance flap.

"LaPorte!" he called. When there was no answer, he called out again.

From inside the tipi, the soft click of a hammer cocking could barely be heard. "Who the hell wants him?" a voice roared back.

"LaPorte!" Blunt called again. "Get your ass out here."

There was a hasty rustling of buckskin shirt and trousers, and the soft murmur of a female voice. "Shut up!" Blunt heard the man say. Moments later, the flap was thrown aside and LaPorte plunged through the opening. The man was so massive it appeared to Blunt that the tipi was giving birth to him. "By God, this better be somethin' damn important or I'm gonna have me a scalp!" His words rolled like thunder from his wide bushy head, causing the two drunken Indians to stagger to their feet, standing unsteadily for a brief moment before sagging back to the ground. LaPorte paid them no mind. His face, a mask of angry indignation, changed instantly when he recognized Morgan Blunt. Slowly, a sly smile crept through his heavy beard as he eyed his benefactor and partner in crime. "Well, now. Mr. Blunt."

Morgan Blunt, operating from the strength that financial power afforded, was one of the few men who was not intimidated by Joe LaPorte. He knew that as long as he paid LaPorte handsomely to do his dirty work, the bear of a man was his to command. "Come on out here, LaPorte. I've got a job for you and that band of Blackfeet of yours."

"Shhh," LaPorte quickly responded, his finger over his lips. Looking from side to side to see if anyone had heard, he took Morgan's arm and led him a few feet away from the tipi. "Don't talk about that, Mr. Blunt," he whispered. "I got me a little woman in there. If she finds out I run with the Blackfeet, she'd draw up like a persimmon—and most likely cut my throat to boot." He led Morgan a few feet farther. "Blackfeet ain't looked on too kindly around these parts."

"All right, all right," Blunt replied impatiently. "I've got a job for you, an important job." When he was satisfied that he had the huge man's attention, he continued. "This job can make you five hundred dollars if you do it right." LaPorte's eyes widened with the mention of such a princely sum. "All you have to do is find a fourteen-year-old boy and kill him."

LaPorte wasn't sure he had heard correctly. Five hundred dollars was a staggering amount of money just for killing one boy. "Five hundred dollars," he said, punctuating the comment with a low whistle. "Who is he? What did he do?"

"He's the boy you were supposed to take care of when you killed his father. You've already been paid to do the job, but you killed a half-breed boy instead." Blunt let that sink in before he continued. When LaPorte started to complain that it was not his fault, Blunt cut him off. "Never mind about that. You got paid to do a job and you didn't get it done. Now I'm giving you a chance to get it done right, and make yourself an extra five hundred to spend on your liquor and squaws."

A contrite LaPorte stammered his appreciation. "I'll sure get her done this time, Mr. Blunt. You can count on that."

"And, mind you, I won't tolerate any more mistakes. I want to see the boy's head so that I know you've done the job."

LaPorte grinned. "Yessir, don't you worry. I'll git him this time. Where do I start lookin' for him?"

Morgan then related all he knew about the possible whereabouts of young Jim Tracey—his escape from St. Louis after "murdering" Tyler Blunt, and Morgan's suspicion that he might now be using the name of McCall. "The little murderer had a taste for the frontier, and I know that he's bound for this part of the country. If I was you, I'd keep an eye on those two buzzards over there." He nodded toward the two trappers tending their mules some distance away. "The boy was running with them before. He might be planning to join up with them again."

"You must want this boy bad." LaPorte could plainly see the fire in Morgan's eyes when he talked about the boy. "How did he kill your brother?"

"With a knife," Morgan replied curtly. "But that's not important—it was murder, and I want him dead, I don't care how long it takes you. Find him!" Morgan held his temper in check, as he reminded LaPorte, "The sooner you find him, the sooner you get five hundred dollars."

"I'll find him." LaPorte needed no further incentive. The thought of that much cash was enough to make his mouth water. There was very little cash money west of the Missouri. Most everything a man needed had to be bartered for. He would soon be a very rich man.

Frank took the lead as they set out that morning. His horse, a dirty buckskin he called Tater, always wanted to be out front anyway, so he usually gave in to the ornery beast and let Buck follow. It had been three days since they left Laramie, and Frank had a worrisome feeling that kept gnawing away at his brain. More than a hunch, it was a sense some mountain men develop after years spent in the high country. It was hard to explain, like the time near Popo Agie Creek when a band of twenty Blackfeet snuck up on him and Buck just before daylight. They hadn't seen or heard anything, but they knew the Indians were there. And if they hadn't relied on their instincts, their hair would most likely have been waving on some Blackfoot buck's lance.

Frank had that same feeling now. Buck hadn't made any mention of it so far, but Frank noticed that his partner had paused several times during the day to look over their back trail. He decided to wait until they stopped to eat and rest the mules before expressing his concerns to Buck. When they had reached a line of trees that bordered the North Platte, he signaled Buck to follow him down a draw that ended at the river's edge.

Buck pulled up behind him and dismounted. Before Frank could comment, Buck asked the question, "When are we gonna git rid of whoever the hell's been tailin' us all the way from Laramie?"

"I was just about to ask you the same thing," Frank replied.

The natural thought was the possibility that some other free trappers were dogging them to see where they planned to trap. Buck had not been shy about bragging about their harvest at the rendezvous, and it had not been an especially productive year for most of the trappers. While it might be mentioned that one intended to trap in a general area, a man never pinpointed exactly where he was going to set his traps. By this time, nearly every beaver stream in the Rockies was well known, and every trapper was searching to find that one river, that one valley, that no one had trapped yet. For that reason, Buck and Frank were not surprised that someone might be following them.

"Whadaya wanna do?" Buck asked. "Lose 'em now? Or wait fer 'em to catch up?"

"Well, I dang shore wanna lose 'em before we git to South Pass, but why don't we just set here a while and see if they'll come on in. We might can persuade 'em that it'd be unhealthy to follow us."

"What if it's a bunch of Injuns lookin' to carve out our gizzards and steal our stock?"

Frank shook his head. "If it was a sizable bunch of Injuns, they'da already jumped us."

While the pack animals pulled at the grass near the riverbank, the two trappers made themselves comfortable under the trees and waited, rifles ready, watching the trail they had just traveled. The afternoon wore on and still there was no sign of anyone.

"Well, hell, whoever it is ain't coming in," Buck finally decided. "And I ain't aiming to set here all day." There was never any doubt in his mind that his intuition had been right. "They're figurin' to follow us all the way to the other side of the pass. Beaver's too scarce to be sharin' our huntin' grounds with anyone else."

They started out again, this time heading up the shallow water for more than a mile before leaving the river and doubling back in a wide circle. Both men were convinced that they were being followed, and their plan was to come up behind their pursuers. After backtracking about two miles, they cut back to cross their original trail. A few minutes' study of the tracks told them that what they had sensed was indeed fact. Two additional sets of hoofprints were intermingled with those of their own mules. "One man, leading a packhorse," Frank stated, and Buck agreed.

Prodding their mules into a faster gait, they retraced their steps until they came to the spot in the river where they had waited. The stranger's tracks followed theirs into the river. Keeping to the trees, they rode along the riverbank, their eyes alert, rifles in hand. When they approached the place where they had left the river, Buck suddenly signaled Frank to stop. A giant hulk of a man sat on his horse in the middle of the river, studying the tracks that led up from the water.

"LaPorte!" Frank muttered to himself.

Buck moved up quietly beside his partner. "What the hell does that coyote want with us?"

"Well, it ain't likely he's looking for beaver. That devil don't trap anything except humans," Frank replied. It had never been proven, but was widely suspected that the evil LaPorte came by the pelts he traded primarily by stealing and murdering the poor souls who had actually waded the icy streams. The issue to be decided now was whether it was best to face him down or try to lose him in the mountains.

"If LaPorte is trailing us, it ain't fer no good reason," Buck said. "I'd just as leave git to the bottom of it right now."

Frank agreed that that might be best. They tied the pack mules in the trees and rode to intercept LaPorte when he came out of the water. The huge man was so absorbed in studying the bank for tracks that he didn't notice the two trappers waiting for him until his horse climbed up from the water.

"Whoa!" he roared, startled by the sudden appearance of the two he had been tracking. Taken aback only briefly, he quickly recovered his customary smirk. "Well, if it ain't Buck and Frank. Fancy running into you two varmints."

"Fancy my ass," Buck retorted. "You've been tailin' us ever since we left Laramie."

LaPorte snorted a laugh. "What the hell would anybody wanna tail you two birds for?"

"That's what we aim to find out," Frank answered. "I don't see no traps on that packhorse. What do you want, LaPorte?"

LaPorte's gaze shifted from Frank to Buck and back again. "Maybe I just wanna join up with you boys."

"Wouldn't that be precious?" Buck replied, his tone flat and sarcastic. "The answer to all my prayers."

LaPorte's brows knotted, his eyes narrowed, and he quickly tired of playing the word game. "I heared you boys take on a new partner now and again. Where is that young boy that was riding with you two at rendezvous? Is he gonna meet you someplace?"

Frank cocked his head to one side and squinted at the dangerous giant of a man. "Now that's the second person that's asked us about that young boy this week. We ain't seen him since Green River. How come ever'body's wantin' him of a sudden?"

"Oh, I got a message for him. His daddy wants him," LaPorte said, a wide smile across his face.

Frank didn't blink. He wasn't sure LaPorte had the mental acuity to deliver a pun. One thing he was sure of, though—LaPorte had no honest business with the boy. "That boy's gone back East."

LaPorte sneered at Frank. "Maybe he is—maybe he ain't. I'll find him if he's west of the Missouri. I got friends that'll help me find him. It's dangerous country for a boy." The sneer faded from his face. "It's also dangerous country for two old coots like you two. You never can tell when a war party might strike your trail."

"I've had about enough of you, LaPorte," Frank said. "Now 'spose you just git your sorry ass out of here so my mules can git your smell outta their nostrils."

A quick spark of rage flashed in LaPorte's eye. He jerked the pistol from his belt and pointed it at Frank's belly.

Buck had already sidestepped his horse around to a position behind LaPorte. "Wonder how big a hole this here buffaler gun would make at this close range," Buck commented casually.

LaPorte froze. Slowly he withdrew the pistol and stuck it back in his belt. He didn't utter a word. He didn't have to—his face said it all. He had been bested this time, and he didn't like it. Scowling darkly, he wheeled his horse and galloped away toward the north.

"Enjoyed the visit," Buck called out after him. "Don't be a stranger now." To Frank, he said, "Goin' back to his Blackfeet."

Frank nodded soberly. He watched the departing man as he galloped out through the cottonwoods and disappeared over the top of the bluff. "I think we just made a bad mistake there—I'm thinkin' you shoulda shot him. We'd best watch our backs."

They decided it was best to stay right where they were for the rest of the day and make a show of setting up camp. It didn't figure that LaPorte was going to give up on them just because they had confronted him. Evidently he had reason to believe they knew something about Jim. Well aware of LaPorte's capacity for dirty dealings, they decided the thing to do was sneak out after dark and try to lose him.

Their caution was unnecessary, for LaPorte had decided the two old trappers had no notion where the boy was. When he galloped away from the riverbank, he pointed his horse directly north, heading for Blackfoot country and his friend, Lame Fox. He was going to need some help if he was to earn his five hundred dollars, and Lame Fox could send out the word that he was looking for a white boy. It might be impossible to find one young boy, even a white one. An entire tribe would be hard to find in the territory west of the Missouri. He had told Morgan Blunt that it might take some time, but Blunt just ordered him to find the boy, no matter how long it took. Winter would be setting in before long, and LaPorte wanted to find Lame Fox's camp before the first snows came. It was his intention to look for the boy at Fort Union, at the mouth of the Yellowstone, and at Fort Cass, at the mouth of the Bighorn. Both trading posts were places where a young man looking for a place to hide might show up.

Frank and Buck made their way through South Pass, then north to trap the western slopes of the Wind River Range. When winter set in, they would camp at the Forks of the Snake—or maybe join Bridger's bunch on the Yellowstone. Though they kept a sharp eye for the likes of Joe LaPorte and hostile Indians, they saw no more of the loathsome Mr. LaPorte that fall.

* * *

The object of LaPorte's search, young Trace McCall, was even then no more than fifty miles away as the hawk flies. His eyes trained on a thicket of scrub trees and brambles, he waited, not moving, as his friend Black Wing cupped his hands before his lips and expertly produced the mating call of a bull elk. They had left their ponies tied below and climbed high up through the mountain meadows, Black Wing calling out as they went. This late in the fall, the bulls were seeking out their mates, and soon the mountain air was filled with the bugling of the big beasts.

Now Trace caught sight of a big bull's antlers thrashing through the brush of the thicket. Black Wing bugled again, and the bull turned in their direction, furious—positive that some stranger was trying to mate with his cows. He snorted frantically, overcome with jealous rage, and squealed and whistled at the would-be intruder. Other bulls on the far side of the meadow echoed his warnings, and soon the clamor was almost deafening.

Black Wing looked back at Trace and they both smiled. "You'd better shoot straight or this one will chase us all the way back down the mountain," Black Wing said.

"If we don't shoot straight, you might have to mate with him. You're the one doing the bugling."

An agitated bull could be dangerous, especially if wounded, so they positioned themselves to shoot from two sides, aiming for the lungs. Trace could have easily shot the bull from a comfortable distance with his rifle, but he had decided it best to save the little powder and lead he had left. Consequently, it was necessary to get in close to make their bows effective.

Suddenly there was an explosion of cracking limbs, and the bull elk burst through the thicket, six or seven hundred pounds of hurtling rage. *Thung! Thung!* Two bowstrings released. The elk continued charging for another twenty-five yards before abruptly crashing to the ground, his forelegs folded underneath him.

The two boys looked at each other and smiled their approval. Buffalo Shield would be very proud. The village was moving to winter camp and the elk's meat and hide would be needed. Trace was well pleased with himself. The prospect of spending the coming winter in Dull Moon's warm tipi greatly appealed to him, and any thoughts of St. Louis and the Blunts were far from his mind.

Hamilton Blunt looked up from his desk when his brother entered the room. "Well?" was his only greeting, even though it had been well over a month since Morgan had left to meet LaPorte at Fort Laramie.

Morgan, equally as brusque, answered. "I saw LaPorte. He knows what to do."

Hamilton, never a man of patience when it came to waiting for his orders to be carried out, was not satisfied with his brother's answer. "Well, was there any sign of the boy?" Morgan shook his head. "Had anyone seen him?" Again Morgan shook his head. "Did you tell LaPorte to get off his behind and go out and find him?"

"Dammit, Hamilton, I put LaPorte on it! Nobody's seen the little son of a bitch since summer. You're talking about thousands of square miles of prairie and mountains out there. He ain't gonna find him overnight. It might take some time, but LaPorte'll find him. A young white kid out there by himself will show up sooner or later." Morgan settled himself in a chair opposite the desk. "I'll be going back out there in the spring. I'll bring his scalp back for you." A hint of a sneer formed at the corners of his mouth. "It'll make a nice little wristband for your bride."

Hamilton failed to appreciate his brother's crude humor. "You need to watch your mouth, Morgan." He brooded over the information just given him for a few moments before speaking again. "I want his head," he said softly.

"My goodness, am I interrupting something?"

Both men turned quickly as Julia came silently through the door. "No, of course not, dear," Hamilton quickly replied. "We were talking business, that's all."

She graced them with a smile, making a special effort to seem cordial toward Hamilton's moody brother. In truth, she was not pleased to see Morgan back in St. Louis. The man made her uncomfortable. With his ever-present leer, he seemed to regard her with contempt. When she had spoken to Hamilton about Morgan's seemingly hostile attitude toward her, he said that it was largely her imagination. She feared that Morgan harbored ill feelings about her—and maybe even held her responsible for Tyler's death.

It had been a horrible nightmare for her, recalling the circumstances of Tyler Blunt's death. It had been so terribly difficult for her to accept the fact that her son Jim was capable of something so heinous. Hamilton had tried to spare her as much pain as possible when he explained how Jim had cold-bloodedly stalked Tyler and stabbed him from behind. Hamilton had even tried to accept some of the blame, saying that he should never have sent Tyler over there to try to persuade Jim to come and live with them. It grieved her to think about it. Jim had always been such a kind and loving boy. What would his father have thought? That notion caused her to experience a tiny twinge of guilt, and she unconsciously glanced down at the satin dress she wore. It was a sight different from the homespun she'd worn when John was alive. *I don't have any reason to feel shame,* she told herself. *John would be pleased that Hamilton was here to take care of me.*

Gathering her wits about her, she effected a warm smile. "Well, brother Morgan, I'm happy to see you made a safe journey back." Morgan didn't reply, but continued to sneer. She turned quickly to her husband. "Hamilton, would you speak to Frances? I want to bake an apple cake, and she insists that you gave her orders to keep me out of the kitchen." If Julia could have had her way, Frances would no longer be in Hamilton's employ. But Hamilton would not even discuss the possibility of firing Frances. She had taken care of him and his house for years now, and she looked upon Julia as little more than a nuisance living in what she felt was her own house.

Hamilton Blunt favored his bride with a benevolent smile. "Why don't you tell Frances what kind of cake you want? She'll bake it for you. You know I don't want you to soil your pretty hands by slaving in the kitchen." Hearing a contemptuous snort from Morgan, he quickly cut his brother short with a searing glance. He got up from the desk and, taking Julia by the arm, escorted her to the door. "Now why don't you go on down to the parlor and I'll join you for some coffee in a few minutes, as soon as Morgan and I finish up a little business here."

Making an attempt to be cordial to her brother-in-law, she called back, "Morgan, will you be joining us?"

Hamilton answered for him. "No, Morgan's going down to the freight yard." When she left the room, he closed the door behind her and turned to face his brother. "You make sure that damn half-wit LaPorte knows how important it is to eliminate that brat of hers?"

"He knows," Morgan said with a shrug. "Besides, he wants the money."

"Dammit," Hamilton spat, "I can't have that boy showing up around here again. People might start believing his side of the story."

"Hell, why are you so worried? He'd be a damn fool to show up here again. Anyway, he ain't gonna do much talking after LaPorte and his boys find him."

Hamilton's concern that Trace might return and go to the sheriff with his version of Tyler's death was muted when winter set in for good during the following weeks. Travel to or from the western frontier had halted completely. It would be some months before the trails were passable for even mule trains to get through.

Far across the frozen plains from St. Louis, in a sheltered valley in the Big Horn Mountains, Trace McCall contented himself to spend the long winter with his Crow family. Snug in the warmth of Dull Moon's tipi, he sat with Buffalo Shield and listened to the old man's tales of the history of his people, working on the horn bow he was making. The buffalo had been plentiful and their food stores were ample. Trace and Black Wing would not have to leave the safety of the valley until the weather was good enough to hunt in the mountains once more.

Chapter 9

Joe LaPorte sat in the back of the disabled prairie schooner, its broken wheel causing the wagon to sag toward the right. Four mules lay dead in their traces where his Blackfoot war party had shot them down. While his Indian friends plundered through the sacks and barrels thrown from the wagon, LaPorte thumbed through a cloth-bound family album that contained a stack of letters.

LaPorte stared at the pages of words, all of them meaningless to him since he could not read. Still, he leafed through them as if hoping to find some clue that might indicate that the young man lying dead beneath the wagon was the boy he searched for. Some were written in large, bold strokes, some in a more delicate script. He glanced down at the mutilated body before him and shook his head in disgust. This was not the boy. Angry, he threw the letters aside and climbed out of the wagon to join in the whooping and laughing of the circle of warriors as they indulged in the slow torture of the young man's wife.

She had been a pretty little thing, and there had

been quite an argument before he could convince his Blackfoot friends that she must be killed. Lame Fox's nephew, Two Humps, wanted very much to keep the woman. But LaPorte insisted she had to be killed. He couldn't leave witnesses alive. Otherwise, he would not be free to come and go in the white man's forts. It was Lame Fox who saw the logic in this and ordered his nephew to take her life.

She was almost dead now, her homespun dress soaked with blood, as she knelt on the ground, her chin resting on her chest. Her screaming had stopped long before as she waited for the blow that would take her away from this world of suffering. When it came, she made no sound other than the rush of her final breath. She sagged to the ground, the axe still buried in her neck.

Four years was a long time to search for one white boy in a wilderness that stretched beyond the Rocky Mountains. LaPorte was halfway convinced that Jim Tracey—or McCall, whatever his name was—no longer existed. No doubt he had fallen prey to a war party and his bones lay bleaching in the sun somewhere in the vast regions of endless plains—or perhaps he hadn't come west at all. LaPorte had long since given up on earning the five hundred dollars that Morgan Blunt had dangled as enticement to find and eliminate one fourteen-year-old boy. After four years, the boy was closer to a grown man than he was to a kid. How would he recognize him if he saw him? Still, Morgan Blunt journeyed out from St. Louis to find LaPorte each spring, admonishing him to find the boy. LaPorte had taken the lives of several young white men who had the misfortune to be traveling alone, yet none was the boy he so desperately searched for.

He opened the flat tin box and looked again at the money inside, a sizable sum saved up to start a new life beyond the mountains, no doubt. There was not much else of value to be gained by the murder of the young couple—a small amount of powder and shot, some flour, some salt pork, a bolt of cloth, and a few trinkets. LaPorte toyed with the idea of taking this young man's head to Morgan Blunt and claiming it was that of Jim Tracey. He was tired of waiting for the reward Blunt had promised him. It was unlucky that the man's hair was dark brown; Blunt had specifically told him that young Tracey's hair was sandy. "Damn!" he uttered in disgust and turned to fetch his horse. He called to Lame Fox, "If your boys are through having their fun with the woman, let's get out of here."

It had not been a rewarding spring for Buck Ransom and Frank Brown. There were too many trappers in the mountains, and there were not many beaver streams that had not been trapped out. Some of their old friends had already given up on trapping as a way of life. To make matters worse, the price of beaver plews had dropped even further since the year before. Five years ago, a prime beaver pelt brought six dollars; last year it brought three. Sublette predicted that in a year or two you wouldn't be able to give one away. Silk, he lamented, was what had killed beaver.

"Well, I reckon we're gonna have to give up on beaver," Frank said as they discussed the gloomy outlook. "Buffalo hides is the thing now."

"Give up?" Buck retorted indignantly. "Why, I reckon not! Beaver'll shine agin. Just wait till them silk hats start coming apart in the rain. They'll be wantin' beaver right enough."

"I swear, Buck, sometimes I wonder if you ever notice what the hell's goin' on around you. We ain't never had such a skimpy load of plews before, and this close to rendezvous." Without thinking, he looked from side to side before adding, "And we had to come this far up in Blackfoot country to git these."

They had both seen sign during the last couple of days, most likely hunting parties passing through the mountains. And just the day before Frank had been forced to lay behind a creek bank, neck-deep in icy water, to avoid being seen by a party of about twenty Blackfeet. For safety's sake, it was time to cross back over to the western side of the mountains and start working their way down toward the Green River.

After looking over their packs to make sure everything was tidy, both men climbed aboard their horses. Buck took the lead as they filed out of the shallow gorge where they had camped for the previous two days. He had just cleared its rim when a musket ball whistled past his nose. By the time he heard the shot, he had already jerked his horse back down into the gorge again. He heard his pack mule scream behind him as an arrow buried itself in the animal's neck.

Frank wheeled in beside him, bending low in the

saddle. "Head for the creek bank," he yelled and raced for cover with Buck on his heels. Behind them, the air quickly filled with musket balls and war whoops.

"Blackfoot!" Buck yelled as he whipped his horse frantically. The race was on, the Indian ponies swiftly closing the distance between them. Buck drove his horse recklessly over the rough gullies that wound down to the creek bottom. When he was within a dozen yards of Buck's pack mule, one Blackfoot tried to get a shot off with his bow, but the roughness of the terrain spoiled his aim and he gave it up. Driving hard, the warrior instead caught up to the pack mule and grabbed the animal's tail, hoping to slow the mule down. Buck pulled his pistol out and blasted the warrior off his pony. This caused the rest of the war party to pause momentarily before charging after them again. It was all the time the two trappers needed to reach the safety of the sandy creek bank.

They slid off their horses and quickly hauled them down behind the high bank. Buck tied the animals in a patch of willows while Frank scrambled back up to the lip of the bank to hold off their attackers.

"Give me your rifle," Frank barked, "and hurry up with them mules!" He fired, killing a charging young buck with a ball in his chest. As the warrior fell, Frank grabbed Buck's rifle and killed the warrior directly behind the first one. This stopped the charge while the savages reconsidered swarming the sharp-shooting trappers. Frank quickly reloaded both rifles. "Buck, what the hell are you doin'?"

"Just hold on, dammit! I'm trying to git this dang arrow outta my mule's neck."

"Damn that mule! You're gonna be tryin' to pull arrows outta your ass if you don't git up here and help me!"

Buck crawled up beside his partner. He took his rifle from Frank and reloaded his pistol. "What are you frettin' about, Frank? You stopped 'em, didn'tcha?"

"We thinned 'em out a little. They're setting behind that bluff, tryin' to decide if they're gonna give her another try or wait till dark."

"Hell, they ain't gonna come at us agin," Buck said. "That ain't their style. They've done lost three. They'll be waitin' till dark to try to sneak up on us."

"Maybe," Frank allowed. He never took anything for granted.

"They've had enough," Buck insisted. "I know Blackfeet. They ain't willin' to risk any more necks."

No sooner had the words left his mouth when the savages rose up from the bluffs and mounted another charge upon the two trappers. "Oh, shit," Buck blurted and fired, taking out the lead rider. Frank waited a few seconds, giving Buck time to reload, before he picked the closest brave and cut him down, reloading himself as soon as he had pulled the trigger. In seconds, Buck was ready to fire again. Firing at staggered intervals, they were able to inflict heavy losses upon the Blackfeet. When their leader called the attack off, there were four more warriors lying dead before the creek bank.

"You all right?" Frank asked when a lull in the fighting occurred.

"Reckon so," Buck answered. "They shore tore up this cottonwood over my head, though." He motioned toward the shattered tree trunk with his head while reloading his rifle.

Frank glanced up at the splintered bark only inches above Buck's head. "There's more than a few old fusees in that bunch. Somebody's got a decent rifle." He squinted toward the bluffs where the band of Blackfeet had once again retreated. "I reckon they won't be trying that no more. Nuthin' to do now but sit tight until dark. Then we'd best git our asses out of this place."

Buck nodded. Frank had just about summed it up. The spot they had landed in by the creek was defensible against a frontal charge, like the two they had successfully repelled. But he knew that they would be sitting ducks if they stayed there much longer. Even if they defended both sides of the creek, they were still vulnerable from the upstream and downstream sides. Their only hope was to slip out under cover of darkness.

On the far side of the bluffs, Lame Fox was visibly distressed. After seeing their firepower, he had thought it unwise to rush the two trappers the second time. But LaPorte had persuaded him to take the risk, and now he had lost seven of his bravest warriors. LaPorte himself had not participated in the headlong assault, preferring to remain hidden in the bluffs, taking shots from a distance. He could not, he insisted, afford to be seen by the two white trappers in the event that Lame Fox's warriors were not successful in overrunning them.

"Their guns are too strong," Lame Fox complained. "It was not a wise thing to do. Now I have lost seven warriors, and the white men are still alive."

"You should have kept going," LaPorte replied coldly. "You almost had them when you turned back. They can't reload but so fast, and your warriors were almost on top of them when you quit."

Lame Fox did not take the criticism kindly. "Their guns are too strong," he repeated, openly irritated. "They are better than the few old muskets we have."

"We don't wanna let those two old buzzards get away. They've got rifles—pistols too—and powder and lead, and horses. You need that stuff." *And I need those two scalps,* he thought to himself. Ever since his confrontation with Buck and Frank four years before on the North Platte, he had been waiting to catch the two of them when he had Lame Fox's warriors with him.

Lame Fox certainly desired the guns and powder, but the fire that burned in him now was for his seven dead warriors lying between the bluffs and the creek bank. They must be avenged. He would wait for darkness, when his warriors could surround the two white men and slip into their camp under the mantle of night. Upon LaPorte's suggestion, however, he sent warriors out right away to station themselves upstream and down, as well as behind the trappers on the other side of the creek.

Frank lowered his head a bit when he heard the solid *thump* of another arrow embedding itself in the trunk of the tree above him. "There's one of 'em down there somewhere near the bend of the crick. If he shows his pretty head, I'll light up his ass for him."

"Well, they're on both sides of us now. Keep your eye peeled 'cause there'll be some more workin' around behind us." He took his knife and worked a little more dirt away from the shallow trench he had fashioned, in which he planned to lay his rifle. "I'm sorta surprised they didn't git a little discouraged when we thinned 'em out like that. Somebody must want our scalps pretty bad."

Frank agreed. "They must. Too bad we're gonna have to disappoint 'em."

They settled back and waited. Both men knew they were pretty much painted in a corner with little chance of slipping out with their horses and mules. If it was the horses the Blackfeet were after, the two might be able to slip out on foot. But then it would be only a matter of time before the Indians tracked them down. Without admitting the possibility to each other, both men resigned themselves to meet the fatal end that many trappers came to in this wild country. At least they were prepared to make it a costly victory for the savages.

The afternoon wore on, and the shadows began to lengthen. The two trappers lay quietly behind their dirt fortifications, one on either side of the creek. The still of the afternoon was broken only occasionally by a grunt or a whispered comment by one of the men—or the urgent whine of an arrow passing overhead. When the sun started its descent behind the mountains, the silence was broken by the singsong chant of Lame Fox's warriors on the far side of the bluffs.

"Sounds like they's gittin' wound up to go," Buck said.

"I reckon," Frank replied. "You wanna stick it out here or make a run fer it?"

"I'd just as soon stick it out here as long as there's light to shoot by. When it gits too dark to see, maybe we can slip out while they're slippin' in."

They waited, fully aware that their chances of slipping by the Blackfeet in the darkness were not very good.

The singing that had continued uninterrupted during the late afternoon suddenly stopped. Moments later, the crack of rifles and shrill war cries split the air. Frank and Buck bolted up, ready to repel the attack, each man frantically searching the bluffs before him, trying to find a target. But there was no sign of anyone. Still the shooting and yelling continued behind the bluffs, as if a major battle was taking place. Baffled, Buck crossed back over to Frank's side of the creek. "What in tarnation are they doin'?" In only a few moments his question was answered.

Suddenly a handful of Blackfeet came charging over the bluffs. Frank and Buck readied their rifles. "Hold on a minute!" Frank yelled, for the Indians were not making a charge toward them. They were running for their lives.

"What the hell?" Buck said. The trappers wasted no more time talking but opened fire on the fleeing

Blackfeet and managed to reduce their number by two more before they were out of range. There was no time to rejoice, however, for a party of fifty or more Indians appeared at the top of the bluff, racing down after the routed Blackfeet.

"Crow!" Frank announced. "No wonder they're running." Both men had the same thought—just when things looked as bad as it could get, they suddenly got worse. Though they were spared by the Crows' onslaught, their lives were equally in danger from the very same band of warriors that continued to thunder after the Blackfeet. There were more than twice as many Crows as there had been Blackfeet, and Crows were not overly friendly toward white men at the present time, either. The trappers rapidly reloaded their rifles.

"Maybe we can sneak out of here before they see us—they'll be so busy chasin' their old enemies they ain't gonna pay no attention to us," Buck suggested.

"I don't know," Frank replied. "If they ain't seen us, it might be smart to just lay low here till they're gone." He crawled up to the top of the bank to get a better look at the running battle between the two Indian forces. In little more than a moment, he eased himself back down behind the bank. "It's too late. This stew's still cookin'."

Buck crawled up to have a look for himself. There, on a low rise overlooking the bluffs, half a dozen Crow warriors sat on their ponies, the rest of their party having disappeared over the rise after the retreating Blackfeet. The Crows were involved in an animated discussion, with one of them periodically pointing toward the two white men. Buck had a pretty good guess what the conversation was about. He slid back down the bank. "Well, partner, I thought we was in the clear, but I reckon we're gonna be here a while yet."

"There are only two of them," Yellow Bear insisted. "I say we go down and kill them."

Buffalo Shield glanced at Trace briefly before turning back to see how their chief would answer Yellow Bear. He had thought about the possibility of this confrontation with white men ever since he had taken Trace to live in his tipi. It had been a concern of his that the boy, though almost thoroughly embracing the Indian way of life, would have a difficult decision to make when this time came. Trace was now fully accepted by the band of Crows as one of them. But would his white blood dominate when it came to the question of fighting his own kind? He watched Trace closely as the boy walked his pony close up beside his adopted father.

Red Blanket was not as eager as Yellow Bear. He looked around him at the bodies of dead Blackfoot warriors. After a moment he spoke. "I see the bodies of nine of our enemies lying on the ground. I think we'd better think some more before we charge those two white men, or our own dead will be lying with the Blackfeet."

Yellow Bear was beside himself. Two of the cursed hair-faces were boldly making a stand in the heart of Crow hunting grounds. "Are you saying that we should ride off and leave the evil dogs in peace?"

Red Blanket was patient with his fiery warrior. "I didn't say we should leave them in peace. I only said that we should think before we fight them. I think we must wait until the others return. Then we can surround them. What do you say, Buffalo Shield?"

"I say we should join the others who are chasing the Blackfeet and leave these two in peace. After all, they have killed many of our enemies, and they have killed none of our people."

Yellow Bear became enraged. "Buffalo Shield speaks like a woman because of his white son." His face was dark with anger as he stared defiantly at Buffalo Shield. "I will not leave these dogs in peace. They are our enemies. I, Yellow Bear, will ride against them alone if none of my brothers have stomach for the fight."

"These white men have committed no crime against us," Buffalo Shield insisted. "If they kill our enemies, are they not our friends?"

Before Red Blanket could answer, Yellow Bear shot back, "The white man is no friend to any of our people! He is in our land, killing our game. They must die! If we let them live, more will come."

Red Blanket listened patiently to the argument between the two warriors, knowing in his mind that he would not be swayed by either. What Buffalo Shield said was true—the two white men had done them no harm. But who could say that tomorrow these same two men would not aim their rifles at Crows? It was better not to trust the whites. "I think it is best to kill the white trappers. We need their horses and guns. We will wait until the rest of our warriors have returned."

Trace backed his pony up a few paces. More than an interested spectator, he had listened intently to the discussion between the chief and his warriors. A hailstorm of thoughts was swirling inside his brain as he realized the significance of these moments in his life. For now he must choose—Indian or white? He had had recurring thoughts of this possibility during the last four years, but he had shunted them away in the back recesses of his mind, not wanting to think about it—hoping the moment would never come. He had had no contact with whites these past years, except on those occasions when the village traveled to Fort Cass to trade their pelts for supplies and ammunition. Even then, he had remained in the background, and the traders never suspected that he was not a Crow. He had hunted with his friend Black Wing, and he had fought with him against the Blackfeet and the Gros Ventres. He had found peace within himself while living with the Crows. But something inside told him that the blood he felt racing through his veins was white blood.

Now, listening to talk of killing two trappers, his mind was in turmoil, creating confusion. Thoughts of his father filled his mind now—and the vivid image of that time, four years ago, when he had found his father and Henry Brown Bear slaughtered by the Blackfeet. He knew right then that he could not participate in the killing of these white trappers. For a brief summer, he had been a trapper himself. And, but for the unfortunate meeting on the Platte that had taken Rufus Dees's life, he would be trapping now.

Trace reined his pony back a few more paces, separating himself from the Crow warriors. He looked toward Buffalo Shield, who was even then searching the boy's eyes, then back at Red Blanket. "I cannot do this thing," he said. "These trappers are the same blood as my father and mother. If they were evil men—if they had committed a wrong against the Crow people—then I would not hesitate to fight them. But these men have not harmed us. I won't raise my hand against them."

Yellow Bear scoffed openly at the young white man. "It is as I said from the first day Buffalo Shield brought this whelp into our village. He could never be a Crow. He is white, like the two curs down there."

Ignoring the insults of Yellow Bear, Buffalo Shield moved up beside Trace. Placing a reassuring hand on Trace's arm, he said, "I understand what is in your heart. It's all right. You don't have to join in the fight."

"If he does not, then he must be driven from the village," Yellow Bear said, his voice filled with venom, "or killed along with his white friends."

Red Blanket raised his arm, demanding silence. "Long Rifle will not be harmed. He is a friend. It is his decision to make if he fights the white trappers or not." He was about to say more when he was distracted by movement near the creek bank.

"The white men are trying to sneak away!" The shouted warning came from a young warrior behind

Red Blanket. All eyes turned immediately to the creek. One of the trappers was leading his horse through the willows on the other side of the creek. The other was not far behind him. They had not reached the end of the willows when the rest of Red Blanket's Crows suddenly appeared before them, returning from their pursuit of the Blackfeet. Their escape cut off, the two trappers had no choice but to return to their positions on the creek bank.

Trace's heart caught in his throat. During the brief moments when the trappers were scrambling back to cover, he got a glimpse of them out in the open. He recognized them immediately—*it was Buck and Frank!* Confusion swirled his emotions for only an instant. Now it became crystal clear what his choice must be. It was no longer a simple decision not to join in an attack on two white trappers, for now the trappers were no longer nameless, faceless trespassers. Buck Ransom and Frank Brown were his friends. There was no choice before him.

He pulled his pony even further back and his eyes sought those of Buffalo Shield. The man had been a father to him for the past four years. He shifted his gaze to the open, honest face of his friend Black Wing. His gaze was met with one of equal intensity, questioning the steely determination he now saw in Trace's eyes. There was a long moment of silence as his Crow brothers waited for him to speak. When he finally spoke, it came from his heart.

"I know those men," Trace began. "They are my friends. They once helped me when I was alone and desperate." He looked directly into Red Blanket's eyes. "I ask that you leave them in peace."

"Ha!" Yellow Bear grunted, and would have added scathing words to his contempt, but Red Blanket silenced him with a raised hand.

"The white men do not belong in our land. They have no right to take our game. If we let these men go, then more will come. We cannot permit this." Red Blanket turned to Buffalo Shield, knowing the old warrior's affection for the tall young man. "I think your white son has a decision to make."

Trace had thought at first to make a plea to let Buck and Frank go. But he realized it was not as simple as that. For now it was plain where his allegiance stood, and it would only be a matter of time before another such situation presented itself, requiring him to choose again. He was a white man. He could not fight white men. He turned to Buffalo Shield.

"The time has come for me to go back to the white man's world. I feel a deep sorrow in my heart to leave you, my father, but I hope you will understand. I cannot kill my friends."

Buffalo Shield sadly shook his head. "It is for you to decide. You must go where your heart tells you."

"Take his weapons!" Yellow Bear said and pulled his pony around as if to block Trace's path. "He will use them to shoot Crow warriors."

Trace's feeling of remorse was overcome by a sudden anger. Yellow Bear had antagonized him since his first day among the Crow, and he truly despised the fiery warrior. "You might take my rifle, but I promise you, you'll get a lead ball first," he said, his voice low and even as he raised the Hawken to aim at Yellow Bear's belly.

"Let him go!" Red Blanket roared.

Yellow Bear, aware of the rifle's firepower, reluctantly backed away and let Trace pass. When the two of them were shoulder to shoulder, the sneering warrior uttered a low warning. "Before this night is over, I will have your scalp on my lance, white dog."

As the first of the returning Crow warriors galloped up the rise, Trace slowly walked the paint down toward the creek below the bluffs, past Buffalo Shield, knowing that the old warrior would probably watch his back in case Yellow Bear decided to put an arrow between his shoulder blades. As he passed his Crow father, they exchanged glances and Buffalo Shield nodded sadly. The pain Trace saw in the old man's eyes was but a reflection of his own reluctance to leave a way of life that had taught him to live as one with the mountains. Black Wing turned away, refusing to look into the eyes of his friend. As Trace descended the bluff, he could hear some of the returning warriors asking where Long Rifle was going. *Back to the white man's world,* he thought, *and probably to my own funeral.*

"Now what?" Buck asked when he spotted the lone rider descending the bluff.

Frank, following Buck's line of sight, stared at the Crow warrior approaching them at a walk. "I don't know. He ain't carrying no white flag. Maybe he's just showing the rest of 'em how brave he is."

Buck snorted in reply. "Well, I reckon I can hang

a little medal on him for his bravery." He raised his rifle and sighted down on him.

"Hold on a minute," Frank said, his curiosity aroused. "He don't act like he's fixing to try to count coup or nuthin'. Maybe he's wantin' to talk."

"Probably wants us to surrender right peaceful-like so's they can scalp us without losing any warriors." He continued to hold the rider in his sights. "First queer move he makes, he's a dead Injun."

"Hold on, Buck." Frank stared hard at the rider. There was something familiar about the way he sat his pony. Then he noticed the long shock of sandy-brown hair. "That ain't no Injun!" he blurted out.

Their curiosity fully taking over, both men squinted in the late afternoon shadows in an effort to identify the approaching rider. As the rider neared the creek, he made the sign of peace. When he was within earshot, he spoke.

"How did you two old buzzards get yourselves in a fix like this?" It had been a while since Trace had spoken English, and the words felt strange on his tongue.

Still puzzling over who was addressing them, Buck replied, "It were easy." His rifle still trained on the rider, he asked, "And who might you be?" He was suspicious of any white man who rode with a band of Indians.

"I swear, Buck, your memory ain't no better than your manners. Hold your fire, I'm coming in."

"Well, you just come on then, but you'd be advised to keep your hands where I can see 'em, mister." Buck had seen his share of tricks played by Indians, and by white men who rode with them. He wasn't about to be taken in by this sassy young buck.

While Buck had been doing all the talking, Frank had been studying the young stranger intently. When the young man guided his horse over the bank and down into the creek bottom, Frank muttered, "Well, I'll be . . . is that who I think it is?"

Trace grinned and nodded. "Yep," he said as he slid off his pony and stood before them.

"Jim! Well I'll be go to hell," Buck chimed in, his eyes wide in amazement. "Boy, we been lookin' fer you fer four years. We 'bout decided you'd gone under."

Even under the precarious conditions, Trace couldn't help grinning. The two old trappers forgot the band of Crows above the bluffs for a moment and stared in disbelief at the tall young man standing before them. Dressed in moccasins, leggings, and breechclout, he was a far cry from the skinny fourteen-year-old they had stumbled upon back at Pierre's Hole. Standing face to face with him, Frank had to look up to meet the young man's eyes.

"Damn, what they been feedin' you? Last time I seen you, you weren't no higher than this." He held his hand up to his chest. "Was he, Buck?"

Buck just stood there, grinning and shaking his head back and forth in bewilderment. Then both men descended upon Trace, laughing and pounding him on the back. The celebration was short-lived, however, broken up by the shrill sound of a war whoop. The three of them turned to see the Crow warriors amassed along the edge of the bluffs. The reunion would have to wait as the reality of their peril was thrust back upon them.

"What are they thinkin' up there?" Frank wanted to know.

"Right now they're deciding whether or not they're gonna rub us out or let us go," Trace replied.

"Us?" Buck asked. "Ain't you ridin' with them Crows?"

"Was," Trace said. "I reckon I had to make a choice, and I guess I found out I ain't a Crow after all."

"So that's how it is," Frank said. "Well, welcome back, son, but you picked a helluva time to turn back white—just in time to go to your own funeral. You might be smart to ride on back up there and tell 'em you're on their side. There'd be no hard feelings—would there, Buck?"

"Well, I guess not," Buck said, "but I'd shore admire havin' that there Hawken on our side."

Trace smiled. "I've already made that decision. I reckon it'll be the three of us." That settled, the three partners dug in, and prepared to repel the attack they felt certain was coming.

They weren't kept waiting long. The sun was now below the hills and the creek was cloaked in shadow. It would be dark soon. Red Blanket split his band into three groups—one group broke off and rode upstream, another galloped off toward the lower bend of the creek. That left most of the warriors to mount a frontal attack.

"He'll wait until it gets darker and then try to slip in close," Trace said. "That bunch will try for the horses when Red Blanket's warriors attack us from the front." He had ridden with Red Blanket's war parties many times. He knew the chief would come in under the cover of darkness to reduce the risk of taking too many casualties. He also knew that Red Blanket respected the mountain men's skill with their rifles and believed the darkness would work in his favor.

"You gon' be able to shoot at your Injun friends?" Frank asked Trace. "You spent a long time with 'em."

"I don't know," Trace answered honestly. "I wish I didn't have to." He hesitated before finishing. "But I reckon if they're shooting at me, I won't have much choice."

While the three trapped men watched, Red Blanket split his group yet again, sending half of the remaining warriors galloping off downstream after the first bunch. "I reckon that bunch'll be crossing over to come up behind us," Buck said. "They're gonna be sneakin' up on us from all sides." He looked over at Trace. "I reckon it were your unlucky day, running up on us and endin' up in this kettle of stew." Trace didn't reply. He was busy seeing to his rifle and bow.

Frank was quietly studying the line of warriors left sitting their ponies, patiently waiting for the light to fade into total darkness. Red Blanket had divided his war party until there were only a dozen braves between them and the hills beyond. When he had made up his mind, Frank spoke. "I reckon it 'pears we're caught down here in this crick. If we dig in here, we'll make 'em pay, but we'll end up with our scalps loose." He got up and, staying in a crouch, moved over toward the horses. "I don't cotton to waitin' around here for them devils to come lift my hair. Let's ride the hell outta here."

Buck saw the smaller force of warriors facing them and came to the same conclusion Frank had. "By God, you're right. We can bust through that bunch and hightail it up in the hills. If we're lucky, we can take out three or four of 'em."

No one took the time to evaluate the plan. It was better than sitting where they were. They scrambled to the horses and readied them to ride. There was a brief discussion of the wisdom of keeping the pack mules, but neither man was willing to part with his hard-earned plews.

It was already dark in the willows by the creek as they led the horses as quietly as they could manage, stopping just below the edge of the bank. Behind them in the western sky, a long line of gold- and red-tipped clouds provided the only light. "See that cut in the hills yonder?" Frank asked. "We'll head fer that. If I recollect, that leads up a draw that comes out on open prairie. When we ride—and I mean ride like hell—stay in a line. In this half-light, they won't be shore what's coming at 'em."

"I'll go first," Trace volunteered. "My pony is fast, and I don't have to lead a mule."

"All right, then," Frank quickly agreed. He would have suggested that anyway, but he was glad Trace volunteered to take the point. "So's we don't waste shot aiming at the same folks, I'll look to my left.

Buck, you shoot to the right. We'll blow a hole right through them devils."

Trace had a deeper reason for wanting to lead the breakout. He had made a choice as to which side he must fight on, but he had no desire to bring any harm to his Crow friends, especialy Black Wing and his father, Buffalo Shield. As he watched from the cover of the creek bank, he noticed that Black Wing and Buffalo Shield had positioned themselves at the far end of the line of twelve warriors, opposite Yellow Bear. Trace would lead Buck and Frank straight toward Yellow Bear.

"All right, Trace," Frank whispered, "let's git the hell outta here."

Trace leaped upon his pony and charged up out of the creekbed. Frank and Buck, already mounted, sprang up behind him, and the sprint was on. They tore across the darkened flat before the bluffs, Trace leading, riding low on his pony's neck. Buck followed close behind, with Frank bringing up the rear. Luck was with them, for the Crow warriors were taken by surprise. They had given no thought to the possibility that the cornered trappers would mount an attack. Total confusion spread among the waiting warriors. At first Red Blanket thought there was a single rider galloping toward them in the darkness. When he realized there were more than one, it was too late to alert his braves. He yelled to the others to shoot, but by that time, Trace was almost upon them, heading right at Yellow Bear.

Yellow Bear, struggling to hold his startled pony, fought to bring his musket to bear on the charging rider that was suddenly bearing down on him. He fired the weapon, but the shot was yards wide of his target. He didn't even see the war axe that bounced off his skull, knocking him off his horse and leaving him senseless on the ground as two more horses and two mules thundered by him. Behind him, Trace heard the reports of two rifles, followed by cries of pain, and he knew Buck and Frank had both found their marks. He felt a slight twinge of guilt when he heard the shots, but he didn't have the time to worry about it.

The initial breakout was successful, but now it became a question of pursuit. Although taken completely by surprise, Red Blanket quickly rallied his warriors to give chase. His band, having been split to surround the creek bank and too far away to be of any help now, was reduced to nine warriors. Two of these, Buffalo Shield and his son, Black Wing, were less than enthusiastic about overtaking Trace. Red Blanket was smart enough to realize that, and it weighed heavily on his mind as he raced headlong after the fleeing white men. In effect, he knew he had only seven braves against three sharp-shooting mountain men, odds that he did not relish. The three, only vague shadows bobbing up and down in the darkness now, were running toward a long draw that no doubt provided any number of likely ambush spots. He had lost two warriors for certain, and Yellow Bear might be dead as well. If he continued to follow these white men up that dark ravine, he would be lucky to lose only three more. The stakes were too high. After only about ten minutes' chase, he called out to his warriors to let them go, even though they were clearly gaining on the three fleeing white men.

When his braves gathered around him, Red Blanket spoke. "It is foolish to ride into the dark after them. Their guns are too strong. I could not be your chief if I led you into a slaughter. We'll let them go for now. Maybe we can find their trail tomorrow."

Buffalo Shield said nothing, but when he turned to meet the gaze of his son, he saw the hint of a smile on Black Wing's face.

Chapter 10

They didn't stop once they reached the relative safety of the draw, but pushed their horses on up through the ravine toward the rolling hills beyond. Once they had cleared the ravine and realized they were no longer being chased, they slowed their tired horses. They continued on late into the night as the moon climbed up over the eastern mountains, illuminating their path through a rolling plain of treeless mounds. Toward morning, they came back to the mountains.

"Whadaya say, Frank? Rest 'em here before crossing over to strike the Green?" Buck nodded toward a collar of cottonwoods that indicated a stream of some kind.

Frank was of like mind, as he usually was with Buck. The two of them had been together so long that Jim Bridger used to joke that if one of 'em farted, the other one said, "Excuse me." "Yeah," Frank said. "We can git the stock outta sight in them trees—maybe git a little rest ourselves."

With the horses safely out of sight, the three weary souls stretched out on the ground to catch a couple of hours' sleep. They had ridden hard through the night and felt confident that they could afford the time to rest. At first light, Frank woke up and climbed up the hill behind the stream to take a look around. After studying the trail they had ridden the night before, he decided they had lost the Crows, for the time being at least. When he came back down, Trace and Buck were awake. Trace was busy building a fire, and Buck was applying grease to the wound in his mule's neck.

"Damned if I don't believe we lost them Crows," Frank announced. "There ain't no sign of nuthin' clear to the other end of this valley."

Trace looked up from the solitary flame he was nourishing with dried grass and a few small twigs. "I don't think they'll bother chasing us anymore. Red Blanket was already gettin' nervous about being so far away from our village when we ran up on those Blackfeet shooting at you and Buck."

"What was he doin' down this way, anyhow?" Buck asked. "I didn't expect to see no Crows in this part of the mountains."

"We were looking for a Snake war party that stole some of our horses," Trace replied. "We heard those Blackfeet shooting at you and thought we had caught the Snakes."

"Well, we'll just cross over the mountains and follow the Green on down to the rendezvous, and let them Crows and Snakes and Blackfoot chase each other. I'm damn tired of being the one they wanna play tag with."

After they had breakfasted on some jerked venison, they got under way again—this time at a somewhat more leisurely pace. The sun was high in the sky, and there was still no sign of anyone following them. That night they made camp on the Green River.

Frank stretched out beside the fire, his head resting on his saddle. He watched with interest as the tall young man, still dressed in leggings and breechclout sat opposite him cleaning his rifle. Full grown now, Trace was a hell of a sight removed from the boy who had left them after the rendezvous in '35. He and Buck had often talked about that boy, wondering what had become of him, especially after LaPorte and that Blunt fellow had come asking about him. That was mighty peculiar, and Frank would have liked to hear the story. But it was a common rule among mountain men that a fellow's business was his own, and what Trace had done back East was nobody's concern.

As always, the same thoughts Frank had ran through Buck's mind, too. And Buck, being less concerned about the mountain man's code of ethics, blurted out the question. "What in tarnation would a skunk like Joe LaPorte be lookin' fer you fer?"

Trace was surprised. "Joe LaPorte? Who's Joe LaPorte?"

"You mean you don't know?" Frank jumped in, since Buck had bluntly provided an opening. "Like Buck said, he's a lowdown, back-shootin' polecat, and he was askin' all around about you a few years back."

Trace slowly shook his head, trying to remember if he had run across anyone by that name. "I don't know him." He hesitated a moment before asking, "Was anyone else asking about me?"

"Feller by the name of Blunt," Buck replied.

Trace stiffened. He didn't say anything, but it was obvious to Buck that he had hit a nerve. There was a long moment of silence while both trappers fixed their attention on him, waiting for his reply. "When?" Trace finally asked.

"Hell, every year, I reckon. This Blunt feller, he shows up at Laramie every summer with a string of mules packed with trade goods, most of it whiskey, from what I been told. He don't trade at the fort, though—turns his goods over to LaPorte and LaPorte traipses off with 'em up-country somewhere. Blackfoot country, I expect. But this Blunt feller, he always asks around if anybody seen that young boy that trapped with us, summer of '35." Buck paused to scratch his whiskers. Looking at Frank, he said, "Come to think of it, though, I don't believe he asked about the boy this past summer, did he, Frank? Maybe he give up lookin' fer you."

Still, Trace offered no illumination on the puzzle, but it was plain to see he was giving it plenty of thought. His curiosity thoroughly aroused, Buck continued to press. "This here Blunt feller, he's kin of your'n?"

"Hell, no," Trace quickly replied.

Buck's patience gave in to his curiosity. "Well, what's he lookin' fer you fer?"

"I killed his brother."

"Oh," was all Buck said—one of the rare times when Frank could ever remember his longtime partner being at a loss for words. Trace then related the story of his unfortunate encounter with Tyler Blunt, and his mother's marriage to Tyler's older brother.

"You mean this Blunt feller that comes out to Laramie every year is your stepdaddy?" Frank asked.

"Hell no!" Trace spat. The sound of the term reviled him. He had never given any thought to the idea that Hamilton Blunt was now, in fact, kin. "I imagine that if one of the Blunts comes out in this part of the country, it would be Morgan. His brother, Hamilton Blunt, he's the one who married my ma. He wouldn't dirty his fancy britches riding a horse all the way out here."

"So that's why you sorta disappeared for so long," Buck said, "hidin' out with a band of Crows."

"I reckon," Trace replied. "It just sorta worked out that way. When I left St. Louis, I was on the run, but I reckon I really had in mind finding you and Frank."

"Well, I'll swear . . ." Buck started, letting the thought trail off. "But if it all happened the way you say, you was just defending yourself. You ought not have no worry about the law."

Trace shook his head slowly. He had thought this over many times, wondering what his fate might have been had he gone to the sheriff and told his side of the story. He always came to the same conclusion—that he did the right thing when he ran. "Who's the sheriff gonna believe? Me or Hamilton Blunt? I'm sure Hamilton Blunt wishes I was dead. He damn sure looked disappointed when I showed up alive back in St. Louis."

Frank shifted his chew of tobacco to the other side

of his mouth and spat into the fire. After waiting to hear it sizzle, he said, "I believe you're right, Jim. I don't think this Blunt feller is sending the likes of Joe LaPorte lookin' fer ya just to tell ya all's forgiven and to come on home."

"I reckon you ought to know I don't go by Jim Tracey no more. I'm going by Trace McCall now," Trace told them.

There was a brief moment of silence while Buck and Frank considered this. Then Frank said, "All right, Trace it is. You stick with Buck and me and you'll be all right. 'Sides, I don't figure anybody'd recognize you now. You've sure changed a helluva lot."

The three partners started out to find the rendezvous the next morning, following the river until they came upon the meeting place of the annual event. They found it just about two miles north of the mouth of Horse Creek. Trace recalled the rendezvous he had been to four years before. This camp seemed far less rowdy. Indians—Snakes, Nez Perces, and Flatheads—were still there to trade for powder and balls, blankets and trinkets. Their tipis were set up on one side of the river, spreading out for about a mile on the grassy bottom.

As they rode through the sprawling camp looking for a place to unroll their packs of beaver plews, Buck and Frank were met with shouts of welcome here and there from old trappers dressed in buckskins worn shiny and black from long seasons in the mountains. After promising to come back later to visit and swap lies, they rode on. "Mighty poor-lookin' plews," Frank commented to Buck. "I thought our lot was skimpy, but I swear, this is the worst-lookin' harvest I've ever seen."

Buck didn't answer for a moment, distracted by two Nez Perce women riding by on their ponies, dressed in their finest fringed buckskin dresses, with bright silk handkerchiefs tied in their hair. Their friendly smiles held him captive until, laughing shyly, they suddenly bolted toward the lower end of the camp. Tearing his gaze away from the two departing beauties, Buck turned back to Frank. "Yessir, they's poor-lookin', all right. I reckon you could say we done pretty good compared to most. There's too dang many of us going after the same few beaver that's left. But beaver'll shine agin."

After a few days in camp, Buck would wonder about his hopeful prediction. The price of beaver was down from the year before, and the price of goods that the beaver would buy was as high as ever. Buck and Frank were able to trade their plews, but the money was pitifully shy of what they had hoped for. As a result, there was very little left over for fun and frolic after essentials were bought. It was the same for the entire encampment. Trace was disappointed to find that the horse racing, and gambling, the drinking and wild celebration of the first rendezvous he had attended were almost nonexistent now. There was some drinking, however, and some friendly Indian girls—and the opportunity to relax and sleep without one eye open for possible attack.

Trace was little more than a spectator in this camp, having no pelts to trade. He was in need of some things—his supply of ammunition was critically low, even though he had used his rifle as sparingly as possible since his last visit to Fort Cass with Buffalo Shield and Black Wing. For most of his hunting, he had relied on the horn bow that Buffalo Shield had made for him. Now that Trace had returned to the white man's world, Buck insisted that he needed some britches and a shirt, so he arranged for a Snake woman to make them. Trace didn't like the idea of having to accept charity, but Buck assured him he would take payment for the buckskins in some way later on. Uncomfortable with owing any debt for any period of time, Trace rode out from camp to hunt. In two days' time he had replaced the hides that had been used for his clothes as well as providing fresh deer meat for the camp.

One week after they arrived at the rendezvous, a large, powerfully built man rode into the upper end of the camp. His face hidden behind a bushy black beard that was crusted in places with dried tobacco spray, he dwarfed the small Indian pony he rode. His eyes darted from side to side as he made his way through the groups of old Indians sitting under the trees, smoking their pipes. He leered at the women busily scraping hides or carrying wood. The people he passed returned his gaze with notable lack of welcome. For, in truth, this man had no friends in this camp of trappers.

From their campfire near the bend in the river, Frank spotted the latecomer to the rendezvous. "La-Porte," he mumbled.

Hearing him, Buck roused himself from his position stretched out under a tree and sat up to see for himself. After a moment, he said, "It's him, all right." He glanced over at Trace, who was a dozen yards away, kneeling by the water with a fishing line he had rigged up. "Trace," Buck called, "come on over here a minute." When Trace looked around, Buck motioned with his hand.

He tied his line to a tree root and walked over to the fire. Buck pointed to the dark figure making his way along the riverbank, weaving through the campfires of Indians and trappers. "You recognize that man?"

Trace stared hard at the man pointed out. "No, never saw him before."

"That's Joe LaPorte, the thievin' bastard that's been askin' about you."

Trace studied the huge man carefully.

Frank chimed in. "That there's Blunt's man—does all his dirty work for him, I reckon. There ain't a meaner man in these mountains. He'd just as soon kill ya as look atcha."

"Well, how come somebody doesn't stop him?" Trace wondered.

"Cause so far, nobody's caught him at his devilry, but everybody knows he's a lowdown murderer, him and his Blackfoot gang. Trace, you'd best just lay low and stay away from that man."

It was too late, for LaPorte's dark, ferretlike eyes had already lit upon the tall young man in the new buckskins, and his steely gaze riveted upon the three men. *Ahh, Ransom and Brown,* he thought to himself and smiled. *So the damned Crows didn't get you after all.* He was especially interested in the young stranger with them. It was hard to say at that distance, but he would bet that he was around eighteen years of age, and that would make him about right.

LaPorte's heartbeat quickened with the thought that his persistence might have finally paid off. Years had passed with no sign of the Tracey boy, but LaPorte knew he would eventually show up. He was ready to collect on the five hundred dollars Morgan Blunt had promised—especially now, since his former Blackfoot allies had said they were done with him. Lame Fox had lost too many of his warriors in the ill-fated attack on the two white trappers and had barely escaped the Crow war party. He and LaPorte parted company the morning after their flight from Red Blanket's warriors. Lame Fox led what was left of his war party back north of the Yellowstone to lick his wounds. Things didn't look too promising for LaPorte after that. But now maybe his luck was changing—five hundred dollars' worth of change.

"Uh-oh," Buck muttered, "he's coming this way." He motioned for Trace to stay back. "You just sit back there and let me do the talkin'." Frank moved over away from the fire so he could have a clear field of vision. Trace complied with Buck's instructions, but he felt no fear of the huge man.

"Well, if it ain't Mr. Brown and Mr. Ransom," LaPorte said as he pulled his pony up before them, his voice laden with sarcasm. "Heard you boys had a little trouble over near Wind River."

"That so?" Buck asked. "Now I wonder who told you that."

"Word gits around," LaPorte replied, his gaze searching past the two old trappers to the young man behind them.

"What the hell do you want, LaPorte?" Frank demanded.

"Why, I was just being neighborly." His evil grin was a thin disguise for the contempt in his heart. "I just stopped to see how you boys was doin'." His gaze suddenly remained locked on the boy. "And what might your name be?"

"His name might be President Van Buren, but it ain't none of your business, now is it?"

Trace saw the cold spark in LaPorte's eye when the big man shifted his gaze back to Buck. "Don't push your luck with me, old man. I just might decide to eat your gizzard." The two locked eyeballs for a long moment before LaPorte, noticing that Frank's hand rested on his pistol, slowly smiled. "I don't know why you boys is so unfriendly." He backed his horse away, watching them closely as he did. "I'll be seeing you," he said as he turned back toward the main camp. There was a sly gleam in his eye as he gave Trace one last look.

"Damn," Buck said, when LaPorte had disappeared behind one of the Snake lodges, "why ain't somebody done shot that man?" He turned to face Trace. "Don't ever turn your back when that varmint's around. I don't like the way he was eyeballin' you."

Trace could not deny feeling a quickening of his blood when LaPorte had leered down at him with dark eyes that seemed to penetrate his very soul. If there was such a thing as an evil spirit, and Trace believed that there was, then he was halfway convinced that he had just met the evil one's messenger. LaPorte was massive, powerfully built with thick neck and shoulder muscles like a bull buffalo. Trace, though young in years, was confident in his own strength and ability, and he would cower before no man or beast. Still, he would take Buck's advice and avoid LaPorte if possible. Buffalo Shield had taught him that though a man might not fear the great grizzly, he would be foolish to fight him hand to hand.

Several hundred yards away in the Snake camp, Joe LaPorte sat in a circle of braves, watching with an amused smile as they drank from a jug of whiskey the big man had brought. Married to a Blackfoot woman, LaPorte had very little use for the Snakes. And had they known of his alliance with their enemies, the hated Blackfeet, they might have been at his throat instead of gulping the evil firewater he offered.

While his newly made friends finished off the jug of Morgan Blunt's cheapest whiskey, LaPorte's eyes were occupied with the comings and goings of the young Snake girls in the camp. One side of his mouth curled into a lopsided grin as he thought of the money he had in his pockets—courtesy of the young couple in the covered wagon who had had the misfortune to cross paths with LaPorte and his Blackfoot savages. That money could buy him a lot in this camp, and his grin broadened when he thought about the young man who had finally showed up after four long years, and all the money that would come when LaPorte delivered his head to St. Louis.

Chapter 11

"Boy! Have you done took leave of your senses?" Buck was fairly flabbergasted, standing on the riverbank above the young man in the water. "Ain't no tellin' what kind of sickness you can catch, jumpin' in that river buck nekkid."

Trace laughed and continued splashing around in the clear cool water. "I ain't naked. I got on my breechclout."

"Same as being nekkid," Buck insisted. "Jumpin' in the river without his clothes on'll weaken a man fer shore."

"Hell, Buck, you spend half your life wading around in beaver streams," Trace said.

"Not without my britches on, I don't. You better come on outta there and get some clothes on."

Trace laughed again and waded toward the sandy bank. "I was just taking a little bath. Don't you ever feel like you need to clean up?"

"Lord no. It's a dangerous thing to expose your skin to the elements, unless you're a damn Injun—they don't know no better." He handed Trace his shirt and stepped back to give him room to scramble up the bank.

Slipping the buckskin shirt over his head, Trace said, "You ought to try it once in a while, Buck. It'll make you feel like new."

"I swear," Buck scoffed, "you picked up some mighty queer notions livin' with them Crows." He was about to continue his lecture when he was distracted by something behind the boy. "Well, lookee here," he murmured.

Trace turned to see a young Indian girl approaching them. She looked to be no more than sixteen or seventeen. Trace found himself staring in admiration at the girl's graceful yet purposeful stride as she made her way around the hummocks and gullies by the riverbank. It appeared that she was heading straight for them. Trace pulled his moccasins on, never taking his eyes off the approaching girl. "Snake," he heard Buck say, though he was not really listening. He was captivated by her simple elegance, mesmerized by the way the fringes on her buckskin dress gently swayed back and forth in rhythm with her step.

"Well, good morning, missy," Buck said when the girl walked right up to them and stopped. "What can we do for a fine-lookin' lady like yourself?" When she responded with no more than a quizzical expression, he spoke to her in her own tongue.

Though able to converse fluently in the Crow dialect, Trace knew only a few words of the Snake language, so he could not follow the conversation. Already enamored with the girl's large dark eyes and the smooth cheekbones that reminded him of golden velvet, he was impatient to know the purpose of her visit. "What's she saying, Buck?"

Buck spoke to her again before answering Trace. When she responded, he laughed and turned to Trace. "I think she must be a little tetched in the head," he teased. "Maybe I best send her on back where she come from."

"Why?" Trace demanded, his eyes never leaving the girl, who was gazing intently at him now and smiling.

"Because she said she come to see you," Buck replied, grinning from ear to ear. "Said she'd been a'watching you."

"Me?" Trace choked out, and before he could ask more, the girl said something else, diverting Buck's attention.

Buck listened, smiling broadly at the Snake maiden, then translated. "She says you're a fine-lookin' young man, so I reckon the poor girl's eyesight's gone bad on her, too." He was thoroughly enjoying Trace's discomfort. "She said to tell you to meet her in the trees behind that knoll over yonder when the moon gets up."

"Why?" Trace blurted out, that being all he could think of to say at the moment, while his entire being was still captivated by the sweetest face he had ever seen.

Buck burst into laughter. "Why the hell do you think? I swear, I didn't think I was gonna have to learn you ever'thing." He glanced back at the girl—she was laughing too. "To talk is what she says. When the moon comes up, she'll be waiting. Don't want her pap to see her running off to meet you in the daylight." He waited for Trace's reply. When Trace seemed unable to speak for a moment, Buck asked him, "Well, are you aimin' to meet her?"

Trace nodded vigorously, then stammered, "Damn right."

Buck grinned his approval and looked at the girl. She smiled and nodded. The rendezvous confirmed, she favored Trace with a warm smile, turned on her heel and departed. The old man and the boy watched in fascination as she retraced her steps, the little fringes on her dress swaying to and fro.

Trace was thunderstruck. How could she have been watching him? He had certainly not been aware of it. And why had he been so dumbfounded by the mere appearance of a girl? There were many young girls in Red Blanket's village, and he had enjoyed idle flirtations with a couple. But none had rendered him simpleminded and foolish as this young Snake maiden had. "Dang," he sputtered, "I don't know more than two or three words of Snake. There ain't gonna be much talking."

Buck chuckled, "I reckon 'yes' is the only word you'll need."

The rest of that day passed slowly. Trace tried to entertain himself by sauntering through the rows of traders' tents, watching the last of the bargaining between the traders and the trappers and Indians. He also caught sight of LaPorte as the sinister giant entered a saloon tent near the far end of the encampment. Trace carefully avoided that tent, but he roamed the rest of the camp as he pleased, determined not to cower behind Buck and Frank. He had found it necessary to get away from his two older partners anyway, to avoid the incessant teasing. Thoughts of the girl filled his mind all afternoon, and he soon came to believe that night would never come. But finally, and mercifully, the sun dropped below the hills in the west as the cookfires began to glow.

Trace ate, although he had very little appetite. His stomach had suddenly become nervous and not at all receptive to salt pork and pan bread. It didn't help to meet the mischievous eyes and innocent grins of Buck and Frank every time he glanced up at them.

"You know, Frank," Buck began, "the last time I seen anything that nervous was that time above Three Forks when we come up on that rabbit that hopped over that dead log and found hisself settin' next to a rattlesnake. You remember that?"

"Uh-huh," Frank replied nonchalantly. "I remember. As I recollect, we et rabbit *and* rattlesnake for supper that night." He reached for the coffee kettle and swished the grounds around before pouring himself a cup. "'Course, ol' Trace here, he's done been bit by something a sight more deadly than a rattlesnake. He's got a right to be nervous."

"And it's a helluva lot more deadly when you ain't ever been bit before," Buck added, causing both men to chuckle.

Trace flushed, thankful that it was getting too dark for it to be noticed. "You two old fools don't know whether I been bit before or not." He got to his feet.

"I got better things to do than set around here listening to you two jawing and emptying that jug."

"I'm shore of that," Buck chided, still laughing. "The moon'll be up in about half an hour. You better be gittin' your weapon primed." He took another long pull from the jug.

He left the two of them still cackling over their bawdy jokes and walked by the campfires of the few trappers who had also situated themselves at the lower end of the great encampment. He nodded to an occasional trapper as he passed small groups of old-timers, swapping tales around the fire. Their bellies were full, their pipes lit, and the air was filled with the odors of roasted meat and strong tobacco. Off toward the center of the camp, the sound of singing and muffled laughter carried on the gentle evening breeze. Soon he was beyond the last campfire and striding across the grass of the valley floor.

After a few minutes' walking, he had left the camp behind him. He stopped to look at the moon, large and yellow, rising over the hills behind him, and he realized he was trembling with an anticipation he had never felt before. Suddenly he felt foolish. *What the hell am I doing out here?* he thought. *Acting like a lovesick prairie dog, sniffing after some sassy little tail.* He almost decided to turn around, thinking of the aloof posture he and Black Wing had strived to maintain before the young Crow girls. Then he thought again of the Snake girl's little fringes swaying as she walked. *What the hell! That would really give Buck and Frank something to jape me about if I turned tail and ran.*

A few minutes more and he was approaching the

slopes of the low hills and the clump of trees that had been pointed out by the girl. The shadows were deep under the tall pines, a cloak that forbade the bright moonlight's entry. *What if I'm the butt of a big joke,* he wondered, *and she ain't even here? What if she—and Buck—are setting behind one of those trees, laughing their heads off?* He entered the quiet darkness of the shadows.

"Jim Tracey." It was a man's voice. He spun around, barely in time to see a giant shadow lunging toward him. Too late to dodge his assailant, Trace dropped to one knee and tried to brace himself. He caught a brief glint of moonlight reflected in a shiny knife blade as it flashed over his head. A fraction of a second later, he was bowled over by the impact of the man's heavy body. Over and over they rolled, down the slope. Trace fought desperately to keep the knife blade from finding purchase in his stomach as they struggled and cursed. From the crushing weight of the big man's body and the stench of his breath, Trace knew it could only be LaPorte. The momentum of their desperate struggle carried them down until they crashed against the trunk of a large pine, causing them to disengage.

Trace scrambled to his feet and drew his own knife from his belt. His assailant was equally as fast in recovering from their tumble and was soon upon him again, charging like an enraged buffalo. Trace easily avoided the big man, stepping aside and administering a slashing blow as LaPorte's huge body surged past. LaPorte roared—in anger more than pain, for the blow had not been a serious one.

LaPorte was too big and powerful, and Trace knew that his best chance was to stay on his feet. He could not afford to let the bigger man wrestle him to the ground, so he waited while LaPorte paused to catch his breath. LaPorte, laboring from exertion, was nevertheless confident of his physical dominance over his young opponent. The boy was tall and muscular, but he had not filled out as yet. In spite of the blood running down his arm, he was enjoying the slaughter he was about to complete as he stood facing Trace.

"Your name's Jim Tracey, ain't it?" LaPorte growled between gulps of air. "You little whelp. Your hide's worth five hundred dollars to me. You might as well tell me your name. You don't wanna go to hell with a lie on your lips, do you, boy?"

"You can go to hell," Trace replied, slowly shifting his weight from one foot to the other, his knife ready to strike.

LaPorte wanted him in close, where he could use the advantage of his strength and size. "Come on, boy, fight like a real man." Trace continued to bide his time. "You know, I was s'posed to take care of you four years ago, when me and my boys killed your pa. Them Blackfoot, they had a time with your old man's body, but it was my shot what brung him down."

The shock of LaPorte's words exploded inside Trace's head. He had always assumed that his father's death was the result of bad luck—a chance meeting with a Blackfoot war party. LaPorte's taunting boasts were sufficient to light a fuse in the young boy's mind. Blinded by the rage that suddenly overflowed within him, Trace rushed headlong into the sneering giant. Although this was the result LaPorte had hoped for when he baited the boy, Trace was quicker than the huge man anticipated. He felt the sting of Trace's knife as it split the skin of his abdomen, searing its way up under his ribs.

Again LaPorte roared. This time he feared he might be mortally wounded. But like the grizzly he resembled, his wound only made him more dangerous. Cursing and grunting, he clamped Trace in a deadly vice, crushing the air out of the boy's lungs. Trace fought to escape the powerful arms, but he was helpless against the wounded man's grip.

"Damn you," LaPorte gasped, spitting bloody foam with each word, "you may have kilt me, but I'm takin' you to hell with me."

He rolled Trace over, pinning him to the ground. Trace tried to pull his knife out of LaPorte's ribs but his arms were pinned beneath him, trapped by the big man's massive weight. His face contorted with the pain from the knife buried under his chest, LaPorte raised his knife hand to deliver the killing thrust. Driven by pure determination and sinewy strength, Trace wrestled one arm free and caught LaPorte's wrist, blocking the brute's attack.

For the moment, they were at a desperate stalemate. Half on his side and crushed under LaPorte's weight, Trace was unable to free his other arm. He strained against LaPorte's wrist, the knife blade only inches from his chest, while LaPorte clamped down on his throat with his other hand—a hand like a vise that gripped tighter and tighter until Trace could no longer breathe. Still he fought to hold on, but the horribly contorted face of LaPorte began to blur and Trace knew he was close to losing consciousness.

Seconds before sliding into total darkness, Trace heard the sound of a hollow drum, followed by a loud grunt from his assailant. Again the dull thud of the drum, and suddenly the hand clamped around his throat released and LaPorte rolled over on the ground. Confused and gasping for breath, Trace rolled away from LaPorte's body and tried to get to his feet, but he sank back to one knee, too weak to stand. His head was still spinning, and he was unable to grasp what had taken place. When his head cleared a bit, he saw a shadowy form standing over LaPorte's body, holding a large tree limb. It was the Snake girl.

Then he was startled to hear someone running through the brush behind the girl, and Frank's voice came through the darkness. "Are you all right, Trace?"

"I guess so," Trace replied, his voice hoarse as he rubbed his aching throat. He got to his feet and approached the girl, who was still holding the tree limb in her hand and talking excitedly. His knowledge of the Snake dialect was sketchy, so he relied on sign language to convey his thanks, signing it several times, but she gave no indication that she understood. When she continued to chatter frantically, Trace turned to Frank for help. "What's she trying to tell me?"

Frank, still panting from his sprint through the

bushes, took a moment to catch his breath. "Dammit, I'm too old to be running like that." He held his hand up to quiet the distraught Snake girl. Turning back to Trace, he said, "I'm sorry I didn't git here sooner, boy. I shoulda knowed there was somethin' queer about this little meetin'." He said a few words to the girl in her tongue, then translated her excited chattering for Trace. "She says she didn't mean you no harm. LaPorte told her daddy that he wanted to play a joke on a friend of his'n. All she was s'posed to do was tell you to meet her in the woods, and he would give her some beads and vermilion, and her daddy some whiskey."

"You mean she wasn't gonna be here at all?" Trace asked.

"Reckon not." Frank exchanged some more words with the girl, who had calmed down by this time. "She says she decided to sneak out and see the joke played on you, and when she come up through the woods, she seen LaPorte 'bout to murder you."

Trace considered Frank's words for a few moments, then asked, "How do you say *thank you* in Snake?" Frank pronounced the words, and Trace turned to the girl and repeated them. She nodded and hung her head shyly. "Ask her name," Trace said.

"Her name is Blue Water," Frank translated. "Says her daddy's name is Broken Arm."

"Blue Water," Trace repeated. "I owe her my life."

"I reckon," Frank agreed, " 'cause that big son of a bitch was damn shore about to put you under. And I was a step too late to help you." He glanced at the

Snake girl and then back at Trace. "I got to thinkin' about you traipsin' off in the dark like a lovesick buffalo, and that lowdown skunk just lookin' to catch you away from camp."

"He killed my pa," Trace said, his voice low, barely above a whisper. "He was with that bunch of Blackfeet that jumped Pa and Henry Brown Bear." He looked over at the huge body for a moment, thinking how close he had come to death, realizing what a valuable lesson he had learned that day. No matter what might be said or done to him in the future, he promised himself he would never again lose his head in a fight. It had almost cost him his life this time. His thoughts were interrupted by the touch of Blue Water's hand on his arm.

"I must go now. I'm glad you were not killed," she said, as Frank translated. She turned to leave, but then paused. "Do you have a wife?"

Frank answered her, and she nodded and smiled before disappearing quickly into the shadows. When she had gone, he translated the last bit of conversation for Trace. "What did she wanna know that for?" Trace asked.

"I don't know, but if I was to guess, I'd say you ain't seen the last of that little gal." He reached down and grabbed LaPorte's hands. "Come on, let's drag this damn buffalo out in the open so's we can get a look at him."

"What are we gonna do with him?" Trace asked. He was unsure whether or not they should report his death to someone in the camp.

Frank looked with some amusement at the boy.

"Why, hell, whadaya wanna do with him? Give him a funeral? We could notify his next of kin, but I don't know how to git in touch with the particular family of polecats he come from. Now, grab his other arm."

Frank propped his rifle against a tree, then reached down to take hold of LaPorte's arm. Suddenly the huge renegade's hand lashed out like a striking rattlesnake, too fast for Frank to react. Recoiling from the sudden flash of the blade in the moonlight, Trace was stunned to see the knife buried deep in Frank's belly. In that horrible instant that seemed frozen in time, Trace's brain recorded a scene that he would never forget. Frank, doubled over in pain, clutching at air as he crumpled to the ground—the great bear-like monster seemingly roaring back from the dead, the side of his face covered with blood—and Trace's knife still embedded under his ribs, as he reached for Trace's throat.

Caught in the monster's crushing grip for the second time, Trace fought for his life, his hands the only weapon left to him. Unable to break LaPorte's death grip on his windpipe, Trace struggled to get a hand on the knife buried in the man's abdomen, but LaPorte managed to hold him away from it. Straining face to face, Trace looked into LaPorte's searing eyes—wild and glazed—as if the man was already gazing into hell. Trace had the desperate feeling that he was fighting a man already dead, a demon determined to take him to hell with him. Summoning strength from deep within, Trace fought back, equally determined to prevail. Gradually he forced LaPorte's arms back until he could almost reach the handle of the knife protruding from the monster's gut. Just as his fingertips brushed the butt of the knife, LaPorte, in one final act of defiance, called upon all of his brute power, pushing Trace back again, releasing one hand, and ripping the knife out of his abdomen. Roaring with pain and anger, he raised the bloody knife and struck downward toward Trace's back.

Inches from Trace's shirt, the blade was suddenly frozen as LaPorte's wrist was seized, stopped cold in Frank Brown's hand, and held there immobile. "I've had about enough of you," Frank muttered between clenched teeth. With his other hand, he stuck the barrel of his pistol against LaPorte's eye and pulled the trigger.

Trace wrenched free of the dead man's grip and fell back onto the ground, LaPorte's blood spattered across his face. Coughing as he strained to catch his breath, he hurried to Frank's side. Frank, having expended the last of his strength to dispatch LaPorte to hell, sank back exhausted. "I think the bastard kilt me," he said with great effort, as Trace frantically pulled the bloody buckskin shirt away and tried to stop the bleeding. From the other side of the trees, he heard Buck call out, "Trace! Frank!"

"Over here," Trace called back, and moments later Buck came plunging through the thick brush.

"Ah, damn . . ." was all he could say at first when he saw his old partner lying on the ground, his head supported on Trace's arm. "Frank, damn . . ." Words failed him for once in his life.

"Shut up, Buck. It's bad enough without you gittin' all slobbery over me." Although he was in great pain, Frank could not help but chide his longtime friend.

Buck dropped to one knee to examine Frank's wound, then glanced at Trace and asked, "You all right?" When Trace nodded that he was, Buck immediately started gathering Frank up in his arms. "Help me carry him. We've got to git him back to camp."

After Trace and Buck carried their injured partner back to the river and made him as comfortable as possible, Buck did the best he could to clean Frank's wound and try to stop the bleeding. Frank stubbornly fought to stay awake, firm in his belief that once he went to sleep he might never wake up. Buck fussed over him, arguing that he needed rest in order to slow down the bleeding, but Frank refused to cooperate.

"Trace," Frank rasped, "you'd best go back out there and find that bastard's horse before one of them Injuns gits it."

Trace was surprised. He hadn't given a thought to confiscating LaPorte's property, being more concerned with Frank's welfare. It had been one hell of an ordeal for him as well. He had almost met his maker twice in one evening at the hand of LaPorte, and he could still feel the vise-like grip that had threatened to crush his windpipe. "To hell with his horse," he mumbled.

"Frank's right, Trace. That's the way of things out here. It don't belong to nobody else, and you and Frank damn sure worked for it. Don't make no sense leavin' it for somebody else to find." Buck took Trace by the arm and walked him to the edge of the clearing, where his words could not be heard by Frank. "I swear, it looks bad, Trace. That bastard gutted poor Frank right proper. I ain't got much hope for that wound to heal."

Trace felt a deep compassion for Buck, and he sincerely wished he could offer some hope for Frank's recovery, but he was no more optimistic than Buck. "There ain't nothing we can do for him but try to make him as comfortable as possible—then just wait and see."

"I reckon so," Buck said, sighing loudly and shaking his head. "You'd best go on and find that horse."

Trace hesitated. "Are you sure we wanna do that? Ain't you afraid there'll be some trouble when everybody sees we've got LaPorte's horse and goods? They might think we just murdered him for his plunder."

"Ain't gonna be no trouble," Buck hastened to reply. "Ever'body'll most likely be damn glad somebody finally put him under. Besides, these trappers know murder ain't me and Frank's style. If anybody wants to know, I'll tell 'em what happened. LaPorte finally jumped on the wrong trapper, and he got his ass kilt for his trouble. 'Course, we could go over yonder and dig a great big hole in the ground—throw ol' LaPorte in it with all his rifles and plunder—hell, even shoot that big gray horse of his'n and throw it in too. But what good would that do anybody? Just be a waste, that's all. Now you go on, and I'll stay here with Frank."

Buck pulled the saddle off of LaPorte's horse and emptied the dead man's pack on the ground. Among the items laid out for inspection was a little embroidered bag with the initials *L.C.M.* stitched on it. "Well, ain't that sweet?" Frank clucked, propped up against a tree, watching Buck. "Wonder what poor bastard lost his scalp for that?"

When Buck felt the weight of it and heard the distinct clink of metal when he picked it up, his interest was spiked for sure. He opened it and counted out thirty gold coins. "Dadburn, Trace, you've come into a fortune."

Trace had stood apart from Buck while he searched through LaPorte's possessions, examining the rifles and pistols, powder and ball, plus some odds and ends like tobacco and jerky. Now Trace realized that they considered LaPorte's property to be his. The thought of taking a dead man's things, like buzzards over a carcass, didn't sit well on his conscience, but he agreed that it made little sense to leave it to someone else. "I don't want all that stuff," he said. He was especially thinking about the big buffalo gun that had killed his father.

"It's yours to do what you want with," Buck said.

"We're partners, ain't we?"

"Why, shore we are, boy, we done told you that," Buck replied.

"Well, then, I say the stuff that's usable belongs to the partnership. The gold coins get split ten apiece—and the horse goes to Blue Water for saving my neck."

That settled, the gear was packed away with the rest of their supplies and Trace saddled the spotted gray again. Buck, watching the boy saddle the horse, warned, "You best be sure you let ol' Broken Arm know why you're givin' that horse to Blue Water, lessen he thinks you wanna marry her."

"I will," Trace assured him.

Trace could almost feel every eye upon him as he led the big gray horse through the gathering of Snake lodges. Even though these Indians were friendly toward the trappers—at least for the present time—and had come to rendezvous to trade, Trace still felt as if he was walking through a hostile camp. In every direction he looked he was met by a blank stare, for they all knew the big spotted gray. When one old man glanced up from the pipe he was busy carving, Trace stopped and, talking in sign, asked the location of Broken Arm's tipi. The old man pointed to a lodge several yards away where a warrior sat, eating from a large iron pot hanging over the fire.

The Indian continued to eat, dipping into the pot and retrieving long strips of boiled meat, watching the approaching white man intently. When Trace led the horse up before him and stopped, Broken Arm got to his feet and offered the customary greeting of friendship, although there was no outward appearance of welcome in his stern expression.

Trace returned the greeting and, by signing and the few words of Snake dialect he remembered, told Broken Arm that he had brought the horse as a gift for his daughter. He emphasized that the gift was for Blue Water, and not for Broken Arm in exchange for his daughter. For it would have been an insult to offer only one horse for a girl so beautiful and virtuous.

"Ahh," Broken Arm responded, somewhat relieved. Then, looking back toward the entrance to the tipi, he called out, "Blue Water, come." He offered Trace some food while they awaited the appearance of his daughter. In a few moments, a woman appeared at the entrance, but it was not the girl. The look of distress on Trace's face made the woman smile. She looked back inside the tipi and said something. A moment later, Blue Water stepped out into the sunlight.

Trace felt a flutter deep inside his chest and he sensed a flush creeping up behind his ears. She seemed even more radiant than she had been the day before, when she had come to his camp. He knew then that rewarding her for saving his life was not the real purpose of his visit. In truth, he simply had to see her again.

Blue Water smiled shyly at him, then lowered her gaze to avoid meeting his eyes. Her mother stood beside her beaming proudly as they waited to hear what the young white man came to say. Broken Arm told his daughter that the horse was a gift for her. She understood the intent of the gift and, raising her eyes, nodded to Trace, her eyes looking directly into his for the first time.

Trace felt his knees weaken as he met her gaze. Her eyes, soft and dark as a young fawn's, set his thoughts whirling, leaving him flustered and barely able to concentrate on Broken Arm's words. The Snake warrior was speaking to him in broken English. "Word come you kill LaPorte. LaPorte big medicine. How you called?"

"Trace," he replied.

"Trace," Broken Arm repeated the name several times until it felt comfortable on his tongue. Then he smiled and nodded vigorously. "Now Trace big medicine."

The news of LaPorte's death had already circulated throughout the Indian camps, although there had been no fuss or cries from anyone discovering his body. Trace supposed that Blue Water must have confessed her late-night rendezvous. It was obvious that her father trusted his daughter's word, for he showed no anger toward her. And he seemed satisfied that Trace had no intentions toward Blue Water beyond rewarding her for her bravery. As common courtesy demanded, he insisted that Trace sit with him and eat. Trace would have preferred to decline the older man's offer, but to do so would have been rude, so he sat.

At her father's bidding, Blue Water offered the pot of boiled meat to Trace, her eyes steadily gazing into his as he picked a strip of meat out of the thin mixture. He was sure there was a more intimate message in those deep eyes. Or was it just his imagination? A fantasy born of his own desire? His mind was in a state of confusion. At his young age, he could have no thoughts of "trapping a squaw," as the trappers termed it. And yet his mind was filled with thoughts of this bright young girl and with a strong desire to be near her. He wanted to express his feelings toward her somehow, but his nerve failed him and he could not find his tongue. So he sat there feeling dumb while Broken Arm talked about the season and the buffalo and several other things that Trace would not remember. Blue Water, meanwhile, went into the tipi and returned with an otter skin that she had evidently been working on for some time. Seated off to one side, so she was always in Trace's line of vision, she worked away silently and steadily, seeming to pay the fumbling white boy no mind. Every time he stole a glance in her direction, however, she caught him at it and met his gaze with her soft, smiling eyes. Finally he took his leave of the family, still unable to speak directly to the young girl.

"Well, when's the wedding?" Buck wanted to know as soon as Trace returned. He was in the process of trying to spoon-feed some thin soup to Frank.

"What wedding?" Trace snorted, doing his best to appear nonchalant. "I gave her that ol' horse because she did me a favor. I told you that."

Buck laughed. "I know what you told me, but I can read sign."

Seeking to change the subject before Buck got wound up, Trace didn't rise to the bait. Instead, he said, "The Injuns already knew about LaPorte when I went over there this morning. I reckon the girl told 'em."

"Maybe," Buck replied, "but I doubt if she wanted to let on to her pa that she snuck out last night. 'Course, you bringin' her a horse sorta gave it away, I reckon."

"What about the other trappers?" Trace asked

again. "You think there'll be something said . . . you know, about us having all of LaPorte's plunder?"

Buck shook his head. "There won't be nuthin' said when somebody gits around to finding ol' LaPorte over yonder. Bridger or Sublette might ask me about it. I'll tell 'em the right of it and that'll be the end of it."

Feeling somewhat reassured, Trace decided to stop worrying about it. He helped Buck repair some of the packs, replacing worn straps with new hide. He didn't notice their visitor until he heard Buck announce her arrival. "Company's a'comin'," Buck sang out softly in a mocking tone.

She rode the big spotted gray along the riverbank, over the same hummocks she had walked the day before. She rode straight up to Trace, and stopped before him. He stood up to meet her, ignoring the grinning faces of his two partners. She held out her hands and offered something to him. He glanced down and at once recognized the otter skin she had been working on that morning. Speaking in a soft voice that was almost melodious in its lilting tone, she placed the fur in his hands.

Buck translated. "She says she saw that you carried a bow as well as a rifle, so she made you this here otter skin bow case and quiver."

She watched Buck carefully while he spoke. When he finished, she looked back at Trace and nodded her head vigorously. "I make you," she said, stumbling over the words.

Trace was speechless, staring down at the case, which was decorated with beads and porcupine quills. It was a beautiful piece of craftsmanship. Buck spoke to the girl for him, telling her that Trace was honored to receive it and would be proud to use it. She said something else, looking at Trace while she spoke, then she turned her horse and rode back the way she had come.

Trace was at once distressed. Why hadn't he said something? He desperately wanted to tell her how much he hated to see her go. When he turned back, he was met with Buck's slyly grinning face again. *Damn!* he thought, *I'm gonna learn to speak that tongue.* "What did she say?"

"Nuthin' much," Buck said, thoroughly enjoying the tormented expression on Trace's face. "Oh, she did mention that she was aiming to water her new horse upstream by the willows around the bend, where the water is fresh and cool. About sundown, she said."

Broken Arm called to his daughter when she returned to the lodge. "I see you have been riding your new horse. Is he a good horse?"

"Yes," she replied, "he's strong and much more gentle than I would have expected to have been ridden by such a man."

Broken Arm nodded. "That's good. I'm glad he is a strong horse." The polite conversation out of the way, he approached the subject he was really intent on discussing. "Have you finished the bow case and quiver you were making?"

"Yes, I finished it."

"I would like to see it. I looked in the tipi for it,

but I couldn't find it." His eyes held hers as he spoke, and she knew he had probably guessed where the otter skin was.

"I gave it to the young white man. I noticed that he carries a bow, and I thought his gift of a horse was too much to give for no more than I had done."

"Oh?" Broken Arm responded. "I think he feels that you saved his life. So I'm sure he thought the horse was an appropriate gift." He searched her face intently, trying to read her feelings. Remembering the long, stolen glances she had taken when the white man sat with him, he feared that she had become infatuated with the young trapper. Broken Arm did not hate white men, but he did not trust them either. And for that reason, he did not want his daughter to become involved with one. He held nothing but contempt for the women of his tribe who had moved into the white man's tipi, only to be left behind—usually with child—when the trappers moved on. He didn't want that for Blue Water. This young man—Trace, he called himself—seemed to have a good heart, but even if he wanted to marry Blue Water, Broken Arm would not bless the union, for he believed the white man produced an evil seed. One had to look no further than the vile LaPorte to see that this was so.

He studied Blue Water's face and pressed for an answer. "Do you have strong feelings for this white man?"

Blue Water flushed. Then she raised her gaze to meet that of her father. "I think he is a kind and beautiful man, but I don't really know him. It would be foolish of me to have strong feelings about one I don't really know."

Broken Arm nodded and smiled at his daughter, satisfied that she was in no danger of behaving foolishly. Still, he could not be sure of the young man's intentions, so he thought it best to take his family away from this place and return to the upper Wind River country.

As for Blue Water, she was well aware of her father's mistrust of white men. But she could not deny the desire within her bosom to know this quiet young man who stood so straight and tall. For this reason, she had chosen her words carefully when Broken Arm asked her if she had feelings for Trace. She loved her father very much and did not like to deceive him. But she promised herself that she would see the young trapper just this once more. Feelings so strong could not be denied.

The shadows of the willows deepened in the fading light of dusk. A muskrat splashed noisily at the water's edge, unaware of the young man sitting silently on the bank. A night bird scolded in a shrill whistle, startled by the furry rodent's splash. Then all was quiet again. Unmoving, he waited, listening. He had sat there since the sun first dropped behind the hills, and he now thought that she might not come at all. He cocked an ear to one side, thinking he had heard something, but it was only his pony, swishing his tail at an insect. Several more long moments passed. It was then that he heard her. This time he was sure, as he heard the soft padding of a horse's hooves on the sandy bank and then the low whinny of his pony's greeting. She had come!

In a few moments, Trace saw Blue Water as she entered the grove of willows. Cloaked in the shadows, she led her horse directly toward him until she was almost upon him. When he rose to his feet, she was startled, but only for a moment.

"I did not see you," she explained. Then, realizing that he could not understand her words, she made the words in sign.

He tried to think how to say he was sorry he had frightened her in sign, but he could not. So he simply nodded his head and smiled. She returned his smile, and the warmth of it was enough to melt his heart. She pulled a blanket from behind her saddle and spread it on the ground beneath the willows. Then she knelt down on her knees and beckoned for him to join her.

Facing her, their knees almost touching, he could feel the closeness of her body even before she took his hands in hers. Just from the gentle caress of her hands, he feared his head would start spinning, intoxicated by the faint scent of woodsmoke in her hair. He wished that he could tell her the feeling in his heart at that moment, but even if he had known the words, it would have been impossible. Somehow, he felt that she knew his heart anyway. Her eyes told him that she was experiencing the same passion.

She spoke softly in her native tongue while she explored his body with her hands, lightly caressing his face and neck, his shoulders and arms—wanting to know him. She smiled as he responded, exploring her body, lightly caressing her neck and shoulders, her breasts and the soft curve of her thighs. Time stood still, and there was nothing else in the world, just the two of them in the soft night. They both seemed to know when it was time. Gentle blossoms of moonlight floated upon the ripples of the water, unaware of the raw violence of this wild country and the dangerous times for two young people in love. As the benevolent moon shone down on their naked skin, they came together in youthful, virginal passion.

When their passion was spent, they lay in each other's arms until sleep closed their eyes. Finally knowing the secret of that great mystery that every young boy dreams about, Trace drifted off to sleep, content and yet finding it hard to realize that it had actually happened. When he awoke, she was gone.

He reached out for her, but no one was there. It was still dark, the moon hanging low on the far hills now. Soon it would be morning. Looking behind him, where she had tied her horse, he saw only his paint, nibbling on the tender willow bark. He sat there for a few minutes, thinking about what had happened that night. He had never dreamed that it would be so tender and passionate. Now he had some thinking to do. His whole world had suddenly changed. He was not sure he could leave her.

He looked down and rubbed his hand across the blanket she had spread, trying to hold the image of her soft body in his mind. He would have to return the blanket in the morning. She had not wanted to wake him when she stole away. Maybe he should wait to give her the blanket, as she might not want her father to know she had slipped out to see him. *Of course she wouldn't,* he thought. *She's not sure I'll do the honorable thing by her.*

He untied his horse and rode back to camp, dismounting before riding in. There were still a couple of hours before daylight, and he didn't want to wake his partners. After unsaddling and hobbling the paint, he took a moment to check on Frank. Finding that Frank was sleeping peacefully, he rolled up in Blue Water's blanket and was soon asleep, dreaming dreams of a beautiful young Indian girl.

"Ain't that a pretty sight," Buck said, standing over the sleeping form of his young partner.

"Just like a babe in swaddling clothes," Frank agreed weakly, doing his best to be cheerful.

"If I was a bettin' man," Buck went on, "I'd bet ten prime pelts that our young friend cut meat last night." He laughed. "Look at the expression on that face. I swear, I wonder if I looked that happy after my first time."

The object of their entertainment stirred, and in a moment, was wide awake. "What are you ol' buzzards standing over me for?" he groaned.

"My Lord, boy, it's most past sunup. We thought we was gonna have to load you on a pack mule," Buck scolded, then, "Where'd you git that fancy red blanket?"

"As if you didn't know," Trace answered. He roused himself from his bed and started peeling off his buckskins while he walked to the water's edge.

Before Buck could protest, he plunged into the cold current. When he surfaced, it was to find the old trapper standing there with a look of consternation upon his face.

"I swear, Trace, I wish you wouldn't do that," Buck complained. "You're gonna find out one of these days that you've done come down with something. And it'll be on account of them dang baths you take all the time."

Trace grinned. He couldn't explain to the two gruff old trappers how alive he felt on this morning—a morning that was different from all mornings that had passed before. He climbed up the bank, shaking the water from his long sandy hair. "I'd best see about taking that blanket back," he said.

"That'll take some doin'," Buck said.

Trace didn't understand. "Why?" he asked.

" 'Cause that whole band of Snakes packed up and left during the night," Buck answered. "They're long gone."

"Gone?" Trace's heart sank. "Whadaya mean, gone? Hell, they can't be gone—not all of 'em."

"Ever' last tipi, horse, and dog," Buck said.

Trace's bright new world came crashing down around him. His immediate thought was to saddle his horse and ride out after them. Buck, being able to see the picture more clearly than the lovestruck young man, endeavored to put the issue into perspective for him. It took both men, and a lot of talking to convince Trace that it was useless to pursue the Indian girl.

"She knew her people were pullin' out last night,"

Buck said. "Hell, I knew it. They were packin' up yesterday, gittin' ready to leave—I figured today—but I reckon ol' Broken Arm decided not to wait for daylight."

"That's a fact, Trace," Frank offered, groaning with the effort to raise up to speak. "She didn't have no notion of stayin' behind. If she did, she'da brung her trappings with her. I suspect she left that red blanket just so's you'd remember her."

It took a while before Trace allowed himself to be convinced that what he thought was his first real love was, in actuality, no more than a roll in the hay for her. Still, he refused to accept that notion completely. One little corner of his brain would hang on to last night and remember the passion that had clearly been there in the young girl's eyes. She had truly loved him then. No one would ever convince him otherwise.

Now, however, he had no choice but to accept the fact that she was gone. And later on when his bruised heart had recovered, he would understand that Blue Water's place was with her people, and not with him. The young recover quickly from injury—physical as well as mental—so he soon forgot the pain it caused. But he would never forget the night he spent with the girl.

Over the next few days, the rendezvous sputtered out, with most of the trappers already on their way toward the fall hunting grounds. Buck could not deny a feeling of impatience, born from many years of the same routine, but he knew it was out of the question for Frank to travel. His partner was so torn up inside that he awoke each morning with traces of blood around his mouth and in his beard—from only the slight movements he might have made during the night. Though they didn't talk about it anymore, all three men knew it was just a matter of time. Frank tried to persuade Buck and Trace to leave him there by the river and go on toward the Yellowstone country, as they had planned. But Buck and Trace refused to leave him.

It was hard for Buck to watch Frank's deterioration. He knew Frank needed nourishment to recover, but Frank became violently ill each time he tried to put anything in his stomach. Consequently, he wasted away, day by day, until it got to the point where he barely moved, lying in his blanket and mumbling about old trails and people long gone. It totally unnerved Buck, and he would sit for hours just watching him. Near the end of the week, Frank took another turn for the worse.

He had begun babbling, talking wildly about Indians robbing their traps and stealing their horses. When Buck tried to hold a cool rag on his forehead, Frank pushed it away, calling Buck a murdering horse thief. When Buck persisted in laying the rag upon his forehead, Frank suddenly pulled his pistol out of his belt and pointed it at Buck's head.

"Now, by God," he said, holding the pistol surprisingly steady for one so weak.

A quick move by Trace was the only thing that saved Buck's life. He knocked Frank's arm up just as he pulled the trigger, and the ball sailed harmlessly over Buck's head. The sharp report of the pistol seemed to jolt Frank back to his senses, although it was plain to see he didn't understand what had happened. "Buck," he said, his voice weak again, "what the hell are you doing?"

Buck, thoroughly shaken by the incident, nonetheless answered him calmly. "Nuthin', Frank. I was just trying to lay a cool cloth on your head."

Frank didn't resist when Trace gently removed the pistol from his hand and tossed it toward his saddle. Looking at Buck, Trace shook his head sadly, and together they eased Frank down on his blanket. Both men knew their companion was dying. It could not be long now. They made him as comfortable as possible, hoping he would rest quietly through the night.

"It looks mighty bad," Buck whispered when it appeared that Frank had drifted off to sleep. He shoved his hat back and scratched his thick white hair, troubling over what they should do. Unable to think of anything more they could do that might ease Frank's dying, they prepared to turn in. They decided to take turns keeping watch over Frank in case he got wild again during the night.

"You get some sleep," Trace said. "I'll take first watch and wake you in a few hours."

Frank seemed peaceful enough, although his raspy breathing sounded labored and painful. Trace shook Buck awake sometime after midnight, and Buck took over the vigil. Satisfied that Frank was resting peacefully, Buck poked up the campfire a little and propped himself against a cottonwood. A few hours before first light, Frank suddenly sat upright and blurted out in a loud and distinct voice, "Buck! Goddamn you!" Those were his last words. He sank back on his blanket and was gone.

Frank's outburst awakened him and Trace sat up to find a shaken Buck Ransom. "What is it?" Trace blurted.

"It's Frank. He's dead . . . I swear . . . he's dead." Buck shook his head from side to side, unable to believe his own words.

Trace got up and walked over to kneel beside the still form of the old trapper. He pulled the blanket away and gazed thoughtfully at Frank's wasted body, now too small for the buckskins that draped him—a body always lean and hard, now pitifully frail from his illness. He felt Frank's neck for a pulse and was startled by the coolness of the old man's skin, a clammy, terminal chill that told him Frank had indeed departed. His death mask was one of anger, unlike the living version of the man. "I'm afraid he's gone, all right," Trace said, turning to Buck.

Buck seemed strangely wary of the body, as if he wanted to keep a safe distance between him and his late friend. His reluctance to approach Frank in death struck Trace as especially odd, since the two had been so close for so many years—so odd, in fact, that Trace started to question him about it, but then decided the old man was just stunned by Frank's passing. "I reckon we'd best get him in the ground."

"I reckon," Buck answered. "I'll git the shovels, you wrap him in his blanket."

Trace was still puzzled by Buck's seemingly detached attitude and he wondered if the old trapper was simply trying to deny the profound grief he must surely feel. "I can get the shovels, Buck. Maybe you might want to say a few private words to him."

"No," Buck immediately snapped. "I'll git the shovels, you git him ready."

Trace stood there for a long moment, searching Buck's face for explanation. Finally he said, "Buck, what the hell's wrong with you? Frank's your friend. Don't you want to say good-bye to him?"

"He layed a curse on me," Buck replied, his voice so low that Trace almost didn't catch it.

"He what?"

"Put a curse on me with his dying breath," Buck insisted.

Astonished by Buck's outrageous remark, Trace pressed him for an explanation. Buck then related the events of the previous night when Frank had risen from his blanket and said, "Buck, goddamn you." Those were his dying words, Buck insisted, and everybody knew the potency of a deathbed curse. Trace, finding it difficult not to laugh at the simple old man, attempted to persuade him that Frank had no earthly idea what he was saying. And at that particular time, he was most likely already departing on his dark journey. After all, Frank had been babbling nonsense for days before. He didn't know what was dropping from his mouth. Buck was not convinced, feeling that a curse on a dying man's lips was not something to be taken lightly.

Exasperated, Trace shook his head. "Buck, for God's sake, what in the world would Frank wanna put a curse on you for? You were the only real friend he ever had."

"I don't know," Buck replied, thinking hard. "There was that time on the Little Missouri when I dropped his powder horn in the river."

Trace gave up. "Go get the shovels and let's put him in the ground." He went back to prepare the body while Buck trudged off to fetch the shovels that had once belonged to Trace's father.

They buried Frank under some cottonwoods close by the riverbank. There were no rocks handy to pile on the grave, so they dug it extra deep and smoothed it over with sand, hoping to disguise it sufficiently to protect it from scavengers. When Frank was finally in the ground, the reality of his death struck Buck for the first time, and he realized that he would have to make the rest of his life's journey without the one man who had always been at his side. Trace was sure he detected a tear in the old-timer's eye as he stood over the grave. So he discreetly stepped away to tend to the horses so as to give Buck a few moments to say a last good-bye. He could see the old trapper's lips moving in a final farewell, although he was too far away to hear the words.

Leaving the Green River rendezvous, Buck and Trace rode in a single file, each leading a pack animal. They would head toward the Yellowstone country for the fall trapping season, although both men sensed that this rendezvous might well be the last. Beaver was down. Even Buck no longer insisted that it would shine again, and without his longtime friend, he had very little enthusiasum for trapping.

But they set out to make the fall hunt anyway, because there was nothing else to do. They were trappers, after all, and the mountains were where they belonged.

Chapter 12

Buck and Trace left the rendezvous on the Green River two somber and heavy-hearted trappers. Buck was starting out without Frank Brown at his side for the first time in many seasons. Following behind, Trace was deep in thought as well—thoughts of Frank, but also haunting memories of a smiling Indian maiden with smoky black hair and eyes as dark as night.

They trapped the Yellowstone country in early fall, working their way over to the Musselshell, and back down to the Absarokas. Late December found them near the Wind River country when suddenly heavy clouds moved in, dumping more than a foot of snow in less time than it takes to skin a muskrat. It was not an unusual occurrence in the mountains this time of year. In fact, Buck had been predicting the heavy snowfall for several days, so they were as prepared as it was possible to be. The two of them had made their camp in an abandoned cabin, built by Bridger's men some years before. Now there was little to do but settle in and wait out the winter.

The hard work required to stock their cabin with

firewood and build a shelter for their horses served to occupy Buck's mind much of the time. But Trace could readily see that the old-timer missed his long-time partner a great deal, even though Buck was still convinced that Frank had left him with a bad-luck curse. As evidence of this, he pointed out the scarcity of beaver and the unusually hard winter. He never spoke of it to Trace, but he felt a heavy burden of guilt for having been over at Broadhurst's tent drinking while Frank and Trace were engaged in that desperate fight with LaPorte. Buck would sit watching the fire for long periods, deep in thought. Trace had never seen him like this. To the contrary, Buck had never been one to tolerate a void in the conversation, and if he could not recall a colorful incident to relate, he would make one up. Trace began to worry that Buck was never going to get over the loss of his partner.

As for Trace, the winter did not pose a hardship for the strapping young man. He found that he loved the solitude of the silent white mountain peaks surrounding the little cabin, and he often spent several days at a time away from camp while hunting. Buck soon became accustomed to his young friend's hunting trips, and he was content to stay near the fire and let Trace provide the fresh meat.

Trace found it relatively easy to track elk or deer in the deep snow, and using the skills he had learned from old Buffalo Shield, he was almost always able to get close enough for a shot with his bow. He fashioned some snowshoes out of the pliant limbs of the willows by the stream and tramped high up into the towering mountains, making his camp at night in the snow. Warm in his heavy fur skins, he would build his fire in the snow. As the fire kept sinking, he would keep relighting it, until it would finally settle on solid ground. When it had bottomed out, he had a cozy hole in the snow for his camp. In Trace's mind, there could be no better existence for a man.

The next few years were lean years for the two mountain men. They continued to trap for the small harvest that remained in beaver, as well as for fox, otter, and buffalo. They traded their furs each summer at trading posts like Fort Laramie and Fort Union, and any other place they could swap their plews for powder, lead, caps—Dupont and Galena, a mountain man's lifeline. As they had sensed, there were no more rendezvous after the one on the Green in '39. They wintered at the headwaters of the Yellowstone, at Forks of the Snake, and Pierre's Hole—sometimes with Bridger's men, sometimes alone. Because of the hostile nature of some of the warring tribes during that time, particularly the Sioux, the Cheyenne, and the Blackfeet, they had to move often, constantly watching for war parties. It was rough going. They were among the few surviving free trappers—most had given it up a year or two back. It was a harsh existence, and it molded hard men.

After that first winter, Buck seemed to have put Frank's death behind him, and returned to his more familiar nature—that of a rip-roaring, fun-loving companion. And Trace was happy to see the transformation. Buck even uprooted himself from the fireplace once in a while to accompany Trace on his winter hunts. Although trapping was the life both men preferred, the day finally came when even they had to admit that it was time to try something else. So when spring came that year, they decided to ride down to Fort Laramie, hoping to discover other possible pursuits.

Rocking along in the saddle, his body in perfect tune with his horse's rhythm, Buck allowed his thoughts to wander back to earlier times, when he and Frank first came upon Trace. Looking at the broad shoulders and straight back of the young man ahead of him, he marveled at the changes that had transformed the boy they had taken in. There was nothing reminiscent of the rangy, skinny youngster he had found raiding his beaver traps so long ago. If it were not for the long shock of sandy hair, one might mistake him for an Indian in the way he sat his pony, seeming to see everything around him at once. This quality was the primary reason Trace always led the way now, his eye as sharp as that of any hawk circling high above them in the mountain pass.

By the time they reached South Pass, there were not many additional plews packed on the mules, though they had spent the better part of a month working their way down. The last few weeks had seen little sign of Indian activity, but now, on this last morning, Trace spotted smoke on the horizon to the north of their trail. The two of them paused to consider it, speculating on its origin.

"Looks like somebody ain't havin' a good morning," Buck commented dryly. "I just knowed there was Sioux war parties raidin' around here—I could feel it in my bones."

"Maybe," Trace replied, continuing to study the thin column of smoke rising high in the morning air. "Smoke's too dark to be a campfire and too thin to be a brushfire. Looks like it might be from kerosene or something."

"Could be, I reckon. But it ain't on our trail," Buck quickly pointed out.

"No, but maybe we ought to go take a look. I ain't seen many Sioux with kerosene cans. Somebody might need some help."

"Dammit, Trace, it ain't no business of our'n. We'd best git ourselves on into Laramie."

Trace smiled. He knew Buck would not ordinarily hesitate to give assistance to any poor soul caught in a bind. But he was within a day's ride of a drink of whiskey, and that exerted a powerful influence upon any decision he had to make. "I'm gonna take a look. You can head on into Laramie if you want to. I'll catch up with you."

"Ah, hell," Buck fussed. "I'll go with you, if you're so all-fired nosy. We're more'n likely to run up on a Sioux war party, though." He followed Trace's lead out toward the hills to the north, grumbling to himself as he rode. "Dammit, Frank, I know it's you bringin' us hard luck."

When they got within a mile of the smoke, they slowed their pace and proceeded with more caution. The source of the smoke appeared to be beyond a series of rugged hills that were slashed with many deep gulches. Progress became difficult as they pushed their horses through gullies and over sharp ridges until reaching one last ridge. There they dismounted and, leaving the horses below the ridge, crawled up to the crest.

Below them, they saw the last smoking boards of a wagon bed resting on a broken front axle, the rear axle having been hardly touched by the fire. There was no one in sight, but there was plenty of sign to tell them what had happened. Several pieces of smashed and half-charred furniture were scattered about. A couple of large chests lay opened, their contents scattered over the grass of the ravine floor. There were no bodies to be seen, so the possibility that the owner of the wagon had been taken captive seemed the logical conclusion.

They waited a long time before bringing up their horses and descending the ridge to take a closer look, certain that the raiding party had long since departed. There were a great many tracks around the wagon, but they surmised there were probably no more than a dozen Indians in the war party.

"Well, whoever the poor soul was, looks like they rode off with him," Buck said, scratching his beard thoughtfully. "What in the world was he doin' out here with a wagon, anyway?"

Trace didn't answer. He was studying the broken axle and the way it was wedged against a rock. He picked up a piece of smoking leather, a part of the traces, and examined it closely. There was no indication that they had been cut. Glancing around, he saw other pieces of the harness. The team had been unhitched. An Indian would have simply cut the traces with his knife.

Buck, impatient to leave, summed it up. "Looks like Injuns chased the poor devil till he run up this here gully and broke his axle. Now they're long gone."

"Maybe," Trace answered, "but I don't think so. My guess is he saw the Injuns before they saw him. I think he drove up this ravine to hide and ran up on that rock. The axle broke, so he unhitched the team and hightailed it. I don't think he was here when the war party found his wagon."

"Yeah, there's that possibility," Buck admitted. "I was just about to point that out."

As if to confirm Trace's speculation, first one, then a second mule appeared at the foot of the ravine. Free of harness, the mules walked slowly toward the men, stopping every few yards to pull up a muzzle full of the tough grass that covered the floor of the ravine.

"Forevermore . . ." Buck uttered. "Look what's coming here. Well, I reckon we can use a couple more mules."

"Let's leave 'em alone for a while," Trace said. "We might find this fellow before the Injuns do."

"If they ain't already," Buck snorted.

Trace had a notion that if the mules had been working as a team for any length of time, the loose mules might eventually follow along after the others. Envisioning the scene right after the man drove his wagon up on the rock, he figured that the driver probably unhitched his team and chased them off to keep the Indians from getting them. No doubt he jumped on one of them and made his escape.

Buck wasn't so sure Trace was right. "I don't know 'bout them mules. Now, if the man had a'been driving a team of hound dogs, maybe so."

A search around the area told them where the wagon had entered the ravine, where the war party had approached, and in which direction they had left. But it was impossible to determine where a man on a single mule might have left the ravine. Trace saw two possible outlets that led over rock outcroppings where no tracks would be left. So, in spite of Buck's protests, Trace made himself comfortable while he waited to see what the mules would do.

After about thirty minutes, the two abandoned mules grazed their way up to Trace and Buck's animals. Cautious at first, one of the mules approached the paint and was immediately warned off by the horse. Rebuked, the two orphans backed off about twenty yards and continued to graze for a while. After a second attempt to approach the horses and another, stronger rejection, the mules broke off and headed up a rocky draw at a trot.

"Well, that ain't the way I woulda picked," Trace sighed as he stepped up in the saddle and started out after the mules.

"Waste of time," Buck grumbled, but he followed along behind, leading their pack mules and Frank's horse.

The mules took them on a slow, meandering trail through a gulch and across an open stretch of flat prairie. The general direction seemed to be toward a line of low-lying hills with sparse patches of trees near the base. When the mules stopped to graze again, Trace went on ahead and started to search for a trail. After a scout of no more than half an hour, he found what he was looking for—tracks of two shod animals. From the indentations in the hard earth, he figured they were carrying riders. He waited for Buck to catch up to him.

"Well, I reckon you was right," Buck allowed. "Two fellers rode out on mules—but what are you fixin' to do about it? 'Pears like they got away from the Injuns. Now I expect you and me ought to do the same."

"Aren't you curious at all?" Trace asked. After all, this wasn't exactly the place you'd expect to find somebody driving a wagon. He had a feeling that whoever it was, they were probably lost and maybe desperate.

"Hell, no," Buck snorted. "They oughta had better sense than to be out here in the first place." Although he felt the need to register his objections, he knew that once Trace made up his mind, it was as good as done.

It was a good thing they had picked that rocky gulch out of the ravine, Trace thought, because the men they followed made no efforts to cover their trail after they got on the flat. He could imagine their reckless sprint for the hills that he and Buck were fast approaching. By the time they entered the trees at the bottom of the first hill, it was well past noon. From the tracks that led up through a narrow draw, Trace guessed the men had been forced to slow down to rest their mules, and when he found fresh droppings, he decided it was time to proceed with caution. He studied the slope before them and the lay of the land on both sides. Noting the pattern of the trees beyond, he speculated, "There might be a stream on the other side of this hill."

Buck dropped back with the animals while Trace scouted ahead to the top of the slope. There was a stream on the far side all right, and sitting beside it, looking tired and confused, were the two they had been following. Trace motioned for Buck to come on up. "Well, there sets your two homespuns, all right," he said as Buck settled beside him.

As they had figured, there were two of them—a man and a boy. And from what Trace could see, it appeared they had nothing but the two mules they had ridden—no weapons, no bedrolls, no supplies. They sat huddled together, apparently lost and confused.

Trace looked at Buck, but before he could speak, Buck said, "I know—greenhorns," his face a mask of fake disgust. "You go on down and I'll stay here with the horses till you say come on in."

Trace made his way silently down the slope. The two sat talking, unaware of his presence until he spoke. "You fellers have some trouble?"

They reacted as if he had thrown a handful of gunpowder into a fire. They bolted upright, the man falling against the boy, knocking him into the stream. Trace stood there, amazed by their frantic gyrations, which made them look like two frightened pigeons. "I don't mean you no harm," he said. "I would have given you some warning, but I couldn't be sure you didn't have a gun hid somewhere." He could see that neither had recovered from the initial fright. At least they didn't run. The boy was still staggering around in the stream, trying to keep from winding up on his seat in the chilly water. "Name's Trace McCall," he offered.

The man finally found his voice. "Mr. McCall, I reckon I don't have to tell you, you gave us a start." He wiped his brow with his shirtsleeve, sopping up the cold perspiration that had suddenly formed there. "I'm Jordan Thrash. This here's Jamie. We've just escaped from wild Indians."

Trace studied the two unlikely travelers. Jordan Thrash was a slight man, narrow in the shoulders, with a bony face that bore the lines of many years following a plow. His weather-beaten face was tanned and leathery to a line above his ears. From that point upward, his pate was bald and white, indicating that he normally wore a cap, and not a broad-brimmed one. His boy, Jamie, on the other hand, was fair, with cheeks as smooth as a baby's, not yet of an age to shave. Like his father, Jamie was thin, yet unlike his father, he had managed to hang on to his hat during their flight from the Sioux war party.

"My partner's up on the hill with our horses," Trace said, then he turned and whistled for Buck to come on in. He detected a decided look of concern in the eyes of both Jordan and Jamie Thrash, possibly wondering if they had fallen into the hands of ruffians after a narrow escape from savage Indians. "Looks to me like you folks have lost about everything you own. Buck and I can give you a hand. I don't think you have to worry about those Injuns, they headed due north after they burned your wagon."

"We'd be much obliged," Jordan said, wincing at the fate of his wagon. "Did they burn everything?"

"Nossir. There are some things still scattered around. They just made a mess of most of it. It's hard to say how much they carried off, since I didn't know how much you had to start with." He glanced at the spent mules standing in the middle of the stream. "We can round up your other two mules back there on the flats."

When Buck brought the horses and pack mules down, Trace introduced him to the Thrashes. Still wide-eyed at the sudden appearance of the two mountain men, Jordan Thrash was obviously still not sure he and his son were not in danger. They relaxed a bit, however, when Buck went about the business of building a fire and offered them some salt pork and coffee from his pack. Jordan confessed that they had not eaten that day. A cup of Buck's steaming black coffee limbered up Jordan's tongue, and he began to recount the events that had brought him and his son to this little stream in the foothills.

He had been a sharecropper on a farm in southern Ohio for seventeen years, ever since he and his wife were married. The ground was poor, and he fought it for all that time, trying to scratch out a meager living for the two of them and Jamie, who came along less than a year after the wedding. He considered himself a capable farmer, but some land just won't yield a crop, and the sixty acres he struggled with almost beat him under. He was barely making ends meet when bad luck came to roost on his doorstep a year ago. "My wife, God rest her soul, took sick last fall, and we lost her before winter. Mr. Carver, that's the man who owned the land, sold our farm out from under us not two months after my wife died." He placed his hand on his son's shoulder and smiled reassuringly. "Me and Jamie decided we could find us a farm of our own out here before everybody else got the same idea. Ain't that right, Jamie?"

"I reckon so, Pa," Jamie replied softly, offering a brave smile in return.

Trace looked at the boy, now making short work of a tough piece of fried pork. *Well, you sure got off to a good start,* he thought. *Lost your wagon and most everything else—don't even know where the hell you are.* Jordan looked as if he was used to hard work, but Jamie was going to have some filling out to do. He was a mite frail for such rough country, in Trace's opinion.

"I ain't figured out yet where you two was headin'—way up here this far north of the trail," Buck said. He had been listening silently to Jordan's accounting of their journey up to this point.

Embarrassed, as any man is when caught doing something foolhardy, Jordan reluctantly replied. "Well, we were told we had just missed a wagon train of folks who had left Fort Laramie a week ago, heading for Oregon. So we set out to catch up with them."

"Just the two of ya?" Buck blurted.

"Yessir . . . well, we know it's best to travel in a train. That's why we were trying to catch those other folks." Jordan was wishing the conversation could be changed—he obviously was uncomfortable at having his poor decisions aired in front of his son. But Buck never was known for being long on tact.

"Forevermore . . ." Buck sighed, shaking his head from side to side. "Mister, you ought to have been a riverboat gambler 'cause you're the luckiest son of a bitch I believe I've ever run into. It's a wonder you and the boy here ain't sproutin' arrows like a porky-pine. What were you doin' so far north of the Platte, anyway?"

"Dammit! He told you," Jamie finally interrupted. "We saw the Injuns and we cut off to the north to keep them from seeing us. It don't matter now. We done what we done and now we're here."

Taken aback a bit by the youngster's outburst, Buck grinned. "Right you are, son. I didn't go to ruffle your feathers." The boy was slight, he thought, but he showed some sand.

While there was still some daylight left, Trace and Buck, along with Jordan on Frank's horse, went back and rounded up the two loose mules. Jamie was left to keep an eye on their camp, armed with Frank's old rifle. The mules were still grazing aimlessly over the flat stretch of prairie where Trace had picked up Jordan's trail earlier in the day. It was no chore to round them up, as they seemed genuinely glad to see Jordan and willingly stood still while halters fashioned from rawhide rope were slipped over their heads.

Since it was getting late in the day by the time the two stray mules were secured, they decided it best to wait until morning before going back to salvage what they could of Jordan's belongings. That decided, they returned to their camp by the stream. Jamie seemed relieved to see them back safe and sound, although there had been nothing to cause him concern while they were gone. *Kind of a scary young-'un,* Trace thought. *Some folks would just be better off if they stayed back east.* He wondered if he was that green when he journeyed out here with his father and Henry Brown Bear.

"I'm getting tired of eating salt pork," Trace announced after the animals were taken care of. "I saw plenty of sign on top of the hill. I think I'll follow this stream down a'ways and see if I can run up on a deer." His announcement was met with universal approval from the other three, who also felt a need for a hardy supper. "I'll take Jamie here with me." He motioned to the boy. "Come on, Jamie—maybe we'll get a shot at something." Trace figured the boy could use some training, something that had apparently been lacking from his father.

Jamie looked uncertain, glancing at his father for guidance. Buck didn't wait for Jordan to give permission. "Hell, yeah, Jamie. Go on and show ol' Trace how to bring home the supper. That there rifle belonged to as good a man as ever set a bait stick. And it's a good'un, but it shoots a hair to the left." He laughed and added, "Ol' Trace might not've told you that."

Buck got Frank's bullet pouch and powder horn

and hung them around Jamie's neck. "Now, if we could get you outfitted in some buckskins, you'd look like a genuine Mountain Man. 'Course, you might wanna let your beard grow out." He laughed heartily at his own joke while Jamie blushed, his smooth cheeks glowing.

Off they went on foot, Trace leading as he made his way effortlessly through the brush without disturbing a leaf. Jamie followed, trying to emulate the mountain man. When they had covered about half a mile, Trace stopped and waited for Jamie to catch up to him. "There," he pointed to a place beside the game trail they had been following. "An old buck marked his territory there." Jamie nodded. There were fresh droppings to the right and left of the trail. Trace sensed they were close. "We've got to be real quiet now." He continued walking, his sharp eyes searching the trees before them.

A hundred yards farther down the slope, the stream took a sharp turn, doubling back on itself. Trace stopped and dropped to one knee. He motioned for Jamie, signaling him to be quiet. When Jamie moved up beside him, he tapped the boy on the shoulder and pointed to a stand of willows where the stream turned. Jamie didn't see anything at first, but soon he made out the features of a fair-sized black-tailed buck standing like a statue among the willows, listening.

It was an easy shot, fifty yards, no more. Trace remembered the thrill of killing a deer when he was a young boy so he decided to let Jamie take the shot. He motioned for the boy to ready his rifle. Jamie seemed reluctant, unsure of himself, but Trace urged him to take the shot before the deer bolted. Jamie nodded and brought Frank Brown's Hawken up to aim. Trace stopped him and held a percussion cap up for him to see. Jamie looked puzzled so Trace reached over and placed the cap for him, then nodded for Jamie to shoot. *I reckon he's never fired anything but a flintlock,* Trace thought.

"Aim for a point right behind his front leg," Trace whispered. Jamie nodded and pulled the trigger. *Tchow.* The Hawken belched, hammering Jamie's shoulder. The rifle ball missed the deer by ten feet, rattling through the willows above him. The deer was off at once, bounding over the wide stream in a single leap, only to fall dead on the other side, a lead ball fired from Trace's Hawken deep in his lungs.

"Damn," Jamie uttered.

"You just ain't used to that rifle yet," Trace said. To himself, he was thinking, *I ain't sure you've shot any rifle before.* He couldn't imagine that any boy, even a boy younger than Jamie, didn't know how to handle a rifle—especially if he wanted to make it out here.

The meat from the buck was tough, but it was good, and especially welcome to Jordan and Jamie. They ate their fill that night and again the next morning for breakfast before breaking camp and starting back to look for their belongings. Trace led the procession, with Jordan and Jamie following behind, leading their extra mules. Buck brought up the rear, trailing the pack animals.

They reached the ravine where the wagon had

been burned a little before midday, and Buck and Trace scouted around the area while Jordan and Jamie sorted through the scattered clothes and blackened furniture. When they had salvaged everything that could prove useful, Buck helped Jordan fashion some makeshift packs for his mules, using rawhide and rags for straps.

"We can take you to Laramie—that's where we were heading anyway," Trace said. "I don't know what you plan to do now, since you lost everything. Maybe you can find somebody heading back East from there."

Jordan shook his head, his chin determined. "We'll be heading west, I reckon, just like we planned to do. But we'll go to Fort Laramie first and wait for a wagon train heading for Oregon."

Buck studied the pair of them for a long moment, father and son. Determination would carry freight just so far before a man needed a wagon and supplies. "I ain't trying to tell you what you ought to do, Jordan. But a man needs more than four mules and a few packs of clothes and such to make it to Oregon."

"I suppose you're right," Jordan replied. He was reluctant to say more, but convinced that he was in the company of honest men, he confessed that while he had lost a great deal to the war party, he still had some money. "It was going to see us through the first year in Oregon. Now I guess it'll have to go to buy us another wagon and supplies just to get us there."

That added a sensible amount of weight to Jordan

Thrash's determination to continue on over the mountains, as far as Trace was concerned. They made camp about twenty miles from the spot where they had left the burnt-out wagon. The next day would see them arrive at the twin towers of Fort Laramie.

On the day that Trace and Buck started for Fort Laramie with Jordan and Jamie Thrash, Hamilton Blunt received a visit from his wife in his office in St. Louis.

"Forgive me for bothering you when you're working," Julia said when she opened the office door and peeked in. "I know you don't like for me to come down here, but Frances was baking today and thought you might like some fresh muffins." Lately, he had not been coming to the house for his noonday meal, and she worried that he was not eating properly. She pushed the door wide and entered the room. She saw at once that he was displeased and that her gesture had merely irritated him.

"Julia, what are you doing here? You know damn well I've said I don't like to be disturbed when I'm at the office."

"I know. But you've seemed so distracted lately I thought you might like something nice to eat." Why, she wondered, did it irritate the man anytime she happened by his workplace unannounced? It used to be a pleasant surprise for him. Lately, everything she did seemed to infuriate him, even at home. It had been eight years since their wedding, and there was no denying the changes she'd seen in her mirror since then. But she expected Hamilton to appreciate the fact that she was not a young girl when they married. The years had rounded her slender body a little, the body that he had been so feverish to know, and there were now streaks of gray in her dark hair. But there was gray at his temples and in his beard as well.

"Well, I don't have time to stop for a tea party in the middle of the afternoon," he said gruffly. "You can save the muffins for supper tonight." He got up from his chair to escort her out the door, when the door of the storage room behind his desk suddenly opened.

"Oh!" was all the young woman said when she saw Julia in the room. She started to retreat back into the storeroom, but decided that it might make matters worse. So she stood there, her hand on the doorknob, and tried to affect a pleasant look.

Hamilton looked startled, but for only an instant. "Come in, Miss Pauley," he said and turned quickly to Julia. "I don't know if you know Miss Pauley. She's helping with the books." Without missing a beat, he turned back to the young woman. "Did you find the ledgers you were looking for, Miss Pauley?"

The young woman was too flustered to reply properly, not being nearly as coolheaded as Hamilton Blunt. She fussed with the top buttons of her blouse, which Julia noticed were undone, before she managed a reply. "Yes, I found them."

Julia was disappointed, but far from shocked, to have stumbled upon the first evidence of a suspicion she had harbored for some time now. She knew there was some reason for the distance between her husband and herself during the last eighteen months. It was unlikely that a man of his vigor and lusty appetites could have aged to the point where his ardor had cooled completely. All signs had pointed to the possibility that he had simply tired of her. Now she turned from the girl to face her husband. "I thought Mr. Finch took care of the ledgers."

"He does," Hamilton replied, "Miss Pauley is helping him." There was a hint of strain in his voice even though he managed to fix a smile on his face. "Now, why don't you run along home and let us all get back to work." He glanced at the basket of fresh-baked muffins Julia had placed on his desk. "Maybe Miss Pauley would enjoy some of your muffins," he offered, trying to seem politely innocent.

"Miss Pauley can bake her own damn muffins," Julia promptly shot back. She snatched her basket from the desk, turned on her heel and went out the door. *I'll be damned if I'm going to feed your little plaything while she's servicing you!*

"Well, I think your dumb little wife just got an education," Madge Pauley opined when the door had been slammed shut. She paused a second, then added, "I thought you said you and her were separated."

"We soon will be," Hamilton Blunt said evenly, between clenched teeth. "I am sick to death of that woman."

She moved over to his desk and put her arms around his neck. "A man like you needs a young woman," she said and began tickling his ear with her tongue.

He grabbed her roughly, almost tearing her blouse as he fumbled with her buttons. "Come on," he said, lifting her off the floor, "let's go look for those ledgers." They both laughed lustily as he carried her into the little room behind his office.

Chapter 13

It was close to dusk when they arrived at Fort Laramie, and the gates were just about to be closed for the night. Being in no particular hurry to see the inside of the fort again, Trace suggested that they camp outside so the horses could graze. There would be plenty of time in the morning to take care of the business of trading their plews. This suited Buck in spite of his craving for a drink of whiskey. Jordan, on the other hand, was anxious to learn of any possibility to get outfitted for the Oregon trek as soon as he could. So he and Jamie bid Buck and Trace goodbye and thanked them for coming to their rescue.

"I reckon we owe you our lives," Jordan said as he shook hands with Buck.

"No such a'thing," Buck replied. "You'd a'done the same. That's the way of it out here."

As he and Trace climbed into the saddle again, Buck said, "They ain't no grass left around here. We might as well ride out a'ways till we find better grazing."

The suggestion suited Trace, so he turned the paint's head upriver and led them out. About one hundred yards above the fort they passed a circle of wagons—two big freight wagons and an odd assortment of farm wagons and prairie schooners—a good-sized train. They were formed in a defensive circle, their animals already brought into the center for the night. It was not unusual to see the freighters out here, but Trace and Buck thought it odd to see so many other wagons. On their way through South Pass, they had come across a trail of wagon tracks, which they had found puzzling. It had never occurred to them at that time that the tracks might have been made by ordinary settlers heading west. It was unthinkable to imagine people dumb enough to think they could reach the Oregon territory in a wagon. "Folks ain't got no idea what's between Laramie and Oregon territory," Buck had said. Now, of course, they realized that the tracks they had seen were no doubt made by the very wagon train Jordan had been talking about. And now here was another group of settlers evidently planning to try it. Jordan Thrash wasn't the only crazy person around, it appeared.

About three miles upriver they found a place that suited them, and they made camp for the night. As soon as the horses and mules were taken care of, they had a supper of jerked buffalo. Neither man was in the mood to cook anything, even had there been any fresh meat. Buck boiled some coffee, and the strong black liquid and the jerky served as their feast. The blanket felt good that night.

The members of the wagon train were up and hustling about their chores when Buck and Trace rode by the next morning on their way back to the fort.

The two mountain men could hardly keep from staring. It was the first time they had seen so many white women in quite some time—washing clothes, chasing youngsters, cooking over open fires. It reminded Trace of a carnival. "I swear," Buck allowed, "I thought Jordan Thrash was daft in the head for thinkin' there'd be another bunch of folks out here in wagons."

Seeking to trade their furs, they went in search of Jim Bridger, but Bridger's man, Bordeaux, told them that Old Gabe was not back yet from his camp in the Cache Valley on Bear River. But Bordeaux was the man in charge of trading, anyway, so Trace and Buck exchanged their cargo for shot and powder and some hard staples.

"I'm sorry I can't give you more credit for them plews, boys. There just ain't no market fer 'em no more." Bordeaux scratched his beard thoughtfully as he picked through the furs. " 'Bout the only thing that shines these days is them buffalo hides there. I can do you a little better on them."

Buck shook his head sadly, lamenting the passing of a life he loved. "I 'preciate anything you can allow. I swear, I might have to turn Injun if I can't find some way to make a livin'." He glanced over at Trace. "You might wanna go back to them Crows you was livin' with."

Trace didn't say anything, but just smiled and shook his head. He thought to himself that if he had to turn Injun, he'd more than likely be looking up in Bitterroot territory for a certain band of Snake Indians and a handsome little Indian maiden.

Bordeaux looked from one of them to the other, sizing them up. Then he made a suggestion. "If you two are really looking for a way to make a living, you ought to go out yonder and talk to them folks in the wagons. That is, of course, if you think you can find your way through the South Pass to Oregon."

Buck reared back on his heels. "If I can find my way . . ." he sputtered. "Hell, I s'pect I've rode that territory as much as any white man in the country—except Jim Bridger—and maybe as much as him." He snorted as if to clear Bordeaux's insult from his nostrils. "But what the hell would I want to be a farmer for?"

Bordeaux laughed. "I ain't talking about joining 'em. They've been waiting here for over a week looking for a guide to lead 'em out there. The one they hired was supposed to meet 'em here but he took off with the advance money they give him to buy his supplies with. We've had some trouble with Sioux war parties, and I reckon he didn't figure it was worth risking his hide."

Buck thought about it for a few seconds. The idea had possibilities, but it wasn't without considerable risks. Besides, he wasn't sure a string of wagons could get over the mountains, even without Injun trouble. "I don't know," he pondered. "How much would they pay a man to guide 'em out there?"

"I think they were gonna pay that feller four hundred dollars."

"Four hundred dollars? Who do we have to talk to? I'd lead 'em into hell's front yard for four hundred dollars."

"The feller that seems to be in charge is a preacher—name's Longstreet. Big ol' feller with a long white beard, drives a team of oxen."

They thanked Bordeaux and went outside to talk it over. "Whadaya think, Trace?" Buck asked as soon as they set foot on the hard-baked ground of the courtyard. "It don't sound like it'd be a whole lot of fun being mother hen to a passel of farmers, but leastways we'll be headin' back to the mountains."

Trace considered the possibility for a moment before answering. He had entertained some thoughts about striking out toward the Bitterroots alone. But now that Frank was gone, he felt a sense of responsibility toward Buck. In spite of his feisty attitude, Buck was pushing on in years, although he would flare up madder'n hell if Trace even suggested he was slowing down. "What the hell," he finally decided. "We can give it a try."

Reverend Longstreet stood up to stretch his back. In addition to providing spiritual guidance for his flock of settlers, he was also their blacksmith, hauling his forge and bellows in one of the two large freight wagons in his train. The other belonged to Blunt Brothers Freight Company out of St. Louis and would be returning to St. Louis loaded with buffalo hides—that is, if the owner could negotiate a satisfactory trade with Bordeaux. At the moment, as Longstreet understood it, the trading was not going to Mr. Blunt's satisfaction, for Bordeaux was as hard-nosed a trader as they come.

Longstreet stood there a few moments longer before returning to the chore of mending a cracked axle. As he gazed back toward the massive tower on the front wall of the fort, he saw the two mountain men coming from the passage that tunneled beneath the tower. He had seen them ride past earlier that morning, leading pack mules. Now it appeared they were heading in his direction, so he continued to bide his time, observing their approach. It was difficult to determine at a distance whether these wild men were Indian or white.

"Good mornin' to you, neighbors," Longstreet said. Watching them closely, he waited for them to state their business.

"Morning," Buck replied as he and Trace dismounted. "Bordeaux said we might oughta talk to you, if your name's Longstreet."

"I'm Longstreet. What about?"

"I hear you're needin' a guide to git you folks over the mountains." He nodded toward Trace. "Me and my partner here can git you there if anybody can."

Reverend Longstreet didn't reply at once, taking his time to look the two buckskin-clad mountain men over. They were a contrast in human beings, he was thinking—one short and grizzled, with snow-white hair and beard; the other a young man, straight and tall as a lodgepole pine. There were a lot of unprincipled scalawags drifting across the western frontier. How could a man be sure these men were not two more who would take his money and desert his wagons in some forsaken canyon in the Rockies? "It's a fact we're looking for a guide to continue our journey," he said at last. "Have you gentlemen any references?"

"Have we any what?" Buck asked, unsure what to reply.

Trace stepped in when it was obvious that Buck was stumped. "Mr. Bordeaux will vouch for us. He'll tell you we know the country."

Longstreet studied Trace's face. He liked the way the young man's gaze never wavered when he looked into his eyes. Reverend Longstreet considered himself a fair judge of character, and he sensed honesty in the deep blue of the young man's eyes. Still, he had erred before, so he did not want to make a hasty decision. He was about to speak when the young man's attention was distracted by one of the women of the train walking by.

Trace turned to look at the woman, waited until he was sure, scarcely believing his eyes. "Mrs. Bowen?"

Nettie Bowen turned at the sound of her name. Smiling, she looked to see who had called. Noticing the two men in buckskins for the first time, she glanced at the tall young man, then at the stocky older man, without recognizing either. When her gaze shifted back to the young man once more, her smile slowly expanded as her mouth dropped open and she realized who he was. "Jim? Jim Tracey? Is that you?" Bringing her hands up to her cheeks as if to hold her surprise in, she exclaimed, "Merciful Heavens, I can't believe my eyes!" She rushed to him and ensnared him in her ample embrace, pinning his arms to his sides.

Trapped, he could do nothing but grin and endure. When she released him, she was so excited that she didn't know where to start. Nettie Bowen was possibly the last person he would ever have expected to see west of the Missouri. As for Nettie, she, along with many people back in St. Louis, had assumed that John and Julia Tracey's youngest son was long dead—done in by savage Indians or lost in a blizzard. And here he was, big as life—bigger than life, in fact—grown up so straight and tall that all vestiges of the boy were gone, replaced by the wide shoulders and thickened neck of a man. Little wonder she had not recognized him at first.

"You've got to come with me and say hello to Travis," she went on. "He's not gonna believe his eyes." She stepped back to take in the total picture of him, still finding it difficult to believe she was looking at the same skinny boy she had fed in her kitchen back East.

"Yessum," he said, beaming, feeling embarrassed by the emotion he had generated in his mother's longtime friend. "As soon as we finish talking to Mr. Longstreet here."

Longstreet, who had been grinning to himself as he watched the reunion between Nettie and the young mountain man, spoke up. "This young man and his partner say they could lead us to Oregon, Mrs. Bowen. What would you think of that idea?"

Nettie, still smiling brightly, glanced at Buck briefly, then back at Trace. "I don't know the other gentleman, but if Jim says he knows the way, then I expect he does."

Longstreet studied Trace's face for only a moment more before deciding. "Time's getting by us. Every day we set here waiting is a day lost to the coming winter. I reckon we've hired us a couple of guides." It was apparent, however, that there was still something that bothered him. "One thing puzzles me, though," he looked Trace straight in the eye, "Mrs. Bowen called you Jim. I thought you said your name was Trace. Which is it?"

"Trace," he immediately replied.

Nettie Bowen showed no hint of the surprise she felt when she heard his answer. Knowing the reason young Jim Tracey had fled St. Louis—but firm in her confidence of the boy's innocence—she reacted at once and volunteered, "Jim is a boyhood name they used to call him."

This seemed to satisfy Reverend Longstreet. "Well, then," he said, looking at Buck, "when can we get started?"

"Well, as I recollect, we ain't got no appointments," Buck replied. "As soon as your folks is ready, we'll git on the trail. It's already a mite late in the summer to start out. But I reckon if we don't set on our haunches for too long, we can get over the mountains before the first snow flies."

Trace left Buck to negotiate the financial settlement with Reverend Longstreet and allowed himself to be pulled off toward Travis Bowen's wagon. Holding him firmly by the sleeve of his buckskin shirt, as if afraid he might try to get away, Nettie chattered away. "Travis is gonna fall over when he sees you. Where have you been all these years?" Not leaving time for him to answer, she continued, "I reckon you're mighty surprised to see me and Travis out here. No more surprised than I am to be here, I expect. My, but your mother would be proud to see what a man you've grown into." With that thought, she stopped and turned to look up at him, her smile replaced by a look of concern. "I can pretty much understand why you're calling yourself by some other name. I reckon you know that the Blunts said you murdered that no-good scoundrel Tyler. I didn't believe it for a minute—even if it hadda been murder, it a'been a blessing for the world."

"I didn't murder Tyler Blunt, Mrs. Bowen. He tried to kill me, and I defended myself."

"Well then, that's good enough for me. Your mama didn't raise no liars." The smile returned to her face. "What do we call you, anyway?"

"Trace McCall."

She nodded while she turned it over in her mind. "Good choice," she said. "Your pa and your brother would appreciate it, God rest their souls."

They approached a nearly new wagon with sheets already bleached out by the sun. A slightly built man was bending over one of the back wheels with a bucket of grease and a wooden paddle. Nettie called out to him, and he straightened up when he caught sight of the man walking with his wife. Travis Bowen wore a pained expression as he squinted at the young mountain man that Nettie still held by the sleeve.

"Travis," she said, "I want you to meet somebody." She pulled Trace right up in front of her husband. "This here is Trace McCall," she announced grandly and stepped back to watch Travis's reaction.

Travis nodded and extended his hand, puzzled but patiently awaiting an explanation for the visit. There was something familiar about the tall stranger, but he had no notion at all who he was. When there was no word of explanation, Travis finally asked, "Well, what can I do for you, sir?"

"It's good to see you again, Mr. Bowen." When it was obvious that Travis Bowen still did not recognize him, Trace said in a quiet voice, "It's Jim Tracey, sir, only I don't call myself that anymore."

Travis stepped back, astonished. "Jim? Jim Tracey? Well I'll be . . ." He was at a loss for words for a few moments. Then he guffawed out loud and took Trace's hand again, pumping it vigorously. "My God, I wouldn'ta knowed you from Adam! I swear, what are you doin' out here?"

"Going to Oregon with you, I reckon," Trace managed to get in before Travis suddenly shushed him.

Looking furtively from side to side to see if anyone else had taken notice of the reunion, Travis took Trace by the arm that Nettie had just released and pulled him around to the back of the wagon. "Boy, I'm mighty glad to see you. We wondered about you and hoped you was making out all right. But you've got to be careful." With a nod, he pointed out one of the large freight wagons across the circle. "That wagon yonder belongs to Blunt Brothers. Morgan Blunt drove it out here."

Trace tensed and unconsciously tightened his grip on his rifle. A glance in Nettie's direction told him that in the excitement of the moment, she had forgotten to tell him that fact herself. He felt Travis Bowen's hand on his forearm. "Easy, son. I reckon if I couldn't recognize you, chances are he won't either. But you best steer clear of him. He's supposed to pull his wagon out of our train today—he's only come as far as Laramie with us."

There was no longer any fear in Trace McCall. He had fled when he was a boy only because he was not confident his side of the story would ever be believed and he had no intention of being hung, or rotting in prison, for killing Tyler Blunt. Out here, where a man's rifle was the prevailing law, he saw no reason to step around Morgan Blunt. He told Travis that it was not in his nature to look for trouble, but he would not hide from Morgan.

"I reckon you know Morgan got hisself appointed deputy sheriff. The only reason was to justify killing you if he got the chance. He convinced the sheriff that you murdered Tyler. He's still out to get you, Jim."

"If he is, he's gonna have to do it himself," Trace replied calmly. "His man LaPorte ain't around to do his dirty work anymore."

Travis's face showed his deep concern. He was afraid Trace was not as troubled with the threat as he should be. "You watch your back till we get away from Laramie. I've never seen a man with such a fire in him to get his revenge."

Trace was touched to see such anxiety in the faces of his old friends. To ease their worry, he promised to keep a sharp eye out and to avoid contact with Blunt if possible. To change the subject, he expressed his surprise at seeing the two of them in a wagon train bound for Oregon.

Travis explained that he had decided he could not finish out his remaining years in the employ of Hamilton Blunt. With Nettie's blessing, he had put their little house in St. Louis up for sale and joined Reverend Longstreet's party. There had been more and more talk about the Oregon country, and he decided it was the best chance for Nettie and him to own any real land. "Hell, we ain't young anymore, but we've got a few more good years. No sense in giving them to Hamilton Blunt."

As the conversation went on, Trace was puzzled that there was no mention of his mother. He found that strange, since his mother had been possibly Nettie Bowen's best friend. When he finally asked about her, the question seemed to embarrass Nettie.

"She's fine, I reckon," was Nettie's reluctant response. "I mean, I ain't talked to your ma in some time now. I saw her once before we left at Mr. Trotter's store. That's the last time I talked to her."

This surprised Trace. "You two used to visit every other day."

"To tell you the truth, Jim—I mean Trace—I don't think Hamilton Blunt liked for her to visit with the wife of one of his employees."

That news was disappointing to Trace. He knew that Nettie Bowen was about the only friend his mother had. Glancing at Travis, he was puzzled by the expression on his father's old friend's face. The talk about his mother appeared to distress Travis.

Further thought on the matter was interrupted by the arrival of Buck Ransom.

After Trace made the introductions, the talk turned to the journey that would begin the following morning. Buck and Trace tried to paint as realistic a picture of the rough road ahead of them as they could without being completely discouraging. Buck summed it up by saying, "I ain't never heard of nobody crossing them mountains in a wagon, but we seen tracks over near South Pass—and if anybody can make it, I reckon it'd be us." After accepting Nettie Bowen's invitation to return for supper, Buck and Trace left to close up their camp in preparation for an early departure.

In spite of the caution shown by Travis Bowen, the surprise reunion did not go unobserved. Seated in his freight wagon, taking stock of his inventory, Morgan Blunt felt the blood freeze in his veins when he heard the exclamation from Travis. *Jim Tracey!* He was certain that was the name he had heard—a name he had been waiting to hear for more than four years. Could he believe his ears?

As soon as he had arrived in Fort Laramie with Longstreet's wagon train, Morgan was met with disturbing news. Joe LaPorte had been killed at the rendezvous that summer. Morgan's first reaction to the news had been the anxiety of realizing that his chances of exacting revenge upon the murderer of his brother were fading. It had been years since Jim Tracey put a knife into Tyler's gut, and Morgan was beginning to fear that even LaPorte would never find him. Without LaPorte, Morgan had no ally with the Indians, and certainly no knowledge of the mountains. And now this stroke of luck. If his ears did not deceive him, Jim Tracey had delivered himself to his executioner.

Stunned for only a few moments when he heard the name blurted out of Travis Bowen's mouth, Morgan reached immediately for a rifle from the wooden crate he had brought for trade. Fumbling in his excitement, he tried to calm his emotions long enough to pour a measure of powder down the barrel. Selecting a leather patch, he seated the lead ball and rammed the load home. There was no thought of consequences or injury to innocent parties. He was determined to shoot young Tracey down where he stood, bystanders be damned!

As quietly as he could, he quickly pulled barrels and boxes aside to give him suitable room from which to shoot. Grabbing the edge of the heavy wagon sheet, he pulled it up enough to give him a hole to sight through. "Damn!" he exclaimed, for he was too late. Travis had already led Jim around to the back of his wagon. Almost choking on the bile generated by his intense hatred, he entertained thoughts of sending a rifle ball through the sheets of Bowen's wagon in hopes of a lucky shot. He thought better of it when he spied Buck Ransom approaching from Longstreet's wagon, his rifle cradled across his forearm. "Damn," he uttered once more and sank back on his heels, a scalding mixture of anxiety and frustration churning within his gut.

Though he strained to hear the conversation taking

place on the other side of Bowen's wagon, Morgan could not make out a word. After a few minutes, however, the visit was over, and Buck reappeared, the tall buckskin-clad figure walking beside him. *I would never have recognized him,* Morgan thought as he slowly eased the barrel of his rifle underneath the bottom of the wagon sheet. The cowardliness of shooting Trace in the back did not concern him. Morgan was a big man, and capable of extreme violence, but he had no thoughts of a fair fight. An execution, pure and simple, was what he had in mind. The problem, however, was that Trace walked on the far side of Buck, and Morgan could not get a clear shot. He couldn't chance a miss. Then he heard Nettie Bowen call out the supper invitation, and he immediately drew his rifle back inside, knowing he would soon have another chance.

Back at their campsite, Buck and Trace packed up their plunder and prepared to move their horses and mules downriver with those of the wagon train. It was already getting late in the day by the time they drove their animals inside the circle of wagons. Trace noticed that the big freighter that belonged to Blunt Brothers was missing from the circle. *All well and good,* he thought. *It's best to avoid a confrontation.* The paint was a bit skittish about being hobbled inside the circle of wagons, but he settled down when the pack mules were placed close at hand. After his horse was taken care of, Trace helped Buck set up their camp.

No sooner had they settled themselves when Reverend Longstreet assembled the members of the train to meet their new guides. There were undisguised expressions of concern on the faces of the men, obviously wondering if these two wild figures could be trusted to lead them where they wanted to go, or if they were of the same ilk as the former guide who had taken their money and fled. They were somewhat relieved when Longstreet assured them that Bordeaux himself had vouched for their honesty and capability. The gathering became almost cordial when Longstreet informed them that Travis and Nettie Bowen were well acquainted with the tall young man as well.

"I'd like to add my recommendation that you folks couldn't have hired two better men to guide you," a voice called out from the back of the gathering. Trace turned to see the crowd parting as Jordan Thrash made his way through to the front. "These two sure saved my bacon." He stepped up, grinning, his hand extended. "Looks like I found my wagon train," he said to Buck.

It was not an easy time for Trace, uncomfortable as he was in crowds of women and children. But he stood patiently while Longstreet introduced them, and he endured the stares of the women and children as they openly gawked at his fringed buckskins and the otter skin bow case strapped across his back. The men eyed the Hawken rifle, cradled casually across his forearm. Glancing beyond Jordan Thrash, who was busy meeting his new neighbors himself, Trace spied Jamie standing quietly and watching him.

When their eyes met, Jamie smiled broadly. He appreciated Trace's discomfort.

Buck, on the other hand, seemed to glory in the attention. He posed and preened in all his mountain wildness, duly impressing the homespun congregation. Trace wondered that the people didn't mistake him for Moses himself, come to lead them to the Promised Land. His thick shock of snow-white hair that fell in tangled snarls joining a craggy beard of black and gray, might cause a person of imagination to be reminded of the snow-capped peaks of the Rocky Mountains. Watching him as he performed for the farmers and merchants, Trace could not repress a smile. Reverend Longstreet had his guide all right, and the wagon train had their authenic mountain man.

The introductory meeting lasted for most of an hour before the gathering dispersed to return to their individual wagons for the evening meal. Buck had completely captured his audience with his descriptions of the trails ahead and the dangers that he would protect them from. It was with some reluctance that the folks retired to the cookfires, and Buck had to politely refuse several supper invitations, explaining that he had already accepted one from Mrs. Bowen.

"How long has it been since you've had real cornbread, fried in a pan?" Travis Bowen asked when he noticed the rapt attention with which Trace watched Nettie preparing the food.

Realizing that he had been caught staring, Trace laughed, embarrassed. "I didn't realize how long it had been until I saw Mrs. Bowen mixing it—not since I saw my ma fix it that way, I guess."

Not wishing to open the conversation to any questions about Trace's mother, Travis quickly changed the subject. "I reckon you know the mountains pretty good by now."

"I reckon. Not as good as Buck, though." It did not escape him that Travis was still reluctant to talk about his mother. He guessed it was because she had married Hamilton Blunt and Travis probably thought the subject might make him uneasy. It made little difference to Trace. He certainly did not approve of his mother's choice, but she had been firm in her decision. Maybe it was best for her that Blunt was there to care for her after the tragic death of his father. Trace had decided long before to accept it.

While Nettie went about the preparation of the cornbread, Travis tunneled into the sacks and boxes in his wagon until he found a jug of corn whiskey. Passing it to Buck, he announced, "Here's a little somethin' to wake your appetite up. Brought it all the way from St. Louie—made it myself." He grinned as Buck eagerly grabbed the jug and tilted it. Nettie shook her head in mock irritation as the men passed the jug around. Trace took a small swallow of the fiery liquid, closing his eyes tightly to hold the tears back. When Travis offered it again, he declined, the vivid picture of Buck's drunken binges at rendezvous still fresh in his mind. He was thankful when Nettie Bowen announced that supper was ready and Travis replaced the cork in his jug and returned it to the wagon. Buck's forlorn expression was lost on Travis, but Trace knew that it was painful for the old trapper to see the jug put to bed while still half full.

"I'm sorry I couldn't fix you some fried chicken or something you're not used to getting. I reckon you've had enough venison to last you your whole life." Nettie apologized as she ladled generous portions from the stewpot. "But it's a treat to us. Mr. Bordeaux had some fresh venison that one of his men killed this morning, and I thought it would be more pleasing than salt pork."

"Fresh meat is still fresh meat," Buck countered. "Don't make no difference what kind of critter it was carved off'n."

"Buck's right," Trace said. "We've been living off jerky and salt pork the past few days—the only fresh meat we've had was a tough old blacktail buck we carved up three nights ago. We appreciate a real cooked meal for a change." He graciously accepted the plate offered and seated himself cross-legged on the opposite side of the fire.

"Humph—jerky," Nettie scolded. "A man can't get much nourishment from nothing but jerky."

Buck, his hand outstretched to receive a plate, commented, "Jerky's better than nuthin', I reckon—'course, nuthin's easier to fix."

Nettie did a fine job cooking the fresh deer meat, making it into a stew spiced with some onions, also traded from Mr. Bordeaux. From a barrel in the back of the wagon, she dipped out a ladle full of molasses to sop up with cornbread. Accustomed to much simpler fare, Trace and Buck thought it a veritable feast.

The talk turned to the rugged mountains to be

faced in the weeks before autumn, since there was naturally a great concern about the unknown on the part of the settlers. After talking to Bordeaux, Buck had found that there had already been a few hardy souls passing through Laramie who had struck out for Oregon. Reverend Longstreet's train would not be the first, but they would be among the first, and a lot of folks figured they wouldn't be the last. Buck was interested to know if all the men in the company were prepared to fight Indians if it came to that. He had heard that some religions didn't hold with fighting, and he wanted to make sure this bunch was not of that persuasion.

"I don't wanna worry you, Missus," he said to Nettie, "but them Sioux have been ornery all summer. And when the shootin' starts, I don't wanna look around and find that it ain't nobody but me and Trace with a rifle."

"You don't have to worry about that," Travis said. "Some of the folks is close to their Bibles, but all of us believe in an eye for an eye. We're ready enough to defend what's ours."

"Well, that shines right enough," Buck replied. "I'm hoping it ain't gonna be necessary to have to fight. Most of the tribes we might run into have been pretty peaceful. Long as we stay clear of them Sioux war parties—and the Blackfoot and the Gros Ventres—we'll most likely be all right. We ain't gonna be goin' through their usual territory, but you cain't never tell where you might run into a raidin' party."

"All this talk about Indians makes me nervous,"

Nettie declared as she pulled the coffeepot from the fire. "Have some more coffee."

She had taken no more than a step toward Trace's outstretched cup when the rifle ball snapped past her face. She saw the fringe fly on Trace's buckskin shirt when the ball passed through it, barely missing his shoulder. The crack of the rifle, following an instant later, startled her, causing her to drop the pot of coffee on the ground. Trace was up before the echo of the shot had died away, dragging Nettie out of the firelight and roughly depositing her close to the wagon. "Stay down!" he commanded.

"Thar!" Buck shouted, pointing toward a stand of cottonwoods near the river where he had seen the muzzle flash. He crawled toward the back of the wagon, peering at the darkened trees in hopes of seeing a target.

Someone in the circle of wagons screamed out, "Injuns!" and there was a wild scramble for cover. Women called to their children frantically as men ran for their guns.

"Hold on!" Buck called out. "Ever'body just settle down. It ain't no Injuns." He knew the single shot was meant for one person, and that person was Trace. Trace, with the same thought, was already making his way through the darkness toward the river. "Don't nobody shoot," Buck called out again. He was afraid one of the settlers might accidentally hit Trace. He wasn't sure himself where his young partner was.

There was no doubt in Trace's mind who had fired the shot. Somehow Morgan Blunt had found out he was there from Bordeaux, or someone in the wagon train—it didn't matter which. He had always known that this day of reckoning was bound to come. He moved silently through the scrub brush near the river, stopping every few yards to listen and watch the shadows. Buck had pointed toward a small stand of cottonwoods that stood taller than the skimpy willow whips he was now passing through. Trace circled around the trees, figuring that if Blunt decided to run, he would probably head upstream, away from the wagons. Moving swiftly, hardly disturbing the thick brush near the riverbank, he drew upon lessons learned as a Crow warrior to guide him.

Laying his rifle aside, he took his bow from its case and strung it. Holding the bow and three arrows in his hand, he made his way to the riverbank, where he stopped to listen, his ear close to the ground. He heard the soft pad of footsteps on the hard, sandy bank of the river minutes before he could make out a dark form running toward him. He had guessed correctly that the would-be assassin was coming his way. He notched an arrow and waited. He had to be sure of his target.

Trace had reacted so quickly after the rifle shot that Morgan was still trying to reload his rifle while on the run. It was an unaccustomed role for Morgan, and he was finding it difficult to run and measure powder at the same time. Finally he stopped to complete the reloading. Panting for breath, he fumbled with his bullet pouch to find a lead ball. *Damn,* he cursed himself. *I had a clear shot and missed!* In spite of the coolness of the evening, he found it necessary to wipe the sweat from his eyes.

Kneeling in the darkness some fifty feet away, Trace could see the dark form standing still now, but he could not be certain it was Blunt. It could be Buck, or one of the men of the train. To be sure of his target, he called out, "Blunt!"

The sudden sound of his name caused Morgan to pull the trigger of his rifle before it was reloaded, resulting in a harmless flash of powder. He flung the useless weapon away, pulled his pistol from his belt, and fired in the direction of the voice. There was no further hesitation on Trace's part. He let fly the first arrow and quickly notched a second.

Morgan staggered backward and started to scream, but the arrow slicing through his throat turned his cry of distress into a frantic gurgle. Dropping to his knees, he clawed at the protruding shaft with both hands, trying to dislodge it—until the second arrow slammed into his chest with a dull thud. Falling over on his side, feeling his life drain from him on the sandy riverbank, he made no more than a whimper when the dark shadow appeared over him.

"There was no need for this," Trace stated evenly. "I didn't murder your brother. He tried to kill me. I had no choice."

Morgan was past caring. His throat clogged with blood, he was fighting a losing battle for breath. In his pain-addled brain, the figure hovering over him was the angel of death and he knew he was finished. Trace stepped back and waited until Morgan's last tortured breath escaped his lungs. Two of the three

Blunt brothers had now died at his hand. It was a sobering thought for a man as young in years as Trace. But he had been given no choice in either killing. Moments later, Buck, carrying a flaming torch, arrived ahead of a group of men from the wagon train.

"By God, it's Morgan Blunt, all right," Travis Bowen said, peering over Buck's shoulder.

Buck looked at Trace, standing quietly by, gazing down at the still body of the man who had hunted him for so long. "You all right, son?" Trace nodded. "I reckon you're lucky he warn't no better shot. Hell, he come closer to hittin' Mrs. Bowen than he did you."

Travis Bowen stepped back from the corpse of the man he had feared for so long. There was something more he could tell Trace at this moment, but he wasn't sure if it wouldn't be best to let Morgan's death be the end of it. He decided to hold his tongue.

CHAPTER 14

Reverend Longstreet proved to be an efficient wagonmaster, organizing his flock of settlers for the journey ahead of them in an orderly fashion early the next morning. No one grieved terribly over the sudden passing of Morgan Blunt, for no one in the train except the Bowens knew the man. Though Morgan had traveled with them from St. Louis, he had always remained distant from the others. His wagonload of trade goods was left with Bordeaux at Fort Laramie to be claimed by his brother at such time as the news of Morgan's death reached St. Louis.

As for Trace McCall, he felt at last free of a nagging thought that had dwelt in the back of his mind ever since he had fled St. Louis. With LaPorte gone, and now Morgan, he felt sure that was the end of his having to constantly look over his shoulder. True, Hamilton Blunt was still to be reckoned with. But Hamilton was not the type of individual who would risk the danger and discomforts of the frontier himself. Maybe this would be the end of his troubles with his mother's husband. Even the thought of his mother happily married to Hamilton Blunt was not enough to dampen his spirits on this bright morning, with the Wind River Mountains to the north, and the Wasatch Range on the horizon. This was the kind of country that enlivened a young man's soul. Trace easily understood Buck's eagerness to do any job that would take him back to the mountains. He glanced up at the cry of a hawk circling high above, allowing his mind to wander to thoughts of a little Snake maiden somewhere in that vast land called Oregon. Maybe he would set out to find her when they reached the Bitterroot country.

After discussing the possible trails where wagons might travel, and the disposition of the various Indian tribes known to frequent the country, Buck and Trace had decided to follow the Sweetwater through South Pass, then turn south and strike the Green. They agreed that it would be necessary to turn back north again to skirt the Wasatch Mountains, and perhaps follow the Snake past the Bitterroots. They had trapped most of that country, and Buck knew every place to ford a river and every pass that a team of mules pulling a wagon might cross.

Guiding a train of settlers turned out to be a better occupation than Trace had anticipated. He and Buck rode out ahead each day to scout the day's planned route and select the night's camping site. In addition, Trace hunted almost every day to provide fresh meat for the folks in the train. When there was concern about alerting any hostiles in the vicinity, Trace was as good with a bow as he was with his rifle, so he could hunt without making a noise. Of course, the Hawken allowed him to bring down a deer at a far greater distance, but the skills taught him by old Buffalo Shield enabled him to stalk most animals until he was within easy range of his bow.

After the first night on the trail, Nettie Bowen insisted that the two guides should camp with her and Travis. She was adamant in that it was no trouble for her to cook for the four of them. It was a good tradeoff for Nettie, since Trace always kept them supplied with fresh meat. So from that night forward, Trace spread his bedroll under the Bowens' wagon and Buck slept next to him although he sometimes accepted supper invitations from several other members of the reverend's flock. It was the closest thing Trace had found to being a part of a family since he had chosen to leave the Crow village.

Nettie was always cheerful, no matter the hardships of the trail. In fact, she was almost motherly. Travis Bowen was certainly cordial toward Trace. But sometimes, sitting at night by the fire, Trace would catch Travis staring at him with a far-off look in his eye. When he realized that Trace was meeting his gaze, he would abruptly look away, as if caught napping. If it had happened only once, Trace would have thought nothing of it, but it seemed that Travis was working something over in his mind that troubled him. Whatever it was, he didn't seem inclined to come out with it, and Trace wasn't curious enough to ask.

Jordan Thrash seemed to be a contented man. He had been able to purchase a wagon at Laramie and evidently had enough money left to outfit it for the trip. He smiled and waved each time Trace and Buck rode by. Jamie sat up on the seat with Jordan, taking over the driving only occasionally. It appeared that Jordan didn't trust the boy to handle the mules anytime it was hard going. There were other boys on the wagon train that looked to be close to Jamie's age, but Jamie was pretty much a loner. Trace noticed that he kept to his father's wagon most of the time. Whenever there was a steep climb or a muddy river crossing, Jamie pitched in with the other men and boys, working to keep the wagons rolling. But Jamie wasn't very strong, and Trace felt a little sorry for him.

"That boy is gonna have a hard time of it," Buck stated one afternoon when the train had struggled most of the day to cross a steep ridge. They had to tie off the wagon wheels and sled them down the other side. "He looks plumb whipped. He better hunt, because it shore looks like he can't work."

"He can't hunt either," Trace responded, then related the results of Jamie's attempt to shoot a deer. "I swear, Jordan must have kept him chained to the front porch in Ohio."

"He shore as hell stares at you ever' time we ride past their wagon," Buck said, grinning widely. "I think he wishes you was his daddy."

"The hell he does," Trace replied, then softened a bit. "It's a shame. A boy his age ought to know how to shoot. I ought to take him with me next time I go hunting."

That was all that was said on the matter until two days later, after the wagons were circled and the pilgrims were starting their campfires. Trace took his customary ride around the perimeter of their camp, checking sign, making sure there was no party of hostile Indians waiting. When everything looked to be to his satisfaction, he swung by Jordan's wagon. Jamie looked up as he rode up before them.

"Come on, Jamie," Trace called out cheerfully, "let's go see if we can scare us up a deer or something. Maybe you'll get another shot at one."

Jamie didn't answer but looked anxiously at his father, who was mending a tear in the wagon sheet. Jordan stopped what he was doing and considered Trace's invitation thoughtfully before finally speaking. "Sure, Jamie, go on along. A boy oughta learn to shoot. I can finish up here."

Trace held out his hand. "Here, jump up behind me and we'll go saddle up Tater."

With Trace's help, Jamie scrambled up behind him, and they loped off to the creek bank, where Buck had hobbled the horses. They were still carrying Frank's old saddle on one of the pack mules, so Trace untied it and threw it on the ground before Jamie's feet. "Throw that saddle on him, and I'll get Frank's rifle for you." While he busied himself with fetching the rifle, Trace watched Jamie's efforts out of the corner of his eye. What he saw told him that he might have taken on a bigger project than he had at first anticipated. The boy knew how to saddle a horse, but he had a helluva struggle doing it. Trace walked back with the rifle and stood looking at the horse, now saddled. "I expect you'd best tighten up on that girth. Tater likes to blow his belly up, and you'll most likely wind up riding upside down."

"I pulled it up as tight as I could get it," Jamie answered.

Trace smiled. "Give it another pull." He gave Tater a sharp rap in the belly and the horse exhaled, causing the strap to go slack. Jamie jerked it tight, grinning at Trace.

They rode out of camp and followed the creek for a mile or so before coming to a beaver dam that had formed a little pond. The thought ran through Trace's mind that, if they hadn't been on the trail, he might have come back here the next morning to set his traps. Motioning for Jamie to dismount, he stepped down and tied the horses back out of sight. A quick scout around the beaver dam provided plenty of sign, and not all beaver. There was deer sign, coyote, even mountain lion—everything came there to drink. "I believe we've found us the horn of plenty, Jamie. We'll just sit here real quiet and let 'em come to us."

They found a place in some tall brush downwind from the pond, where they could watch the water hole without being seen. While they waited, Trace gave Jamie some instructions on how best to sight and fire Frank's rifle. "You're sure you're ready to get meat?" Trace asked. " 'Cause if you miss, we won't get no supper. I'm not going to back your shot this time."

Jamie smiled, confident that this time it would be different. "I'm ready."

"You better be sure," Trace teased, " 'cause if you miss, you also have to walk back to camp."

They didn't have to wait long before a group of four antelope walked cautiously down to the water's edge. Trace smiled to himself—he could feel the boy trembling with the excitement of the moment. He had to grab Jamie's arm to keep him from jerking the rifle up too abruptly. "Easy, Jamie, bring it up real slow—you don't wanna scare 'em off. Now aim it like I showed you." Jamie did as he was told. "Take a breath and hold it. Hold that stock tight against your shoulder. When you're ready, squeeze that trigger like it's a spoon in molasses."

The evening quiet was shattered by the report of the rifle and the thundering of hooves scattering in panic, followed by a joyous squeal of excitement from Jamie. One antelope lay dead on the edge of the pond.

"I got him! I got him!" Jamie screamed.

"You sure did," Trace laughed. "Are you sure that was the one you were aiming at?"

"Yes, it was. Damn right it was!" Jamie yelled back, a devilish gleam of joy in his eyes.

Trace got to his feet and, pulling Jamie up by the back of his collar, said, "You killed him, now you go butcher him."

Jamie, the smile still spread across his face, looked at Trace and shook his head. "I don't know how to butcher a deer."

"It ain't a deer, it's an antelope, and you're gonna have to learn to butcher sometime. You might as well start now."

Jamie's smile faded, and he suddenly looked very serious. "I don't want to butcher him."

Trace snorted in disbelief. "You don't? Well, you're gonna."

"No, I'm not," Jamie said defiantly. "The damn thing can just stay there, for all I care."

Trace was confused by the boy's attitude. "You can't just go killing something and let it go to waste. That just ain't right."

"Well, I'm sorry. If I'd known you expected me to carve that thing up, I wouldn't have shot him in the first place. I thought you'd do that part."

Trace was flabbergasted. "Well, if that don't beat all." He stared at Jamie for a few moments, not knowing what to make of the situation. Then the grin returned to his face. "You're gonna skin that antelope or I'm gonna throw your ass in that pond."

"Oh, no," Jamie cautioned. "Oh, no, you're not!" He backed away. "Don't, Trace, I can't get wet."

"You can't get wet? I swear, you're worse than Buck." Before Jamie could run, Trace grabbed him in a bear hug, picked him up and walked to the edge of the pond.

"I'll skin him! I'll skin him!" Jamie screamed frantically.

Trace, caught up in the moment of horseplay, just laughed. "It's too late now." With that, he threw Jamie sprawling into the dark pool of water. Then, for the pure hell of it, he quickly dropped his belt and powder horn and jumped in himself.

Feeling in a playful mood for the first time since he could remember, Trace came up, spitting water and laughing. It had seemed like a hundred years since he had been a boy with nothing on his mind but going for a swim. Jamie, however, did not seem to share Trace's youthful enthusiasm. He was snorting and sputtering, already making his way toward the bank in the waist-deep water.

"Where the hell are you going?" Trace called after him, splashing him with water. "A little water won't hurt'cha." When Jamie didn't respond, and just kept struggling to climb out of the pond, Trace went after him. He caught him by the back of the shirt just as Jamie was about to scramble up the bank.

"Don't, Trace, you'll tear my shirt!"

It was too late. With one mighty tug, Trace pulled the complaining boy back in the water and dunked him under a couple of times before letting him up for air. Jamie came up fighting mad and started flailing his fists at Trace. Surprised, and realizing that Jamie was actually angry, Trace backed away, laughing good-naturedly.

"Hold on," Trace yelled, between fits of laughter while he continued to back away from Jamie's fists. But Jamie, fully incensed at this point, would not back off. Finally Trace had to put a stop to it when one of Jamie's fists caught him beside the jaw. There wasn't much force behind it, but it was enough to cause Trace to decide he'd better disable his attacker. Before Jamie knew what was happening, Trace ducked under the water and grabbed Jamie's shirt by the tails. With one quick motion, he came up with the shirt, pulling it up over Jamie's head so that his arms were immobilized straight up in the air.

Jamie screamed in alarm, and Trace was almost struck dumb for a moment, confused by the strange garment beneath the homespun shirt. Jamie's chest was tightly bound by a broad piece of cloth. That in itself would have been enough to puzzle him, but that was not the sight that shocked him to the point of staring stupidly. One side of the broad cloth had been pulled up under Jamie's armpit, allowing a large, round nipple to protrude from underneath the binding.

The realization of his discovery hit him like a bolt of lightning, and he backed away from Jamie as if she had the plague. "Damn!" was all he could utter for a few moments as he continued to stare from a safer distance.

Jamie began to cry, more in frustration than from fear, as she struggled to cover herself. When she got her shirt back down, she waded toward the bank again. "Get away from me!" she yelled when Trace tried to help her up the bank. Ignoring his extended hand, she pulled herself out of the water, only to slip on the wet grass and slide right back in. "Get away!" she warned and crawled out again, this time on all fours.

"Damn, Jamie . . ." Trace sputtered, climbing out after her. "I'm sorry, I didn't know."

She cut him off. "Now I guess everybody will know." She was still plenty angry and she let him know it. "You had to have your little tomfoolery, didn't you?" She fussed with her shirt, getting madder by the moment. "Now, dammit, I'm soaked, and this damn binding is chafing me. I've got to take it off." She glared at him. "Turn around and don't look until I tell you to." When he had turned away, she quickly removed the wet shirt and began working away at the wet knot that held the binding.

He could hear her muttering to herself, but he couldn't make out the words. He wasn't sure he wanted to know, anyway. His mind was a clutter of confusion, not knowing what to think. "You know, I ain't gonna say nothing to anybody about this, if that's what you want." She didn't answer. He had said that he wouldn't look, but the temptation was too overwhelming to resist one little peek out of the corner of his eye. What he saw sent a shiver down his spine, and he quickly looked away again. Jamie had been successfully concealing two well-formed breasts behind the tightly bound cloth.

"All right," Jamie said. "You can turn around now." She wrung some of the water from her clothes and emptied her boots. Then she went to her horse and climbed up in the saddle. Trace stood dumbfounded, watching her but not knowing what to say. Eventually he deemed it best to say nothing. "I'm going back to camp," she announced in a voice that dared him to protest.

Still unsure as to what he should do or say, Trace just stood there and watched her as she left. For want of anything else to say, he said, "I'll be along behind. I'm just gonna bleed this deer and take him back to camp to butcher."

"It's not a deer, it's an antelope," she said, giving him a cold eye as she turned Tater back toward the wagons.

"An antelope," he repeated, his mind still stunned by the vision of her two lovely young breasts.

He would have jumped on his horse and followed her, but there was little doubt in his mind that she preferred to ride back alone. It was a helluva thing, he thought, running it over in his mind, and he felt a little stupid for not suspecting it before. After all, she didn't seem very strong for her age, and she sure as hell didn't know how to do anything a boy should have known. He had a pretty good idea why she tried to pass herself off as a boy, traveling alone with her father. It would have been a hazardous journey for a girl in a land far from the civilized ways of the East. He glanced back at the antelope carcass. "Might as well carry the meat back to camp," he mumbled aloud. He picked up Frank Brown's Hawken rifle where Jamie had dropped it, strapped it beside his saddle, and hefted the carcass up onto the horse.

Jamie Thrash was distraught to the point of panic. She spurred Tater to a gallop, intent on getting as far away from Trace McCall as she could for the moment. She felt ashamed for having her charade found out, and she was angry with him for forcing her hand, even though she knew he was not to blame. She could also not deny the strange fascination she felt for the tall young mountain man. From the first time she had seen him, appearing suddenly out of nowhere, she had felt a strong attraction to him. It was easy to be with him when he thought she was a boy. Now she only wanted to hide. What must he think of her?

She was sick of this masquerade. It had been her father's idea, anyway. He thought it much safer for her if she was a boy making the lonely trek to the West, avoiding the dangers a young girl might encounter when traveling with boatmen, trappers, and roughnecks. She also knew that her father was not a violent man and, though he would not admit it, would be hard-pressed to defend her honor. So she had gone along with it. Now she wished she could undo it all. Her mind was so clouded with this landslide of thoughts that she wasn't aware of the danger she was riding into until she was suddenly slammed off her horse and landed on the ground.

Stunned, unable to understand what had happened, she tried to get to her feet, but a hand grabbed her hair from behind and jerked her back onto the ground. In the next instant, she was looking up into the faces of two painted savages. When she screamed, they looked at each other, startled. They had assumed it was a boy they had ambushed. They exchanged some words she could not understand. Then, while she was held down by the unseen one behind her, one of the others reached down and ripped her shirt away, revealing her bare breasts. She started to scream again but was slapped hard across the mouth.

The three warriors wasted no time. Binding her wrists with a rawhide thong, they jerked her to her feet while one of them went after her horse. This was a stroke of good fortune, a woman and a fine horse. They had hoped to steal horses from the wagon train, but determined it too well guarded by too many rifles. They were on their way back to their camp in the valley beyond the pass when she came riding across their path.

There was some discussion among the three pertaining to who should have the woman and who should ride the horse. They were on foot because they had planned to raid the white men's horses. Finally it was decided that the warrior who knocked the woman off her horse should rightly have the woman. He should walk and lead the woman. The other two would be allowed to ride the horse. That settled, they started out again.

Terrified and approaching shock, Jamie cried out for Trace, but he was not there, and she was soundly walloped for her trouble. Tears streaming down her cheeks, she was dragged along the ground until she managed to stagger to her feet, trying her best to keep up with her captors. She feared to speculate what her fate might be at the hands of these rough savages as each step took her farther away from her father and the wagon train.

The three warriors seemed to be in a hurry, and it was all Jamie could do to stay on her feet. Already numb to her pain and resigned to her fate, she stumbled along as best she could, suffering the abuse of her captor whenever she tripped or lost her footing. Tales of horror and torture she had heard about the treatment of captives by the Indians raced through her mind, and she questioned her strength to withstand what might lie ahead.

They were crossing a shallow stream that bisected a narrow ravine when the warrior leading her stopped so abruptly that she collided with his bare back. They uttered some brief, excited words, and she looked up to see what had startled them. At the mouth of the ravine, he sat calmly on the paint, directly in their path—tall and straight in the saddle, he cradled his rifle across his arms, watching them patiently.

Her heart screamed out inside her, *Trace!* He had come for her! Then her fears returned. After all, there were three of them, and one of them carried a musket. What chance did he have? The warriors seemed puzzled by the sudden appearance of this silent white man. They eyed him carefully, taking in his strong physical bearing and the Hawken rifle he held so casually. After a long moment, the Indian riding Tater called out something to Trace, making sign with his hands as he did so.

Trace recognized the three warriors as belonging to the Gros Ventres tribe, close allies with the dangerous Blackfeet—some said they were one and the same. His knowledge of their tongue was scant at best, but he knew enough to communicate. He didn't respond at once when the warrior—obviously the leader of the three—asked why he stood in their path. His gaze steady and unemotional, he sized up the opposition he faced before showing his hand. There was something sorely disturbing about seeing two Gros Ventres perched atop Tater. He didn't think Frank would appreciate it one bit.

The warrior asked him again what he wanted. They made no move toward him, but Trace could see that they, too, were sizing up their opposition. Another silent moment passed before Trace spoke. "I give thanks to you for bringing my woman and my horse to me. I was afraid I had lost them."

Their reaction was what he expected. The one who had first spoken jerked his head back in surprise, his eyes wide, not sure he understood what his ears had heard. Then he smiled—a mischievous grin—and said something to his companions in a voice too low for Trace to hear. Turning back to face Trace again, he said, "You make a mistake, white man. The horse and the woman belong to us, and you are blocking our path."

Trace's stoic expression remained unmoved. "I know you want to do the right thing. Release the woman and the horse, and I'll let you go unharmed."

The warriors laughed, and the leader replied, his voice taunting. "Big talk. I look around you and I don't see anyone there with you. There are three of us, all brave warriors. I think we will keep the woman and the horse—and maybe that horse you are riding."

"I'm afraid I can't let you do that," Trace said. "It's a shame that three of you have to die over a horse and a woman. Now take my warning, and leave them and walk away, and I'll spare your lives."

Insulted by the white man's quiet arrogance, the warrior screamed in defiance. "It is I who decides who lives and who dies. I will ride your pony back to my camp with your scalp on my lance!" He was through talking. The two on Tater slid to the ground and reached for their bows. The one leading Jamie dropped the thong and pulled the musket from his back.

"Get down, Jamie!" Trace yelled. There wasn't time for a repeat warning. The Hawken spoke before the first warrior had both feet on the ground, knocking him sprawling into the stream behind them. In an eyewink, Trace dropped his rifle and pulled Frank's rifle up. The second warrior doubled over before he could notch an arrow. Dropping Frank's rifle, Trace pulled his bow from his back. While he calmly notched an arrow, he heard the discharge of the musket and the rattle of the lead ball as it whistled through the brush some three or four yards beside him. Taking his time, he aimed and released his arrow. It struck the Gros Ventre in the middle of his chest, and the warrior sat down heavily on the ground, mortally wounded.

Trace nudged the paint and rode forward at a walk until he was directly over the wounded Indian. Glancing first at Jamie, he asked, "You all right?" When she nodded dumbly, he turned his attention to the warrior dying at his pony's feet. As he would for any animal that was suffering, he dismounted and, pulling his pistol from his belt, put the Gros Ventre out of his misery.

Jamie cried out in surprise when the pistol fired, and drew back for a moment. The sudden eruption of violence had completely unnerved her, even though her senses were already reeling from her treatment at the hands of her captors. Finally she could stand it no longer. She rushed into Trace's arms, locking her arms around his neck and burying her face into his neck. "I thought he was going to shoot you," she whimpered, pressing her body as tightly against his as she could.

"He missed," was all Trace replied. He had purposely ignored the warrior with the musket until last. Recognizing the weapon as one of the unreliable old fusees that the Hudson's Bay Company traded to the Indians, he figured the warrior's aim would not be that accurate. He knew he was far more likely to catch an arrow from one of the other two.

"Forevermore . . ." Buck whispered to himself as he spotted the returning hunters. He got up from his place by Nettie Bowen's cookfire to take a closer look, for at first he could not believe his eyes. He glanced at Nettie, seeing that she too was transfixed by the sight. Walking the paint slowly into the circle of wagons, Trace rode, holding Jamie in front of him. Jamie's arms were wrapped around Trace's neck, her head on his shoulder. He was leading Frank's horse, which carried an antelope carcass, an old musket, and a couple of Indian bows.

"Damn my soul," Buck exhaled. " 'Scuse me, Nettie."

"No offense," Nettie replied, unable to take her eyes off of the two approaching.

Buck walked out to meet them, trying to form a question, but unable to decide what it might be. "Trace," was all he managed before Jordan Thrash came running up.

"Jamie!" Jordan cried out in a panic-stricken voice.

Trace stepped down, still holding Jamie in his arms, realizing it was a most peculiar sight to the growing gathering. He was not concerned with appearances. He would explain all in a few minutes. First he had to make sure Jamie was going to be all right.

"Jamie!" Jordan cried again, and looked from his

daughter to the tall young man still holding her closely, pleading for an explanation.

"She's gonna be all right," Trace said. "She's just had a pretty bad shock." Jordan reached out for his daughter, but Trace gently stayed his arm. "I think it might be best if Mrs. Bowen took care of her." Realizing the wisdom in Trace's words, Jordan stepped back dutifully.

At first Nettie was sufficiently shocked herself, but she did not fail to notice Trace's use of the feminine gender when referring to Jamie. One glance at the torn shirt was enough to confirm it. She didn't hesitate when Trace suggested her help. "Here, darling, you come with me." She reached out for the girl as Jamie reluctantly released her hold on Trace's neck. She led Jamie to her wagon while Trace explained to Jordan and Buck what had taken place.

There was some concern among the people on the train when Trace's accounting of the incident was relayed, especially on the part of Reverend Longstreet. Since he was the captain of the train and consequently responsible for the welfare of his flock, he expressed some misgivings about lingering in that vicinity if there might be a band of Gros Ventres close at hand. It was Trace's opinion that there was little danger of an attack from that source. He was convinced that the three he had encountered were not part of a large war party, but more likely part of a small horse-stealing foray. He and Buck decided to go scout to see if they could locate the rest of the party.

They returned to the scene of Trace's encounter.

Buck, to satisfy his curiosity, dismounted to examine the three corpses lying near the stream. "They's Gros Ventres, all right," was his only observation before remounting. Since the Indians were obviously traveling toward the narrow mountain pass to the south, Buck and Trace started off in that direction.

The sun dropped behind the mountains before they cleared the pass. Even so, they continued until it began to get dark and they deemed it no longer prudent to go on. They made camp under a rocky ledge and dined on jerky. The next morning they found the abandoned camp of the Gros Ventres in a small meadow just beyond the pass. As Trace had suspected, it was a small raiding party, and they had already moved off to the south.

"They'll be lookin' for these three, if they ain't already," Buck said. "From the looks of that camp, they ain't more'n a dozen of 'em, but I expect we'd best get the wagons moving anyhow."

Buck and Trace returned to the train to find Longstreet nervously awaiting them. He had feared that his guides had been ambushed. As soon as the two mountain men were sighted, the cry was heard: "To wagon!" and the train was under way once more.

For the next couple of days, Trace stayed well ahead of the line of lumbering wagons. Things had changed since his discovery at the beaver pond, and for reasons he could not explain, he felt shy and embarrassed whenever he chanced upon Jamie, usually mumbling a brief hello and hurrying on his way. For her part, Jamie quickly recovered from her injuries at the hands of the Gros Ventres and now seemed relieved to be finished with the masquerade she had perpetuated. Having made a new friend in Nettie Bowen, she happily gave in to her feminine side and discarded all the trappings of a boy. In fact, it was quite disturbing to Trace McCall that she had transformed into a rather attractive young lady. He feared that she might cause him many sleepless nights if he allowed her into his mind too often.

Chapter 15

It had been an especially hard day's travel for the folks on the wagon train. They had been caught in a thunderstorm while trying to ascend a long gulch that would lead them up onto a wide flat. The loose dirt of the gulch had turned into a muddy slide in the downpour, causing considerable strain on the mules, as well as on people's nerves. As a result, they had only made four miles that day when Reverend Longstreet called for an early camp by the river.

Nettie declared it a special occasion and fried the last of her supply of dried apples in an effort to bring some cheer to her little family. It was while they were drinking their coffee afterward that Trace caught Travis looking at him with that vacant stare in his eyes. This time Travis did not shift his gaze when he realized Trace was looking him in the eye. He blinked a couple of times and shook his head as if apologizing.

"Jim," he said, calling Trace by his boyhood name, "I reckon I owe you an apology—something I reckon you had a right to know a long time ago. And I'm ashamed to say I was too damned scared to tell you."

Trace said nothing but gazed steadily at his father's old friend, waiting. Travis sighed deeply and continued. "It weren't no accident that killed your brother. Tyler Blunt caved Cameron's head in with an axe. They told your mama he got run over by a runaway team." Trace tensed, but he remained silent, his gaze steady, for he could see in Travis's eyes that there was more to tell. "Tyler told me to go unhitch a team of mules—there wasn't nobody else in the yard. When I came back, I seen Tyler and Morgan standing over Cameron. It stopped me cold in my tracks. They didn't know I was standing by the harness shed and I could hear them talking. I heard Morgan say, 'Well, that takes care of all of 'em. LaPorte took care of his daddy and the young'un. I reckon Hamilton can go after his little sweetpea now.' "

There was no sound other than Nettie Bowen's gasp. Buck's eyes were riveted on his young friend, his coffee cup still poised before his lips. Travis hung his head, deeply ashamed. Though Trace did not blink, his eyes were unseeing, as his head tumbled into a dark spin. All feeling had left his body, and he was suspended in a numbing state of disbelief and shock, the impact of Travis's words striking him like a thunderbolt. The Blackfoot attack was no chance encounter. His father and Henry Brown Bear had been sought out and murdered—poor Henry having been mistaken for him. All at the bidding of Hamilton Blunt. He felt sick deep in his gut as he remembered the image of his father's body, half-sitting against a tree trunk, the skin of his face sagging as a result of his brutal scalping. Then the picture of Hamilton Blunt came to his mind's eye, standing with his arm around Trace's mother, that gloating smile etched across his face. Trace felt every muscle in his body tense.

He could sit still no longer. He almost staggered when he suddenly got to his feet, desperately needing to walk. No one said anything or made a move toward him as he stormed away from the fire and toward the river. He tried to think, to stabilize his reeling mind as he walked along the water's edge, still recoiling from the shock. When at last he felt control returning to his senses, he turned back toward his friends waiting anxiously at the campfire. His brain, having been in such a state of shock seconds before, was now clarified by a single burning hatred for Hamilton Blunt. What kind of monster could orchestrate the slaughter of an entire family over the lust for one woman? *His mother!* He cried out in agony, unaware that he had even made a sound. He forced himself to take control of his emotions. When he was sure of himself, he returned to the campfire.

Travis was trying to explain to Nettie why he had kept his silence for so long, not daring to tell even his own wife. His words abruptly halted when Trace reappeared and he turned to him to plead his case. "Jim, I'm sorry . . . I swear . . ." he sputtered, searching for words sufficient enough to explain his feelings. "I was just plumb afraid of what Morgan Blunt might do—to Nettie or to me. I couldn't stay there and work for them after what I had heard. And I think Morgan suspected I knew too much. I know that's why he drove his wagon out here with us—so he could make sure I didn't say nothing till we was to hell and gone from St. Louis." He looked up at Trace with sorrowful, pleading eyes. "There wasn't nothing I could do to stop the killings—you know I would have—but I only found out after it was too late to stop it. And you were just a boy—you mighta got yourself killed if I'da told you then."

Trace held up his hand to silence Travis. "I ain't blaming you, Mr. Bowen. I reckon I can understand the fix you were in." He turned to his partner. "Buck, I'm going back."

Buck, silent up to that point, slowly nodded his head. "I expect so," was all he said.

"You sure as hell don't need me to help you find Oregon." He glanced at Nettie, who was wringing her hands in anguish. "You're in the best hands I know of with Buck, and maybe I'll see you later on. I'll be riding out at first light."

"I'll be lookin' fer you, partner," Buck said.

Still wound too tight to sleep, Trace decided to take a turn around the perimeter of the camp to make sure all was quiet. He was saddling his horse when he heard his name called and he turned to see Jamie standing there. Instead of her usual attire of boy's trousers and shirt, she was wearing a dress that Nettie Bowen had helped her make. "Jamie," Trace acknowledged.

"Nettie said you were leaving in the morning," Jamie said.

"Reckon so. There's something I have to do."

"Are you coming back? I mean, out to Oregon territory?"

"I don't know," he stammered. "I reckon . . . sometime."

She came closer to him. "I don't want you to leave. I never really thanked you for saving my life, and I want you to know I'm grateful." She gazed steadily into his eyes, and when he could find no words to reply, she stepped forward and quickly kissed him on the cheek. "You take care of yourself, Trace McCall." Then she turned and walked off into the darkness.

Trace was long gone when Buck rolled out of his blanket the next morning. "More Injun than a durn Injun," he muttered to himself as he tied up his bedroll. Although his young partner had slept no more than six feet from him, Buck never heard a sound when Trace saddled his horse and left. He would never admit it, but Buck knew he was going to miss Trace. He'd become mighty comfortable knowing the tall mountain man was watching his back. *He'll be back,* he thought. *The mountains is in his blood.*

Already seven miles behind them and moving fast, Trace held the paint to a pace the horse could maintain while still covering a lot of ground. One thought burned like a hot coal in his brain, and no other thought held any importance, not even thoughts of the young girl whose kiss he could still feel on his cheek. As he rode, he promised his dead father and brother that he would punish the man responsible for their deaths. He had to force himself not to let images of Hamilton Blunt with his mother enter his mind. The thought reviled him so that it physically sickened him. He was not sure he could endure the weeks it would take to reach St. Louis.

Stopping only to rest his horse, Trace drove himself relentlessly, spending long days in the saddle, then starting out again each day in the early light. Approaching the Laramie Mountains, he spotted a party of Sioux and was forced to lay low until they had passed. Then it was back in the saddle and on to Fort Laramie, where he paused but half a day before pushing on east.

Retracing his earlier route from St. Louis, he struck the Missouri at Council Bluffs in time to buy passage on a riverboat bound for St. Louis. He decided to leave his horse in Council Bluffs, so he rode back to the stables where he had first purchased the paint. Gus Kitchel did not recognize the tall young man dressed in buckskins who rode up to his corral, but he remembered the paint. Gus never forgot a horse. He looked Trace over with an eye sharp as flint. Then it suddenly came to him that Trace was the same boy who rode out so long ago.

"Well, I'll be . . ." Gus expelled. "You're that boy that was gonna shoot me over that blue roan."

"I was," Trace replied without emotion. "Now I need to leave my horse with you for a short while." He fixed Gus with a steel-hard gaze. "I like this paint—he's a good horse and we understand each other. I'm not gonna like it very much if he ain't here when I come back for him."

Gus looked up at the young man, who now stood

a full head taller than him, and gulped, "Yessir, you and I understand each other, too. Don't worry, I'll take mighty good care of him."

Trace made no attempt to get to know the boatmen who worked the flatboat downriver, preferring to keep to himself, deep in his own thoughts. For their part, the crew was curious about the silent young man dressed in animal skins, rifle in hand and Indian bow on his back. When spoken to, he responded politely but offered no encouragement for casual conversation. Several times during the trip downriver, when they had made camp for the night, Trace disappeared into the prairie, always returning with game of some variety, which he generously shared with the crew. Since he seemed to want no thanks for his contribution to the camp's mess, they accepted the meat without a show of gratitude. Soon it became expected that he would provide fresh meat, though no one among them thought it wise to approach him on the evenings that he did not.

The boat reached the wharf in St. Louis on a pleasant afternoon in early September. Before it was tied off at the dock, Trace was ashore and on his way toward Milltown. "There goes a passel of trouble for somebody, I'm thinking," one of the boatmen said as they watched the tall buckskin-clad figure disappear into the small crowd that had gathered to watch the boat dock.

CHAPTER 16

Julia Blunt sucked her breath in sharply in reflex to the pain that stabbed at her insides when she got up from her chair. Something was eating away at her. She had gradually been getting sicker day after day, and she feared that she might never recover from the illness—whatever it was. Each day drained her of a little more energy until she felt it was all she could do to make it out to the wide porch that wrapped around three sides of Hamilton Blunt's huge mansion. As ill as she felt, she disdained lying in her bed, especially during the day. Daytime was her best time, because her husband was at work and she was free of his abuse.

Thoughts of her husband caused her to unconsciously reach up to feel the bruise on her cheek. Word had come from the frontier yesterday of Morgan's death, and more than grief, Hamilton's reaction seemed to be anger—anger directed at her, for some reason. He was certain that her son had something to do with Morgan's death. And he had struck her across the face. This was not the first time Hamilton had hit her. He had changed dramatically in the last two years of their marriage. No longer enamored of her body, seeing her beauty fading with age, he constantly berated her for growing older. For the last six months, he had forbade her to leave the house, not even to go to Trotter's Store. Several weeks ago, he brought home a bottle of elixir. He told her he had gotten it from Dr. Wagner, and that it was a health potion the doctor said would restore her youth. Afraid to provoke his displeasure, she took the bitter liquid while he stood over her, watching to make sure she took the full dose. After a few days, she complained that the potion was making her ill and that she wanted to see the doctor herself. Hamilton refused to permit it. Instead he went to the doctor again and got another bottle of medicine that he said Dr. Wagner assured him would make her feel much better. The medicine was equally as bitter as the original potion and offered her no relief. In fact, her health steadily declined. She began to fear she might be suffering from the same mysterious illness that had taken the life of Hamilton's first wife.

Her steps labored—each footfall causing a recurrence of the searing pain in her insides—she walked to the corner of the porch and looked down at the freight office below. It was past Hamilton's usual office hours, but there was still a light on in the back office. She thought nothing of it, for Hamilton often stayed late. In fact, she was grateful for the nights when he didn't arrive until far into the evening. As she looked down, the lamp went out in the back office, and moments later the familiar figure of Madge Pauley came out the front door. There was a time when that might have troubled her, but not anymore. Maybe he would be in a better mood when he came home, and maybe he would feel no need to abuse her.

Julia made her way down the front hallway, holding on to the chair rail to steady her wobbly legs. She could not understand why this recent illness had weakened her so. She had always had a strong constitution, but now she felt as weak as a kitten. As she reached the end of the hall, she found herself suddenly confronted by the solid figure of Frances, holding a bottle and a glass of water.

"I'm not taking any more of that medicine," Julia said defiantly. "It's making me worse than I was."

The stoic expression on Frances's face remained unchanged as she produced a large tablespoon from her apron pocket. "Mr. Hamilton said to make sure you took your medicine," she said without compassion. "He's gonna be mighty angry if you don't take it."

"I don't give a damn if he is," Julia fired back, her eyes flashing, "I'm not taking any more of that vile medicine."

Frances did not move for a long moment, and just studied Julia with cold eyes. Finally she shrugged her shoulders. "Well, I certainly don't give a damn. It'll be your little fanny when Mr. Hamilton finds out."

The thought caused Julia to regret her defiant response. "You don't have to tell him I didn't take it, Frances." The thought of another beating made her shiver.

Frances's chilling glance revealed her complete lack of compassion for the unfortunate woman. "It's my place to tell Mr. Hamilton what he needs to know. I was here long before you came, missy, and I'll be here long after you're gone." She turned and disappeared into the kitchen.

Julia shuddered, partly from her weakened state, partly as a reaction to Frances's sinister warning. From the beginning she had felt the intense hostility and resentment of her husband's housekeeper toward her. She had soon given up any notion of a truce with the belligerent older woman, choosing instead to avoid her altogether. Now she began to think that she actually had cause to fear the woman—that Frances was fully capable of doing her bodily harm in an effort to get rid of her. For her own safety, she went into Hamilton's room, a room they used to share, and took out one of the small pistols from his chest. Checking to make sure it was loaded, she placed it in the deep pocket of her dress and returned to her own bedroom. Perhaps she was overreacting to the dour housekeeper's gruff treatment—possibly it was because of her weakened and vulnerable state—but she felt better with some protection at hand. She would replace the weapon only after Frances had served Hamilton's supper and gone to her own small cottage at the foot of the hill.

Her fear of Frances proved to be unfounded, at least on this night, for she saw the stoic old woman leave the house soon after Hamilton arrived. Standing at her bedroom window upstairs, Julia watched Frances until she disappeared from view. Still unsteady, she sat down on the side of her bed for a moment to calm her racing pulse. Hamilton would be eating his supper, so she had a little time to return the pistol to his room before he came upstairs. It had been more than a year since he had looked for her as soon as he came in from work. He now seemed to prefer his own company, especially on those occasions when Madge Pauley came to his office to "work on the books." For this reason, Julia was stunned to find him standing in her bedroom doorway when she struggled to her feet.

"Oh!" she gasped, almost losing her balance. "Hamilton . . . I didn't hear your footsteps."

He didn't answer right away. Instead he eyed her in the same critical manner a man might examine livestock. When he spoke, his voice was cold, even though he attempted to sound casual. "Come, Julia. I want you to sit downstairs with me while I have my supper."

"All right," she replied, her voice soft and cautious. His invitation surprised her, and she wondered at his mood. He was usually contemptuous at best after a rendezvous with his buxom Miss Pauley.

His critical gaze never wavered as he watched her slowly walk toward him. Julia guessed that he was evaluating the progress of her illness. When she got to the door, he reached out and took her arm to steady her—another surprise, he had not touched her in months. "Let me help you," he said and led her down the hallway toward the stairs. She could smell the sticky-sweet aroma of Madge Pauley's cheap perfume lingering on his shirt, as he walked her to the top of the stairs. Had she not been so ill, she would have been furious. Now she didn't care.

At the top of the long stairway, he paused to let her grasp the railing to steady herself. Still puzzled over his unexpected desire for her company, she permitted herself to suspect that Hamilton might have a conscience after all. Perhaps he was at last showing some compassion for her recent illness, or maybe a portion of guilt for his blatant affair with Miss Pauley. It was while thinking these thoughts that she suddenly felt his foot in the middle of her back a split second before her frail body went crashing down the steps. Her scream was stifled by the impact of each tumbling blow as the breath was crushed from her chest. The sound of her own bones breaking was all that registered in her mind. She came to rest at the foot of the stairs, her body broken and bleeding, unmoving.

Hamilton remained at the top of the stairs, watching her tumble down the stairway until she lay still in a crumpled heap at the bottom. His expression detached and calm, he then took his time descending the stairs. At the bottom, he stood over his wife's body, staring down at her lifeless form. "Die, damn you," he uttered through clenched teeth. "You've been fed enough rat poison to kill a horse." His patience had long since run out. The woman had a constitution like iron, and he had tired of waiting for her body to bend to the deadly potion.

He stood motionless, hidden in the deep shadows of the dark night, waiting until the woman made her way down the long, narrow road that led to Hamilton Blunt's mansion. The woman did not look familiar to him, but she had come from the house, so he assumed she was Blunt's housekeeper. When she had passed, he came back to the road and continued on toward the huge estate overlooking the very freight yard where his father and brother had worked.

It had been years since Trace had last set foot on Hamilton Blunt's front step, and in that time, he had shrugged off his youthful naivete to take on the mantle of a man. There was no uncertainty about the purpose of his mission. He had traveled all the way from the Wasatch with one crystalline purpose—to avenge the slaughter of his father and brother. As he approached the end of his journey, other troubling thoughts pecked away at his resolve. What if his mother truly loved this cold-blooded monster? But if she did, he assured himself, she could not continue to love him when she found out what he was guilty of. Hamilton Blunt simply must be executed. His father's soul cried out for it. Trace was not a shifty murderer. He would not lie in wait for Blunt and shoot him in the back. That would not give him the satisfaction his fury demanded. No, he intended to call Blunt out—settle it face to face. He wanted to make sure Hamilton Blunt fully understood why he was being killed.

He suddenly heard a sharp scream from within the house. Shrill, like a rifle shot. It startled Trace and he paused to listen. But there was nothing beyond that one short scream. It was a woman's voice, and it could only have been that of his mother. Throwing caution to the winds, he ran the rest of the way, bolting up the porch steps in several bounds. Finding the front door unlocked, he burst inside. Before him, at the foot of the stairs, lay the crumpled body of his mother. Beside her stood the man he had come to kill. The sight of his mother's battered and broken body slammed into his brain with a force that stunned him for a few seconds.

Blunt, dazed by the sudden appearance of this tall, buckskin-clad apparition in his entrance hall, was unable to move. Raw fear was a malady that had never struck him before. But recognizing Trace immediately, he now felt fear's icy fingers tightening around his spine. He made an attempt to talk his way out of the sure death that faced him. "Jim," he stumbled over the name, "I'm glad you're here. Your mother's fallen down the stairs. I was in the kitchen when I heard her fall."

Trace made no reply at first, staring steadily at the man he hated so vehemently. His memory of Hamilton Blunt was of a large, dangerous man. The years had changed the perspective. Standing before him now he saw a craven, pathetic coward, unaware that he had soiled his trousers with his own urine. When Trace finally spoke, it was to pronounce a death sentence for Hamilton Blunt. "Your time has come, Blunt. I'm going to kill you for the murders of my father and my brother—and now my mother."

"Wait . . . please, Jim!" Blunt begged. "This was an accident. I swear. Don't shoot me! I had nothing to do with those murders."

"I'm not gonna shoot you—shooting's too good for

the likes of you." He laid his rifle aside and pulled his knife from his belt. "I'm gonna carve you up and watch you die slowly."

Blunt dashed for the door of his study. Trace leaped after him but was too late to get through the door before Blunt slammed and locked it. Filled now with a fury that burned through every sinew of his body, Trace hurled his shoulder against the door, oblivious to the pistol ball that he knew would be coming from inside the study. The door, though solid ash, offered scant resistance to the broad-shouldered mountain man, and it gave way in a splintered explosion. Blunt's pistol ball sailed harmlessly by Trace's ear. Throwing the empty pistol at him, Blunt dashed through the other door, which led to the parlor. Trace easily dodged the pistol and was immediately after him.

For the first time in his life, Hamilton Blunt was terrified. He had always felt that he feared no man. But the sight of this tall warrior, his face reflecting the rage that transformed him into a veritable harbinger of death, completely unnerved him. Trace was a killing machine, as lethal as a rattler. Hamilton's only thought at that moment was to run for his life. He tore through the parlor and into the kitchen. Behind him, he heard the sound of toppled chairs and crashing glass as Trace raced after him. Panic-stricken, Hamilton ran through the dining room, straining to reach the front door and escape into the night. When he ran back through the front hall, he spied Trace's rifle. His heart had almost burst with the terror of the moment, but now he saw his salvation in the form of the discarded Hawken. He snatched up the weapon and whirled around in time to halt his pursuer in his tracks.

"Now, damn you!" Blunt fairly shouted in newfound triumph. "We'll see who walks away from this mess, won't we?" His confidence growing by the second, he cocked the hammer and gloated. "Yes, you son of a bitch, I had your pa and your brother killed—and I damn sure pushed that bitch down the stairs. Now I'm going to get rid of the last of that rat's nest you came from." He smiled as he leveled the rifle at Trace's head and pulled the trigger.

A flash of fire leapt from the muzzle of the Hawken, the boom of the powder igniting, filling the confines of the room. But Trace remained standing. Although he had charged the rifle and placed a percussion cap on it, he was not careless enough to insert a rifle ball in a rifle that he was not ready to shoot. Blunt shrieked in terror as Trace, in a half crouch, and ready to spring, slowly closed in. A rustle of cloth and a scraping on the floor behind them caused both men to pause. Blunt turned to see the outstretched hand of Julia Tracey Blunt, wobbling in one last dying effort as she pointed the pistol. In an instant the pistol flashed, sending the ball into Hamilton Blunt's forehead.

Blunt stood there for several seconds before he sagged to the floor. His eyes were open wide in disbelief, the ugly black hole centered neatly above the bridge of his nose, a thin trickle of blood escaping from it. As he fell, he uttered a low plaintive sigh—

nothing more—and then lay still, the bullet lodged in his brain.

Trace was just as startled by the pistol shot behind him. He whirled in time to see his mother's final act of revenge, seconds before her arm fell back by her side, lifeless. One quick glance at Blunt told him that there was no longer any danger from that source, then he was quickly at his mother's side. But it was too late. She was gone. "Ma," he said softly, knowing there would be no response as he gazed into the face that he had known so well. It was almost unrecognizable now, with her dark, hollow eyes and cheeks sunken and gaunt from her long illness. It was more than he could bear to find her like this. He bowed his head and sobbed uncontrollably. After a few minutes, he raised his head and looked toward the ceiling. "God, how can you let something like this happen? She prayed to you every day of her life. How could you let something like this happen?"

He gently gathered her frail body up in his arms, lest he disturb her broken bones. Her fractured arm hung limply at an unnatural angle as he carried her upstairs to a bedroom. Laying her carefully on the bed, he wrapped the heavy quilt around her then picked her up once more. Standing there in the middle of the large bedroom, his mother cold in his arms, he paused to think about what he should do. Once his mind was made up, he moved quickly. He carried his mother back downstairs and laid her on a sofa while he searched the house for a can of kerosene.

Descending the front steps of Hamilton Blunt's great mansion, he started down the narrow lane with his mother's body over his shoulder. Once a healthy and robust woman, Julia was no heavier in death than a light marching pack on the broad shoulders of her son. Before he had gone fifty paces, flames blossomed from the windows behind him and started licking at the wooden siding of the house. Soon there was enough light from the flames to illuminate the lane before him and cast a long eerie shadow as he continued walking, never looking back. It was the end of a long nightmare for Trace. There were no more Blunt brothers to plague him. It had been a terrible price to pay, for they had slaughtered his entire family. He was the last of his father's bloodline.

As he came to the gate at the bottom of the lane, he was met by a squarely built woman hurrying toward the burning house. Frances had seen the flames from her cottage on the road below. Suspecting foul play, she primed her deceased husband's pistol and set out for her master's house as fast as her stout legs could carry her. Upon encountering the tall man in buckskins carrying a large quilt-wrapped bundle over his shoulder, she knew her suspicions had been correct. She became enraged. Her hopes and dreams of anticipated inheritance when the Tracey bitch finally died were going up in smoke and flames. The long years she had served Hamilton Blunt so faithfully were lost in the fire she could now see lighting up the nighttime sky. And this man, obviously coming from the house, had to be to blame—he carried a bundle, no doubt stolen from *her house! Well, I'll be damned if you're going to get away with it!* she thought.

Trace did not veer from his path when he saw her, but continued upon his intended course. "You! You thieving bastard!" she shrieked. "Stand in your tracks!" She thrust the pistol into his face, glaring at him through eyes narrowed with fury. Suddenly it penetrated her angry mind who this man was—the buckskins, the rifle in one hand, a mountain man—it had to be Julia's murdering son. "I know who you are!" she shouted. He made a move to step around her, ignoring the pistol in his face. "Stand, I say!" she demanded, keeping the pistol on him. Trace slowly shifted his rifle to his other hand. She started to shout something else, but before she could form the words, he suddenly backhanded her with his free hand. She dropped to the ground, out cold. As she crumpled, the pistol went off, sending a lead ball up through a large poplar tree beside the lane. Trace gazed down dispassionately at the unconscious woman, then went on his way to take care of his mother. The small gathering of curious spectators who had hurried to find the source of the flames paid little attention to the tall man with the bundle on his shoulder as he made his way silently through them and disappeared into the night.

The first rays of the morning sun were licking the tops of the tall oaks beside the Milltown road when Trace passed Travis and Nettie Bowen's old cottage. They had vacated it only a few months before, but already it was choked with weeds from Nettie's garden. Trace thought about Nettie and Travis and wondered if they were any closer to the Oregon country they had set out to find. *If anybody can get 'em there, it'll be Buck,* he thought. The picture in his mind brought a sad smile to his face. As he continued on, he looked no more to his left or right, not wishing to burn any of this hateful place into his memory.

Behind him, next to the burnt-out ashes of the house that John Tracey had built for his wife and his two sons, Trace McCall left a fresh grave. He laid his mother to rest near her flower garden, now grown up in weeds, in the shade of the tall poplar. Once the bright and happy home of a hardworking and caring family, it was now a place of sorrow, filled with bitter memories best forgotten. Leaving his boyhood home, Trace next paused briefly in the church cemetery to say a final good-bye to his brother, Cameron. Now there was but one last farewell he was determined to make.

Chapter 17

Trace paused near the crest of the steep slope that descended to a rocky stream below, surveying the scene beyond the rushing water. Although it had been years now, still the image of that day came clearly to his mind's eye. He nudged the paint, and the horse made his way slowly down through the pines, carefully stepping over loose rock and shale. He pulled up short of the huge boulder near the water's edge. It had been from behind this same boulder that he had first sighted the evidence of LaPorte's Blackfoot slaughter. Henry Brown Bear's body had been lying only a few yards away in the shallow water.

He shifted his gaze forward to a large pine on the edge of the clearing, and for an instant the vivid picture flashed before his eyes of his father propped up against the trunk—his body pierced by a dozen arrows, the skin of his face sagging as a result of his missing scalp. Trace closed his eyes, trying to blink the image away. After a moment he glanced at the ruins of the little cabin that he, his father, and Henry Brown Bear had built. The brush had all but taken it over. A casual glance might have missed it entirely.

The impact of returning to this place of horror hit Trace harder than he had anticipated. After so many years, he thought his emotions were hardened to what had happened in the past, but the vividness of what took place here was almost enough to take him back in time—and he once again felt the guilt that had burdened him for being absent when his father needed him most. His rational mind told him that it was not his fault that he had begged to go hunting that fateful day. Still there was a deeper feeling that if he had been there, the three of them might have had a better chance of turning the Blackfoot party back.

"It's done!" he pronounced, shaking himself out of his melancholy. He dismounted and walked toward the two mounds on the edge of the clearing to complete what he had come here to do. Trace felt the need to return to this place to testify before his father's grave that his murderers were in hell where they belonged. Only then could he close this chapter in his life.

He was gratified to discover that the graves had not been disturbed. Though grown over in weeds and brush, his father's grave was readily defined, wider at one end in order to accommodate John Tracey's body, stiffened in a sitting posture. The thought caused Trace to catch his breath briefly before saying what he had come to say.

"Pa, that's the three of 'em—Tyler, Morgan, and Hamilton. I hope it brings you some peace. I reckon you probably already know, but Ma's dead. I buried her beside Cameron. Don't judge her too harshly for marrying Hamilton Blunt—she had no way of knowing. I reckon I'm the only one left now, and I hope you'll understand that I wanna bury Jim Tracey too. It ain't that I'm not proud to be your son. It's just that too much sorrow is riding with that name, and I'd just as soon start over. 'Course, you know I'll never forget you. I'm taking your name and Ma's maiden name as my own. Well, that's about it—that's what I wanted to say."

The last memory of Jim Tracey now buried with his father, Trace McCall stepped up in the saddle and, without hesitation, turned the paint toward the Bitterroots that loomed before him.

Climbing to the top of the ridge, he pulled up to take one last look at the clearing below. Then he looked west, toward the mountains and the fresh breeze that danced across his face. He breathed it deep into his lungs, and he thought about what might lie ahead for Trace McCall. Life was new again. He was back in the high mountains. There had been deep sorrow in his young life, but a man is not made whole without a generous portion of sorrow. It was the healing that built compassion in a man's soul. Trace had lost an entire family, but he had another family. Somewhere beyond the mountains he could find Buck and Jamie—and Travis and Nettie Bowen—or somewhere between this spot and Canada, there was a little Indian girl named Blue Water. The thought brought a smile to his face.

Free to go in any direction he chose, he paused when he heard the far cry of a hawk. Shielding his eyes with his hand, he looked toward the mountains until he spotted it, circling high over a mountain pass. "That's as good as any," he said and turned the paint in that direction.